MW00770721

Bloom *books*

To my readers,

Thank you for joining me on another trip into the story of Mendax, Eli, and Caly. As this series progresses, I am constantly reminded of how amazing and supportive you all are. It's such an amazing thing when a book can bring something into our lives, whether it be new friends, inspiration, or just a bit of joy. You have brought me all of those things while writing this story and I hope it can now do the same for you. There's no one I'd rather take on this journey than you.

Love,

ALSO BY JENEANE O'RILEY

The Infatuated Fae

How Does It Feel?
What Did You Do?
Where Did You Go?

WHERE DID YOU GO?

JENEANE O'RILEY

Bloom books

Published by Bloom Books, an imprint of Sourcebooks
P.O. Box 4410, Naperville, Illinois 60567-4410
(630) 961-3900
sourcebooks.com

Cataloging-in-Publication data is on file with the Library of Congress.

Printed and bound in the United States of America.
KP 10 9 8 7 6 5 4 3 2 1

To you.
I'm sorry. It had to happen.

AUTHOR'S NOTE

So we meet again. *Turns in squeaky desk chair.* This is the part where I warn you about how dark this book is. There are parts of this story that are full of sex, violence…sexy violence, unsexy violence, horrible, awful behavior…sexy behavior… okay, you get the sexy point. All jokes aside, this book contains graphic details of some pretty dark things. Spiders that aren't really spiders, creepy things that made me step away from my writing for a day or two, and a lot more that may be triggering to some of you. If you are questioning it, don't proceed. It's not worth risking your mental health. Hopefully this warning will deter those of you who are uncomfortable with sensitive issues commonly in dark romance books and serve to stoke the fire of you naughty, little heathens that get cranked up by warnings like this. Don't say I didn't warn you.

Jeneane

PLAYLIST

"The Dark of You"—Breaking Benjamin
"Rule the World"—Vision Vision
"Le Noir"—Imminence
"Falls of Glory"—BrunuhVille
"Never Too Late"—Three Days Grace
"Rain"—Sleep Token
"By and Down the River"—A Perfect Circle
"Already Over"—Red
"Another Life"—Motionless in White
"Every Time You Leave"—I Prevail
"Sirens"—Fleurie
"Snakeskin"—Madalen Duke
"Soldiers"—FJØRA & Neoni
"Playground"—Bea Miller
"Vendetta"—UNSECRET featuring Krigarè

CHAPTER 32

"Heroes Fall"—Hidden Citizens featuring ESSA
"Carry You"—Ruelle featuring Fleurie
"Hurts Like Hell"—Tommee Profitt featuring Fleurie
"Goodbye"—Ramsey
"One Last Breath"—Tommee Profitt & Nicole Serrano

CHAPTER 1
CALY

G IVE ME THE BALE OF STRAW!" I SHRIEKED.
The gritty dirt underneath my shoes shifted. I was
struggling, using every fiber of the willpower I still possessed
not to fall to the dusty ground of the barn like a petulant child
and kick my tired feet in the air after the night I was having.

"I'm not givin' ye the straw! There's hardly enough for
the horses as 'tis! Go back inside, ye quick-life!" the red-faced
hostler returned.

"Quick-life" was what some of the fae called humans, and
it was *not* a term of endearment.

"She said you could help me." I winced through my words
as my nails bit into my palm. "I only need enough straw for
one or two beds."

"I heard ye, and I already said no. I've not got enough for
the mares as it is. Surely you seen the lot inside? Half are Fallen!
It's my hide that gets torn open if their horses don't have enough
straw." His scowl further deepened the three lines between his
large eyes. His worn, leathery skin made the expression look
nothing short of painful.

I started to size him up but thought better of it. I was in
pain and exhausted, and though I was incredibly desperate to

get this straw, I wasn't stupid. The brute was huge, and who knew what his powers were?

Aside from the risk of him suddenly turning into a tiger—or any other animal, really—and eating me, word had spread fast about me killing the Seelie queen, and for all I knew, he was a Queen Saracen supporter. Everyone had an opinion on what it was that had caused the queen's human assassin to turn on her. Even more rumors had started flying after word got around about *both* castles' destruction, and some fae were pretty riled up about it.

I pulled my shoulders back and did everything I could to force a little twinkle into my eyes and a charming smile onto my face.

I tried to sweet-talk the man one last time. "The last thing I would ever want to do is get you into trouble or have these horses miss a meal. It's just that all the rooms are full—"

"No." The man cut me off as he continued blanketing the horse next to him.

It was obvious that no one was coming between this man and his straw. On my way to the exit, I made certain to kick over one of the loose bales of hay. "Bite him," I grumbled to the chestnut mare in the last stall.

A gust of icy wind slapped me in the face as soon as I stepped out of the barn. My fingers sought warmth and weapon in the pockets of my oversized tunic, and I curled my hand around my karambit. Okay, it was the severed dragon's claw I'd collected outside Malvar, but it was every bit as useful as a karambit and was shaped the same.

Bits of freezing rain pelted my exposed skin, making soft pops with every drop that hit my head and shoulders while I stood outside the small barn, begrudgingly staring at the annoyingly busy inn.

"Ouch! Ye cow!"

The tiniest smile tickled my lips as I walked toward the curved wooden door of the inn.

As quickly as the smile touched my lips, it fell when I

looked down at the wet, snowy ground. The wind lifted, shaking the creaky wood sign shabbily painted *the Inn Between* that hung from an iron arm above the door.

My tired eyes took in at least a hundred monarch butterflies and luna moths lying wilted and dead in the sludgy ground outside the inn. One, still barely alive, tried to flutter its torn, wet wings. My chest felt heavy and tight, something that was seemingly becoming a constant feeling with my recently restored heart.

I brushed the soft, vulnerable feelings away and gripped my weapon. I couldn't afford to care about butterflies right now. I was too occupied sorting things out with the two most dissimilar men in the world.

I steeled myself, stepped over the dying lepidoptera, and shoved the door open.

"He wouldn't give me the straw," I said through clamped teeth.

"Well, guess you're gonna make do with one bed then, eh? Straw makes for terrible mattresses anyway. Feather is better," rasped the haggard old woman as she moved out from behind the wooden counter.

My thumb smoothed over the black dragon claw in my pocket. "What kind of an inn is this?" I snapped. "How can you not have a spare mattress or a chair? A pile of blankets, for sun's sake?" I pushed my foot into the worn wood floor to stop myself from stomping on it, the noise of the busy tavern overwhelming my already pounding head.

"We're the only inn that's in between the realms, hence our name. It's right on the sign, child." She shook her head, making her dark gray braid whip around to the front of her body. "And before you go tryin' to throw your weight around, quick-life, everyone in this place knows who you are and who you're here with. Doesn't matter a lick when you're between the realms. Tartarus, it doesn't seem like it matters *in* the realms anymore either." The owner snorted. "Can't rule a castle that ain't there, eh? Rumor around here's that the Fallen fae"—she lowered her voice conspiratorially and leaned closer—"plan to bump all the Seelie and Unseelie fae out to the human realm and take the fae realms." She leaned back and arched her eyebrows, waiting for my response.

"You shouldn't listen to rumors," I replied with a sharp glare.

I left the rough-looking woman and started up the stairs around the corner, grateful to be leaving behind the loud lower level that was filled with heavy, robust scents and creatures of kinds I'd never before seen. The aged, wooden stairs creaked as I climbed with purposefully heavy steps. Maybe they would hear me coming and behave—though I knew that wasn't likely.

An irritated sigh left me when I paused at the top of the staircase and stared down the hallway at the door to our room. In contrast to the thump and rattling that was muffled behind it, the other rooms I passed on the way were silent, their residents either asleep or getting drunk at the tavern.

An influx of grunts, swears, and muffles made their way to me in the hallway, where my feet had stalled in front of the door. No wonder the innkeeper didn't want to help me.

"I'm opening the door," I warned loudly.

More shuffling, then silence.

The door's hinges creaked as if giving an audible appreciation for my return.

"So? Are they bringing up another mattress for Lord Smoke-Show to sleep on?" the handsome blond fae asked.

Both Eli and Mendax stood in front of the crackling fireplace, disheveled and out of breath, guilty looks on both of their faces. The two fae seemed out of place in the raggedy room, and not simply because they barely fit inside the homely space. Both men emanated this enormous aura of power at all times. You didn't need to know anything about them or their titles to know they were incredibly important and exceedingly powerful. It was overwhelming just existing in the room with one man capable of shifting the air like that—two made your mind and body act senseless.

4

Another sigh exited my lips as I finagled my way around the large, broad-shouldered bags of muscled pains in my ass to stand in front of the fireplace. I removed my dripping-wet boots and pushed them close to the fire, allowing the heat to reach my cold toes.

"No. There's nothing," I replied.

"Sorry, sunshine. Looks like it's the floor for you," Mendax said, goading Eli. I didn't bother glancing at him to see the smile he wore—I could hear it in his voice. "Don't let the Afters take advantage of you while you're down there."

Goose bumps flourished across my skin at the mention of the creepy ghosts that refused to return to fae hell. I'd never seen one, but what I'd heard about Afters made my skin crawl.

"Me on the floor?" Eli shot back with a sharp laugh. "If anyone belongs on the floor with Tartarus's evaporated ghoul leftovers, it's you, oh shadowy prince of night."

The two men's bickering continued behind me like as I did my damnedest to tune them out and prepare myself for bed. It was like trying to tune out a blender.

We had been traveling for what felt like an absolute eternity, though I knew it had only been a few weeks. We'd slept wherever we could make and tend to a fire, but the weather had taken a turn now that we'd finally moved through Seelie and into the space between realms.

As soon as it had sunk in that Walter was dead by the blade of Queen Saracen—Eli's mother—Mendax had either been silent or tried to hurt Eli whenever he got the chance. He wasn't trying to kill him though, because Eli and I were still tied; if Mendax killed Eli, then it meant that I'd die too.

Which sounded peaceful in this moment.

Eli, understandably, was in no better mood than his nemesis. After all, he had just found out I'd been lying to him for twenty years while also planning the murder of his mother. What was worse for him was that I had finally succeeded. On top of that, his sweet little sister, Princess Tarani, was a leader of the Fallen fae; his best friend and theoretical fiancée—hi, it's me—remained tied to his most hated enemy, and the Fates had summoned the three of us to them in Moirai...with the promise of killing one of us in order to break the bonds between us. Oh, and I was going to kill his father's best friend, the Titan Artemi Zef, while we were there, the man better known to me as dear old Dad. Eli had a lot going on. Well, we all did.

I would finally kill Zef for a plethora of reasons, but among them, he chose my sweet, gentle sister to take the inheritance of his Artemi powers before deserting his entire family. Had he been around to protect us from Queen Saracen, Mom and Adrianna would still be with me today, and none of this would have happened.

My cold toes curled before the fire. So yeah, I'd say the trip had been a wee bit uncomfortable thus far.

I moved from the fire to the bed. If I didn't lie down now, the boys would likely burn it to the ground while they fought over who I would share it with. The narrow mattress dipped as I climbed onto it. I tugged the itchy wool blanket up to my chin and let my heavy eyelids fall shut.

I was exhausted.

I would never admit it out loud, but it was much more of a struggle to keep pace with the oversized fae than I would have thought. I knew they wouldn't think twice about stopping had I asked them to, and suns knew they would carry me had I allowed it. But I would rather have died than slow the journey any further. I had waited a long time to *finally* kill my father. I couldn't wait to watch his awful life slowly fade from his horrible eyes.

The bed dipped again. A muscled arm wrapped around my midsection and pulled me against the front of a very, *very* well-built Mendax. I didn't need to open my eyes to know it was him. The way he assertively grabbed my body and the sultry fragrance of amber and spice with a slight undernote of smoke let me know it was him. I couldn't have fought against the pull my body had toward him if I'd wanted to.

This was the first time he had really touched me since our journey began.

I was still as I took in every dent and valley of his shirtless torso, pressed against my side. The warmth from his body was like a radiator, and I barely stopped myself from snuggling into him with a foolish smile.

"My woman, my bed," Mendax purred. "Sleep on the floor, fox."

"Caly is exhausted. Let her have the bed, you idiot. We can both sleep on the floor. And she is *not* your woman," Eli said. He spoke in his higher-pitched voice, the one that let me know he was about to snap but was trying to keep it together.

I opened my eyes and let out a little petulant giggle. What a stupid situation.

"See? Even she thinks it's funny when you say foolish things like that. She is very much my woman," Mendax rasped in my ear. His blue eyes sparkled with mischief as they latched on to mine, even though the look was meant for Eli.

Eli though, not to be outdone, climbed onto the empty sliver of the bed on my other side. By now, the small mattress had dipped so low, we were almost to the floor. He grabbed my left hand and rolled me until my body was pressed against his.

I snorted as any sane woman would when they had become the tug-of-war prize between two stunning men.

"What in star—" said Mendax.

Eli cradled my head and gave me one of his charming, playful winks. "If *anyone* is going to share the bed with her, it will be her future husband."

I giggled like a schoolgirl. Obviously lack of sleep had done my head in.

In truth, it was nice to feel a bit of playfulness from them after everything. There was an undercurrent of seriousness, but it was covered by a silliness—I'm sure for my sake—that felt like we were all just enjoying a game of duck-duck-goose.

Eli pulled the covers up over us with a smile and leaned over top of me.

The air in my chest lodged itself in my throat. Holy suns,

stars, and every other hydrogen-helium balls there are, what was happening between us?

His thumb lightly stroked the side of my face just before his soft lips grazed mine, asking for permission before pressing into me harder. I melted against him, unable to hide my arousal and surprise at his kiss. Was it from his kiss, or was it from the fact that I could feel Mendax about to maul me in retaliation? The restraint it took for him not to kill Eli did not go unnoticed.

But…what does one do in a situation like this?

"Unless you wish to make the tail end of this journey head-less, I *strongly* suggest you stop touching Calypso, Aurelius," Mendax growled so quietly it made the hair on my arms raise.

All humor and playfulness were gone from his voice.

"It's fine. I'll take the floor. Give me your shirts to sleep on," I said, sensing the severity of this situation—Mendax was not one to be pushed. I moved to lie on my side with my back facing Eli. It somehow seemed the safer position.

"*No*," both men barked in unison as they locked eyes with each other.

"Get. On. The. Fucking. Floor, Seelie," Mendax said, enunciating carefully.

"You sound like a hippo," Eli replied in a similar whisper, completely unbothered.

I snorted.

"What did you call me?" Mendax's low voice filled the small room.

"Look, Caly and I *both* tried to get something else to sleep on from downstairs. They have no other beds available. I even flirted with the old woman at the front desk, and they gave us nothing." Eli took full embrace of being the big spoon and curled up close around my back.

Mendax looked like he was about to flip the entire bed over.

"This is getting out of hand," I started.

Mendax cracked his knuckles so hard, it sounded as if the bones had broken. He moved to stand at the edge of the bed and looked at me for a long moment before he turned around and stalked to the door. Eli and I had both rolled to the right to watch whatever was about to happen. Now I was the big spoon as I looked over Eli's shoulder.

"Thank her," Mendax stated through clenched teeth before looking to Eli.

"What?" Eli asked with a mischievous grin.

"Thank her," Mendax repeated slowly. "Pray and kneel to Calypso for each and every day that you live, because she is the *only*, let me repeat, the *only* thing prolonging your marked little life."

The six-foot-five Smoke Slayer opened the door of our room and left, slamming the door behind him.

Eli rolled back to face me with a victorious smile and began kissing my neck.

"Thank you." He kissed my neck again. "Thank you." Another kiss to my sensitive neck. This one, however, was accompanied by the tip of his tongue.

Eli and I had never been so intimate before, and I couldn't help but feel like it was more about him winning me than actually wanting me.

I could feel his smile pressing against my exposed collarbone.

This felt wrong. I mean, it felt right—so fucking right— but it felt wrong. I didn't want to do this to either of them. I shouldn't have even let it go this far. I needed to remain neutral, no matter how impossible that seemed at the moment. I didn't want to hurt either of them any more than I already had…or was about to.

One of us was still going to die at the end of all this, and that knowledge had morphed into a desire to not miss out on any- thing with either of them—no matter how awkward it seemed.

"Wait, I don't think we should do this," I whispered so softly I wasn't sure he'd even heard me…or if I really wanted him to.

Like the wholesome, charming best friend I had always known him to be, Eli snapped his head up and quickly rolled

9

off me, leaving me cold and somewhat mad at his impeccable fox hearing.

The corner of his mouth lifted. "I'm sorry," he said before biting his lower lip. "I think I got carried awa—"

A horrifying crash thundered up the hallway. It sounded like the inn had caved in on itself.

The two of us bolted upright and looked at the door. Eli was off the bed and standing at the ready before I even finished blinking. The walls of the inn rattled again, sending fragments of plaster and dust to the floor as the door slammed open, barely remaining on its rusty hinges.

Mendax strode in carrying a stained mattress.

Shouts and growls broke out down the hallway as the dark prince threw the mattress to the floor and turned to face the open door.

I clutched the edge of the bed as I peered behind him at what looked like a group of war elves, but I couldn't really see that far down the dimly lit hallway.

Mendax took a step toward the door, turning his head for a second—giving us an expression that made Eli and I exchange looks apprehensively—before he focused on the hallway.

Whoever was in the hallway saw the same look and wisely left.

The prince of smoke and shadows turned his full attention back on us. Eli took a protective step in front of me to block me from Mendax.

"Do not fight with him now, Eli. Our lives are still tied. If you die, I die," I reminded him for the millionth time.

"Believe me, I remember," Eli snapped.

The tension in the room had thickened with a feral spark of danger.

"You. Bed," Mendax snarled, pointing to the lumpy mattress on the floor.

Smoke had begun to slowly cascade from his body in ominous warning.

I moved to the edge of the bed and ran my hand gently

over Eli's back in the hopes of calming him and preventing a fight, only realizing what a stupid move it was after Mendax shuddered while he watched me touch the other man.

Eli clenched his fists as Mendax stepped nose to nose with him before the Unseelie eventually turned to look at me with a pissed-off expression.

I should have kept my hands to myself.

"Both of you take the other mattress," I offered.

"*No*," they said in unison.

Mendax shoved Eli toward the mattress that now lay near the fireplace.

Eli stared at him for a minute, no doubt weighing his decision, before he reluctantly moved to his new bed next to the hearth.

"Feuhn kai greeyth," he said in mock merriment to me as he took one of the blankets off my bed.

"Feuhn kai greeyth," I repeated back to him with a weak smile.

It meant eternal love and friendship in an old fae language. It had been our thing ever since we were little kids.

Mendax growled from where he stood at the edge of the bed before he started to take off his pants.

My pulse sped up embarrassingly fast.

I rolled to the other side of the bed and faced the cream-colored wall, making sure I gave the angry fae plenty of space, and tried desperately not to think about what was underneath his pants.

"How did you get this mattress?" Eli's inquisitive voice carried up from the floor.

The bed dipped again, and I was immediately hyperaware of how small the mattress was. I swear, I could *taste* how masculine and powerful Mendax was as he crawled into bed with me.

His arm wrapped around my middle and roughly tugged me into him, rolling me over so that our faces were only a breath apart on one pillow.

"I wanted it, so I took it," Mendax answered Eli while

keeping his eyes latched to mine. There was a soft look deep in them even though his jaw was set firmly and his grip on me was rough.

"Of course you did," Eli replied. "Caly, if he bothers you at all, say the word."

Mendax snickered.

"Okay, for sun's sake, let's go to sleep. You said we could get to Lake Sheridon tomorrow. Good night," I said gruffly.

Mendax pulled my body closer to his, and like I'd been given a drug, I instantly fell asleep in the protective comfort of his hold on me.

Tomorrow was going to be one of the hardest days of my whole miserable life.

CHAPTER 2
MENDAX

ORANGE RAYS OF MORNING SUN STREAMED ACROSS THE PEPPY fae's face. My smoke pushed at his lips. With every inhale, as his mouth opened, the long fingers of my smoke pressed into his throat. This all could be done and over—I could suffocate him right now. I couldn't believe I hadn't yet. I was acquaintances with Kaohs, the god of the underworld. Maybe he could send Caly back to me if I killed Aurelius and she died because of their tie. A shiver racked my body at the thought of her dying.

Hacking and gasping sounds filled the room, and I realized golden boy had swallowed a good deal of my smoke while I wasn't paying attention. Quickly, I retracted it and closed my eyes.

Caly's supple body stirred next to me. "Eli! Are you okay?" she called to the choking man. She tried to get up and go to him, but my arms remained tightly wrapped around her, as I refused to let her leave me for him.

Still coughing and choking, Aurelius struggled to answer.

Caly tried to shove my arm off, so I pretended to rouse from slumber, sleepily pulling her under me, making certain she felt how my body ached and hardened for her. I dipped my hips just enough to feel myself rub between her legs. It felt like I would die from wanting to sink inside her long before I would die from any decision the Fates made.

She sucked in a loud breath before wrapping her arms around my neck and whispering into my ear, "I know what you did. I was watching you watch him."

I pulled back a little to see her sly smile.

Fuck, she was deviously perfect.

I rolled over and let the goddess leave me to attend to the choking puppy on the floor.

I despised that fae more than anything in this exhausting world. It was because of him and his mother that I no longer had a castle to go home to. They were the ones who had taken the lives of my mother and brother.

Anger rippled through my body as I remembered the way Aurelius's mother had pressed her blade into the top of my brother Walter's skull, sending him to his final resting place in Tartarus.

Aurelius would die somehow. I would kill him in the most painful way possible. I no longer cared if it bothered Caly or not. Watching her fuss over him caused a surge of unfamiliar feelings to course through me. I wanted to rip out the throat of every man who still lived, but that wasn't the unfamiliar feeling. I was scared of losing her, and it made my soul tremble.

I continued to watch the two of them as I got dressed.

It would all be over at the end of today.

Caly's father and the Fates had summoned the three of us to Moirai to stand trial for going against their laws. It was strictly forbidden for a person to be both bonded and tied, but aside from the legalities of the situation, which I certainly didn't care about, the tie to Aurelius and the bond to me were slowly killing Caly. I doubted she was even aware of it with the way I had been continuously pushing my powers into the bond in an effort to keep her as healthy as possible, and I had suspicions that Aurelius was doing something similar with their tie. If we didn't get either the tie or the bond severed today, it would kill one of us before the Fates even had the opportunity to. It needed to be done today, or I would die very soon after, if not by my own blade from the frustration of this endeavor then by giving every last drop of life I had to Caly. The simple thought of leaving her with golden boy was enough to take me down on its own, but if he drained his powers in trying to saving her, then she would die as well. That was the curse of the tie and the reason I always needed to be giving more of myself than him. Our bond didn't operate by jeopardizing her, so I could remove myself, and she would continue on until we met again in Tartarus.

It would be the one and only selfless thing I would have ever done, but still, I would do it for her if I needed to.

"It is time to leave. Be outside in five minutes. Calypso, stay with Aurelius until we reach Lake Sheridon. The weather will be hard for you, and I am *much* colder than he is," I said as I sent an icy glare at Aurelius before walking out the door.

Being a SunTamer, he would always be warmer than other fae, especially a prince of the shadows and darkness like me, and she needed to stay warm. He also needed to stay away from me before I lost control and wound up killing both of them by accident.

On the way out, I stopped by the tavern to see if any Unseelie had found their way to the Inn Between. "A shot of bone nectar," I stated to the orc behind the counter.

"Oi, I wouldn't take that if it was me last day," declared the little fae to my right.

I threw back the white liquid and slid the glass back to the barkeep.

"It quite possibly is my last day," I replied.

CHAPTER 3

ELI

I SHRIEKED AN INCREDIBLY UNMASCULINE SHOUT WHEN CAL PUT her ice-cold hands on my neck. I quickly let out a deep cough in an effort to cover the shrill sound as soon as Mendax turned his melancholy head to scowl at me.

"Your hands are freezing!" I said to her with a cackle.

She was still laughing at the high-pitched sound I had produced prior.

I stopped amid the barren, endless snow and tucked each of her small hands into the most readily available heat on my person: my armpits. She laughed even harder while shouting something about her hands stinking.

"It's warm in my armpits, and your hands are going to turn to hand-shaped blocks of ice in a few moments." I clamped my arms down, locking her in place. Once more, I was startled by how beautiful she was when she stood this close to me. When I looked at her heart-shaped face, it took me back to a better time, when my biggest concern was getting to the human realm to see my human ray of sunshine.

At least I had thought it was a better time and had thought that she was filled with light and goodness. The smile dropped from my face, and I stiffened. Cal had lied to me a lot in those "better times."

I didn't support anything my mother had done to her, *especially* killing Cal's mother and sister, but it was still hard to believe Cal had done what she had to destroy my mother and everything my mother had cared about. In the end, it was still *my mother* Cal had murdered.

"What's wrong?" Cal asked.

"Nothing," I replied with a quirk of my mouth. "We should keep moving. Mendax has already moved pretty far ahead of us."

I gave a convincing enough smile, but we both knew what was bothering me. It was one of the best and worst things about having a best friend like Cal—they knew you in ways you didn't know yourself. We knew generally why the other was upset just by a quick look at their face.

Still, friend or not, she had killed my mother. She had even used my own blade to do it—a feat she had accomplished while I had held my mother back from hurting her.

I would get over what happened. I understood exactly why she had done it, knew all the awful things my mother had put her through. A part of me was even a little proud of Cal. Facing your enemies isn't always as easy as you think it will be; in fact, it's usually harder than suffering at their hands.

I glared at the greasy black hair of the fae who walked in front of me.

Cal was so much stronger than I had ever realized. It hurt that she hadn't let me in and allowed me to be in that part of her world—the part with all the pain and lies. My feelings for her wouldn't have changed, or at least I didn't think they would have. I couldn't help but think things could have been different if only she had let me help her. Perhaps I could have helped Cal not suffer or saved my mother's life. Knowing Cal the way I do, I know why she didn't want to let me in. As tough as she is, she wanted an escape from that world, and I believe—or at least hoped—that I gave that to her, gave her a chance to have moments that weren't consumed by vengeful anger and darkness. She was always the brightest light in my life, and it was comforting to think I may have been hers. Whether that was true or not, I didn't know, and maybe that was just my foolish brain needing to feel that I was still there for her in some way, that I brought *some* type of relief to her.

A shiver took over my body.

"You okay?" Cal asked, obviously having felt it.

I untucked her from my arms and instantly regretted it. "Me? Yeah. I just thought I'd go check with our navigator and ask him why we continue to go in circles," I replied, making sure my voice carried up to Mendax. "Here, take this." I removed my chest plates and secured them to my belt with the rest of my armor. The icy wind hit my back as I peeled both shirts up and shook my head free when they caught on my pointed ears. I bet that never happened to humans with their cute little ears.

"You can't walk around in this weather without a shirt!" she exclaimed.

"I'm fine, honestly. I run hot, sunlight in the veins and all that," I said with a wink as I brushed her off and clenched my jaw to stop a shiver. I didn't know if I had enough power to spare to crank up my internal heat as much as was necessary. The tie between Cal and I was taking more out of me than I had realized. Even though she technically had a *small* drop of Artemi in her veins from her sister's powers, it was only enough to give her some serious pull with the animals. It wasn't enough to give her any amount of extended life or immortality. I knew because it was taking an absurd amount of my own power being sent through our tie to keep her at even a baseline, health wise. She was dying from the bond and the tie, and ironically, right now, it was also the only thing keeping her alive.

The onslaught of snow slowed slightly, changing the surrounding landscape from a blizzard of angry flakes into an eerie and still white blanket. The sudden change stirred some sort of alarm inside me. I knew all three of us had felt it by the slight change in Cal and Smoke-Show's posture. Every one of us felt the unmistakable trace of danger in the air.

It was spooky, the in-between—an uninhabitable space

between the realms that was said to hold the magic that was refused by the other realms. It was almost impossible to find your way back out of the Infinity Forest. Most of the wiser fae would never go this far into the forest; I had previously been one of them. It was amazing the things you did for friends and loved ones.

The simple thought gave me pause—Cal was everything to me, but the line between being friends or more felt so blurry between us. If I was being honest, I didn't know what the perfect label for us was yet, especially after everything I had just learned about her. And just like the Infinity Forest, I had no idea how to get back out. Thankfully, we would find Moirai at Lake Sheridon and would not need to find our way back out. At least that was my hope.

A small spark of gratitude had lit inside me when Mendax had kept his obscenely sharp jaw shut when Cal mentioned that we were going to Lake Sheridon. It didn't seem in his character to miss out on an opportunity to scare her, but he had, and against my better judgment, it made me think a little differently about the Unseelie. He was a horrible, evil monster who deserved his death, but he did appear to genuinely care for Cal.

Deafening stillness encompassed the forest. Not the peaceful kind of stillness that calmed and relaxed but the kind that made the air thick with anxious anticipation. It was the kind of stillness that remained when nothing else survived. The crunch of shifting snow beneath our feet echoed ominously among the snow-covered pines.

I didn't know what the Fates had in mind by sending us to the Infinity Forest, but I knew that it wasn't good.

My head snapped up at a far-off noise.

"What is it?" Cal barked nervously.

"Huh?" I stupidly asked, trying to cover my sharp intake of breath and buy myself time to think of an answer that wouldn't frighten her. As a fox shifter, my hearing was significantly better than either of theirs, and I'd heard her loud and clear, but

I'd also heard something *very* large coming toward us in the distance.

Mendax never looked back, continuing his position as self-declared leader, while my ears strained to figure out what was coming at us. Shit. This was not good.

I stopped and abruptly grabbed Cal's arm. Her wide eyes, full of worry, snapped to mine.

"I need to pee," I blurted.

"Okay..." Cal replied slowly.

"What is the holdup, Goldilocks? Ready to give up and die already? You lasted longer than I expected," Mendax grumbled from ahead.

That chiseled-jawed motherfucker.

"Go pee, you weirdo. Catch up with us," Cal said, walking faster to join up with Mendax.

"No! Watch me," I called out. *What the fuck did I just say?*

Yes. This was definitely a great way to win Cal over.

"What? Ew," she said with a look of disgust that made me want to shrivel into a little ball and burst into flames.

Fuck. This was why I didn't scheme. "I just have to take a leak. Cal's gonna hold my stuff so I don't lose it in the snow," I shouted at Mendax.

"You and your tiny cock are on your own, though you do have my sympathy should you lose it in the snow," Mendax countered with a look to Cal. "Calypso, my pet, leave the weird man with a detachable dick alone and come up here with me."

I tightened my grip on her arm, causing her to look deeper into my eyes as she laughed.

"Just pee behind a tree like you guys have been. There's one right there. What is going on?" she asked, full of confusion.

I lowered my voice. "He—he was saying weird things about my junk the last time we were behind the tree," I declared. *Detachable dick this, you dark-haired shadow muncher.*

She snorted. "What? You are such a liar." But somehow my fib worked; Cal turned toward Mendax. "Just keep going.

We will catch up with you in a few minutes!" she shouted to the irritated Unseelie.

I walked her toward some large, old Scots pines.

"It's true," I whispered, now fully committed. I leaned over to make sure that Mendax had continued walking on ahead. "Every time we go to relieve ourselves, he stares at my dick all weird and says it reminds him of a shade-foot." I almost couldn't say the words with a straight face.

"What the hell is a shade-foot?" She scrunched her face.

"They are like ogres, but they only have one large, stalky leg and one giant foot. They are super fast and lie on their backs with their giant foot up, giving them and everything around them shade." I spotted a bigger Scots pine and grabbed her hand to quickly pull her to it.

The large creature was getting closer.

"You expect me to believe Mendax eyed your dick and said it looked like a *giant foot*?" she asked incredulously.

I snorted and had to pretend to hack and cough in an effort to camouflage my cracking facade. "I think he meant the leg, but yeah, it was super weird. Last time, ugh—uh, no, I'm okay. Sorry, bug in my throat. Last time, he said he had a bit of a thing for ogre feet. They get him all hard and stuff—said he couldn't help it." I shrugged. I was going to Tartarus after this.

"You are such a fucking liar," she said with a laugh, but I could tell I had at least planted a seed of interest.

I held my palms up innocently. "Didn't you see the way he got when we passed that lady ogre at that pub? He practically needed a pillow to hide his chub. Hope you got some big ole piggies in those boots if you want to satisfy smoky the bear," I said with a nod at her feet.

"Shut up. You are so full of it. Hurry up and go! Mendax is probably to the lake by now," she laughed.

A loud, horrible screech ricocheted throughout the forest, close enough to wipe the grin from my face.

"Get in this tree. Go, please," I said, turning her body to face the giant tree trunk. "I know you can climb trees, but do

21

you need a boost?" I stepped close behind her little human frame and put my hands on her waist, ready to lift her up. It felt different than it had when we were children. My hands on her body felt like I was breaking a rule of some kind.

"Eli, what's going on?" Cal asked, a new note of worry in her voice.

The grating scream came again, and I knew she had heard it this time by the way her body went rigid.

"Mendax!" she exclaimed without a second thought.

I watched her, a pit forming in my stomach at a realization. If I hadn't already been setting that bastard up to be eaten by a sickle, the worry in her voice would have really struck something in me. Why did she care so much about him?

"He'll be fine." No, he wouldn't. "Get in the tree, Cal, please," I requested as I boxed her in against the tree. Her back pushed against my chest as she tried to turn around.

The next shriek of the sickle sent a wave of goose bumps up my bare arms.

I would *not* let that piece of shit Unseelie get her killed. This would work out for the best. After this, the bond between Mendax and Cal would be broken, and she and I would be able to leave the in-between without ever even seeing the Fates or her father.

And I wouldn't have to be the one to kill the man that Cal really loved.

"What is that?" she asked, still trying to turn around and face me as I sandwiched her against the tree.

"Fuck, Calypso! *Please* get up this tree. Go to the tallest branch, and you will see *exactly* what creature it is that makes that horrible sound." I was starting to panic.

If she tried to run for Mendax, she wouldn't even make it to him before the sickle got her, and it would be all my fault.

"Please go!" I shouted as nicely as possible. I nearly bit my lip off when she crossed her arms like a petulant child. Her bottom rib pressed against my fingers when I tightened my grip on her waist. She felt light as I lifted her stubborn ass up, pausing when my mouth brushed her ear as I whispered. "If you do not get your pretty little ass up this tree and out of danger in the next three seconds, I will *drag* you up by your pretty little throat. Fucking go." It was taking *everything* inside me not to fling her into the tree in a panic. Her body slackened slightly in my grip, and my eyes widened. "Suns above, you fucking pervert. You *liked* that? You liked me *threatening* you?" Of all the things to get turned on about…

"What? No!" she snapped.

"You did. I could smell it. Honest to sun's fire, Calypso. Not when I give you the shirt off my back or take a dirty mattress on the floor for you, but the first and hopefully only time I threaten you. You are sick. Go." I shoved her up onto a V-shaped branch and followed behind her, using my upper body to pull myself up and block her at the same time.

"I did *not* get turned on by you, and what do you mean you can *smell* me? Who's the fucking pervert now?" she grumbled but continued to climb the absurdly tall tree.

I remained close behind her in case she still decided to run. "Right, I'm the pervert because I'm a fox shifter and I can smell it when you're horny. Shows how much you know about animals' mating behavior, miss scientist. Of course I can smell your arousal." I rolled my eyes dramatically. "And your fear and anger and…sometimes your sadness."

Cal turned her head, eyes the size of melons. The look on her face was almost enough to make me forget we were hiding from a sickle.

"You're serious."

"Use that branch there. Wrap your thighs around it. And yes, you should smell yourself around Mendax." I bit my tongue, wishing I hadn't admitted that out loud. She gave me a sheepish look but continued climbing higher until she reached the tallest, most hidden branch.

"Oh my suns, Eli," she said as she looked down to where the sickle was coming into view.

Cal's mouth hung open as she stared out at the snowy

landscape beneath the tall pine we had sequestered ourselves in. My leg hitched over a wide branch, and I settled myself into the space in front of her. If something happened and it came this way, it was going to have to get through me to get to her. She probably would have fought me for sitting in front of her had she not been in shock after seeing the ice monster that was heading this direction. I had to take an extra long breath before I was able to convince myself to look, telling myself it was for the best.

Cal pressed her chest against my back to look over my shoulder.

"You did this on purpose," she accused. "You heard it coming."

"I did," I admitted. I was sneaky and dirty now, apparently, but I refused to be a liar. "I'm sorry. Mendax will most likely feel no pain if that brings you any comfort. It will be over fast for him."

Her blue eyes looked at me in a way that made me question everything I thought I was sure of. She closed her eyes a few times, fighting the glistening sheen that filled them. If I cared about her any less, I would have stepped down from the competition right then, but I cared about her a great deal more than I probably should have. She had been through enough already. I would do anything to keep Mendax from ruining her life more than it already had been because of my mother. She wouldn't have gone to him had it not been for my mother. She didn't know him like I did. Mendax wasn't in love with her; he was infatuated, and I wouldn't let him hurt her. I just wouldn't.

"What *is* that thing? You have to help him!" She shoved my shoulder so hard, I had to grip ahold of the branch to stop myself from falling out of the tree.

Resolved, I shook my head. "I'm sorry, Calypso, I really am, but no, I won't help him. He *deserves* this death. I know you don't believe me right now, but among a hundred other reasons he should die is that he is incapable of loving you the way you deserve. He is a monster." My jaw felt tight and uncomfortable, and my stomach felt like I had swallowed stones. This was not an honorable way to destroy your enemy. "And now a monster will finish him." My eyes landed on the black-clad fae in the distance. He stood out against the snow like a bull's-eye. I rolled my eyes when the arrogant prick continued walking as if nothing was happening. "That is a sickle."

Snow shivered off the treetops as the spiderlike creature of the in-between let out another horrifying shriek. I'd never seen one in person, only heard the tales of their ability to maim and seen the many paintings around the castle. Seeing it in person was so much worse than I ever could have imagined. Especially when my weak body was the only thing between it and my best friend.

We watched as the sickle's five black eyes landed on Mendax.

He had seconds left to live now.

Why did I feel guilty? He deserved to die. I had outsmarted him fair and square. I had absolutely *nothing* to feel bad about. I knew for a fact he would not have felt any sympathy for me had our roles been reversed.

I straightened and watched as Mendax's black apparel reflected off the tall spikes that covered the sickle's hunched back like tiny mirrors. It's nearly translucent, whitish-pink flesh crackled and snapped like ice as it reared up, displaying six of its eight sharp-as-blades legs, which looked as if they were made of ice, as did the spikes across its neck and back.

"Oh my suns, is that—"

Cal's question was lost in the air as we stared at its translucent belly, where a decent-size man was compacted inside. What looked like a dark-bearded face was pressed against the creature's stomach. From where we sat in the tree, it was impossible to tell if the man was dead or alive in there. Like the nonchalant prick he was, Mendax looked completely confident and unfazed as he held out his right hand and conjured up his infamous black smoke.

My stomach clenched and dropped. It was obvious he

didn't know anything about sickles. That meant this wasn't going to be fair, and I *hated* the way that tugged guiltily at my gut.

With an absurdly high-pitched rattle, the creature dropped its body back down to the forest floor—directly over top of the Unseelie prince.

"Mendax, no!" Cal screamed to rival any banshee I'd ever heard.

Five, milky-coated black eyes shifted to us in the tree. It was only for a fraction of a second before it went back to its task of eating my competition, but it was enough. It knew our location now and was going to move on to us after it finished with this meal.

Another awful, spine-shattering cry sounded, this one shrill and painful to my ears as the sound shot forth from the creature's white-pincered mouth. It moved backward, and a still too-calm-for-the-situation Mendax leisurely pushed himself free of the icy creature just as the sickle shot an arm-length icicle straight into Mendax's chest. Why was he not fighting harder? He fought me harder for a mattress!

"I can't just sit and watch this!" Cal cried out, and yet again, guilt punched me in the stomach for what I'd done.

"Close your eyes. You don't need to watch his last moments. You'll no doubt remember him in a better light than he ever deserves anyway." I reached behind myself and squeezed her thigh.

"We can't just leave him like this!" she shouted but covered her eyes quickly.

I winced. This wasn't like me, and I hated it. My gravel-filled stomach turned again. This was for her, and I would see it through. If she had taught me anything, it was that being the good guy all the time wasn't working for me. I cleared my throat, determined to calm both her and myself. "He's fighting like a warrior," I said, embellishing. He was stuck on the ground, pinned with a three-foot dagger of ice sticking out of his chest, a wet rim of black Unseelie blood surrounding it. Remorse pulled at me so hard, I actually debated going down and helping the stupid bastard. I hated him, and I sure as Tartarus wanted him gone, but at my core, I still hated killing. *I hated it.* I wanted the Seelie and Unseelie to live among each other peacefully, without all the old conflicts and hate, and this went against that. No matter what had transpired, I could never understand how the realms had gotten so divided at the hands of a few cruel and sinister rulers, my mother being one of them.

"What's happening?" Cal shouted, pulling me back to the present.

"Well, uh...he put up a good fight but—" I fumbled over my words as I watched Mendax suddenly spring off the ground like a panther, pulling the icicle from his chest like it was a stray nose hair. I was acutely aware of my mouth falling open as he spun the large ice lance skillfully and wielded it like a weapon he'd trained with since birth.

That was fucking brilliant. He was going to use the creature's own icicle against it. Son of a bitch.

"He's just—he tripped...trying to run away," I said. But he hadn't tripped. The maniac had launched himself at the creature and stabbed it right in its fat, white neck. The sickle squealed but quickly swung its curved arm out to hook on to Mendax's waist. I let out a gasp, knowing that I was about to see the dark fae split in two like a boiled potato.

"What is it?" Cal asked as she buried her face in my back.

Instead of falling into a bloodied heap on the snow, the prince gripped the sickle's arm and began to climb up it. *Climb up it.*

"The fuck?" I muttered as I watched him attempt to pull himself up the razor-sharp, segmented arm. How was he not shredded into a thousand ribbons right now? "Bu—he, well, he just got a...um...rather *embarrassing* hit to the crotch. Should've blocked that one. He's a very slow fighter, isn't he? Ooh, yeah—looks like the sickle got another shot in. No babies coming from him, I'm afraid."

Mendax had somehow managed to reach the monster's

large front pincers. He held on with one hand and slammed the point of the icicle into one of the sickle's many eyes.

"Blast to the face," I coughed in awe. Having always been a participant in the fights with him, it was completely shocking to watch him fight. He was an absolute killing machine.

"Mendax got hit in the face? Was it bad?" She turned around and pushed her face into the rough bark of the tree.

"Yes. *Very* bad—mm-hmm. His face will never look the same," I grumbled. And to think I was even starting to feel guilty for the guy. Now, a part of me was considering rescuing the sickle, for *sun's sake*.

Just when I was about to give in and tell Cal that Mendax was probably—most assuredly—going to make it and then try to kill me, things took a turn for the worse…or better, depending on one's perception of the situation at hand.

Black blood stained the snow as the creature threw Mendax to the ground a few feet away. Before the fae could pick himself back up, the sickle shot out another weapon of ice, which shot straight through Mendax's shoulder, pinning him to the frozen ground. The fae struggled to get up, but the pissed-off creature's spindly legs were already hovering over him. I saw it on the prince's face: this time, he was trapped.

"Fuck…" I swore under my breath. "Call your smoke."

"What?" Cal asked, still covering her face.

"Nothing." I cleared my throat. My knuckles cracked anxiously before I tucked them under my thighs.

Mendax held out his bloodied hand, and relief lightened my shoulders. I guess I didn't want him dead quite as much as I'd thought. Regardless, that was between him and me, and as long as he was tied to Cal and I was bonded to her, either he or I would be dead by the time we met the Fates in Moirai. I would never let him stay alive to ruin her life, but even I would admit that I had seen a different side of him when he was with her. Don't misunderstand me: I loathed him. I had a chest covered in scars that reminded me every time I dressed of the magnitude of my hatred for him. Spending so much time with him had sort of dulled that hate though and given me a bit of insight into his world. Would we hate each other to this degree had our mothers not been enemies and used us as the family attack dogs? Probably not.

His blackened hand trembled, but instead of drawing smoke, it dropped onto the fluffy snow where he was pinned. He was out of fight and powers, and I knew exactly why.

"Suns *damn* it," I said as I stood on the tree branch and climbed around Cal. "Don't you fucking say one word," I barked at her.

Her eyes shimmered with gratitude and more calm than I would have expected. I had to remind myself that Cal wasn't a damsel in distress that I got to save. She had likely been part of more killings than I had, and I wasn't sure if I would ever get over that knowledge.

"I knew you weren't like us." Her bright blue eyes looked sad at the realization. "I'll stay put if you promise not to get us killed."

The words filtered through the branches above me. I was halfway down when I shouted back at her. "Don't you move from that branch until I come back!"

I shifted just before my paws hit the snow. I didn't have enough power for what I was about to do. This was stupid. But I was doing it anyway.

In my fox form, I reached the scene faster than I would have by walking and much quieter than I ever could as a man.

Mendax was on his back, completely under the sickle, still pinned to the ground when I approached. My body tingled all over as I shifted back into a man just as the sickle's mouth was about to close in on Mendax's face.

"Hey, ugly fuck!" I shouted. Both Mendax and the white head of the sickle snapped around to look at me. The movement caused the contents of the creature's round belly to move slightly, catching my eye. The remainder of its last meal was easily visible now as the disfigured body inside was smashed against the thin, see-through walls of its captor's stomach.

"Where is Calypso?" Mendax demanded.

"I should have been more specific with my descriptor. I was speaking to the five-eyed ugly fuck," I responded.

The pointed spikes on the monster's back glinted an icy blue as it turned back to Mendax, apparently deciding I was a waste of time—or, far more likely, much too impressive and terrifying to attempt a fight with.

I focused my attention, and the power of the sun shot forth from my palm in the shape of a small orb. Truthfully, I had been going for something much larger in size, but like any man, it was second nature to exaggerate the size of my balls. I wasn't used to working with my powers so depleted.

Pushing my palms forward, the orb lit up the dull landscape like a firework as it soared toward the monster and landed on its back. The monster's shrill cry rattled my brain, making my ears ring until I could hear nothing at all. It reared back and leapt, easily clearing the distance between us.

"Shit." I took off like a Seelie out of Tartarus, making certain I ran the opposite direction of the Scots pine that was camouflaging Cal.

Somehow, by fate or luck, I managed to stay slightly ahead of the ice spider. At least until I was about thirty feet or so away from where Mendax lay. That was when my body faltered as it slashed my back leg with its sharp, segmented arms. With a grunt, I fell to the ground and turned in an attempt to block the beast as I fell. I had no shirt on, let alone any armor to protect me.

Mind-numbing cold blasted onto my face as its awful pincers latched on to each of my cheeks in a bite. Pressure tugged at my neck as it pulled at my head. I pressed the weird skin and white fur of its hideous face with my palms, but it was no use. I couldn't push it away even an inch, and just as Mendax had fallen under it before, I was almost completely out of power. If I didn't use this last bit, then I would die, killing Cal as well, but if I did use the last of my power…well, I wouldn't have anything else to send through the tie to keep Cal alive either. I supposed this was the destiny I deserved after what I had attempted to do to Mendax.

Before it could bite down any harder, I used the last traces of my power and sent the biggest surge of fiery sun I could muster straight into the creature's face through both my hands. Half a second of a scream left the monster's ugly maw before it combusted in the air with the high-pitched sound of ice shattering against brick.

I leapt up just as wet bits of pinkish-white, leathery skin rained down around me, hitting me in the face with a sickening clap. Keeping my adrenaline-fueled momentum, I stalked back over to Mendax.

"Where is Calypso?" the Smoke Slayer snarled. "What did you—"

I gripped the long icicle protruding from his shoulder and tugged with all my strength. It didn't budge. I tried again, but my hand was still so hot that it only slipped off the end of it, unable to get a grip.

"You should have left me. I would have left you. For a moment, I even thought a little more of you for setting me up. I didn't think you had it in you." Mendax spoke slowly and seriously as he glowered at me. "And for the record, this proves I was correct in my assumption: you didn't have it in you."

This *prick*.

I kicked his shoulder so hard, I felt my own teeth rattle. A crack sounded, and Mendax scrunched his body over in pain— enough for me to get my boot under him with another hefty kick. The bloodied lance made of ice snapped, leaving a large chunk still lodged in the ground and the other part still through his shoulder. He let out a low groan as I gripped the icy stick once again and yanked. It slid from his body with a slick and disgusting sound.

"Yes, for a moment, I almost forgot myself," I responded. "It seems just being in your presence has polluted my character. I don't like you. In fact, I fucking hate you." I stood over the evil fae, comfort at my own words giving me confidence. "I am *not* you, and I am *not* an Unseelie, and for that I am eternally grateful. I don't enjoy hurting or killing. I find no game in trickery or lies, and I don't get off on causing pain. In fact, I dream of a day when all the realms can integrate peacefully and coexist without prejudice. I love nothing more than to laugh and help those who are struggling or in need." I threw the cold sword of ice onto his stomach and turned to walk away. "You will die. It isn't necessary for me to bloody my own hands with guilt to achieve that outcome. Think what you may, but I'm the only one here who has met Zef. Just like Cal and I, her father and my own were best friends before Zef ascended. He left my father the care of watching over them. *You* will die, and I will have clean hands when I marry Calypso in Seelie."

CHAPTER 4

CALY

D ON'T," I SNAPPED AT ELI. MY VOICE BOUNCED OFF THE LIME-stone walls of the cave. My feet were blistered and aching, and my mind hardly felt much better. I could barely contain my terrible mood, and his incessant pokes and prods were not being accepted with near as much patience as I would have wished. I was just in so much pain today for some reason.

The fae weakly lifted his palms in surrender from the ground where he lay. "Okay, okay. I just think that maybe you've let the grief of losing your whole family turn into anger. What if your anger is just sadness that had nowhere to go?"

This was just like him to overanalyze the situation, to try to fix it before any violence or death came to pass. I knew he meant well and was really just upset that he had been there with me the whole time as my best friend but had *no idea* the gravity of everything that I had been going through. He couldn't stand for anyone to be unhappy for long, and knowing that his closest friend was about nine shades morally darker than he had thought made him uncomfortable.

"Leave it alone, Aurelius." I made certain to enunciate his full name so he knew I was done. "I'm killing my father *the second* I get into Moirai, and I'm not waiting a minute longer."

This topic seemed to have been eating Eli alive the entire trip but more viciously the closer we got to the end of our journey. This, like all the other times he'd brought it up, was *hardly* an opportune moment to be discussing whether I should kill my father.

"I'm just saying, maybe you should talk to him first, get some closure before you cut his head off, hear his reasoning. Suns, have you always been this…murdery?" he chuckled.

"I was *your* mother's assassin in the human realm. You *know* I've always been this *murdery*, as you put it," I snapped again, not in the mood to talk and feeling rather lethargic. "Leave it alone. You don't understand what I went through—"

"No, you're right. I don't. *Both* of my parents are dead, so I don't get the option of asking them their reasoning for any of their actions." The masseter muscle in his jaw flared as we glared at each other.

Silence took over the cave once again as we let the conversation die.

We were both far too hungry and weak to be having any type of meaningful conversation. I knew he meant well, but how could he not be more on my side about this? He knew what my father had done to my sister.

"Feuhn kai greeyth," he offered from across the dimly lit enclosure of rock.

The familiar saying instantly grounded me and returned my mind to what mattered. "Feuhn kai greeyth," I returned.

No matter what happened between us, no matter how angry or upset one of us got, how severely one of us had messed up, our love and friendship would surpass it and come out on the other side stronger than ever. Our friendship and love were never-ending and would last forever, in all the phases of life or death.

I was hungry, and nothing good ever came of that. All I wanted to do was lie down on the floor of the damp cave, ignore my stomach pangs, close my eyes, and rest for days.

The three of us had barely made it a few miles toward Lake

Sheridon before we had stumbled across a giant, hollowed-out tree a few feet away from a damp and dark cave. Mendax and Eli could hardly walk, but that hadn't stopped them from somehow mustering enough energy to argue about whether we should stay inside the tree or the cave. Eventually the cave won out after it was reluctantly agreed upon by all three of us that we were cold and in desperate need of a fire, which also was thrice agreed upon would be a terrible idea in a tree. Eli finally gave in, and camp was set in the neat-looking cave.

Over our weeks of travel, more often than not, we had been required to sleep outside. None of us minded. Eli and I had actually come to prefer it. All the other times we'd set up camp, we'd fallen into a familiar rhythm as we completed our designated tasks. Mendax would beat the shit out of a tree or whatever it was that he did when he collected our firewood. Eli would use his SunTamer abilities to start a fire, and I would work on cooking whatever random things we had gathered or Mendax had killed.

This time, things were different. Mendax was too weak to grab more than a few thick branches from the sludgy forest ground; Eli was unable to make a fire and instead collapsed somewhat gracefully on the limestone floor the moment we entered. We had no berries, no meat, no stray roots or patcha (it was a category of wild foods the fae often consumed), nothing, and I was *starving*. For some reason, maybe anxiety, as soon as the fight against the sickle was over, I felt sick and weak. I needed to find something to eat. My bones and joints felt like they were starting to fail me, I was so hungry.

Unfortunately, none of us were in any shape to be wandering around the in-between's forest looking for food. I'd managed to find chunks of flint within the limestone that surrounded us, and after collecting the driest kindling I could locate, I shaved off about a nickel's worth of the flint rock before flipping it over and scraping the rock against my blade until yellow sparks flew. It felt like it took an eternity for the damp kindling to catch, but at least it finally had, and we had a fire now. I had *clearly* grown spoiled with Eli's simple point-a-finger-and-shoot method.

Eli tossed his shirts at me—again—and returned to his previous sleeping position on the ground. He refused to take his shirts back after seeing me shake off my hands *one time* while the fire was getting started. The truth was I was freezing, but I didn't want to constantly be the whining, complaining, weak one of the group. Eli knew my little tells too well, and there was no use in hiding it from him.

So I kept laying the shirts over him like a blanket while he was asleep. I was still cold, especially without the cozy shirt of his that always seemed to be warm, but a different type of coldness seeped through my bones and hid inside my heart when his chest was exposed. I couldn't bear to look at the scars covering the tan skin of his chest any longer. Not when the man who created them lay six feet away from him.

I watched both men sleep. The bright moon reflected off the crisp snow and into the opening of the cave, giving just enough light to watch them. Thoughts of each of them swirled inside my skull like a whirlpool as I pondered what life would be like with one of them dead. My analytical mind pulled and stretched at every fact I knew about the tie and the bond.

I didn't want to be tied or bonded to anyone. I couldn't stand the thought of being responsible for anyone else's life but my own, but especially not these two. Growing up, I'd always felt that I wasn't meant to love anything, that if I did, it was guaranteed a grave ending, and this was just further proof—everything I loved died because of me.

The cold, heavy scent of geosmin permeated my senses. The perfume of dead cyanobacteria and actinobacteria microbes filled the cave, giving it that trapped and musty just-rained aroma.

Mendax's long body lay still on the hard ground. I imagined that was what he'd look like if they killed him—perhaps with more blood. My stomach clenched to the point of pain as the thought ripped through me. Already I had believed him to be dead twice. I knew *exactly* how hard it would be, and it scraped the last bits of decency and independence from my hard shell until my entire soul felt like soft underbelly, like it could no longer survive.

I struggled to stand as a sudden tight, intense pain fought to stop the muscles of my legs—like a cramp but worse. What was happening to my body? I began to fall but steadied myself against the rough wall and continued to make my way to Eli so I could cover him with his shirts once more and hope this time he remained asleep. He was and had always been a real friend to me—my only friend—when I had no one. I couldn't begin to imagine myself having any kind of a life without him in it.

I was the one who should die, not them. What did I have to lose? I was nothing.

The cogs of my tired brain began to turn. I needed to form a plan for when we got to Moirai. If I killed my father before we stood trial in front of the Fates, then they would kill me. Which would leave both Mendax and Eli alive.

I squeezed the small vial adorned with white-gold vines that hung like a memory and a noose around my neck. It contained my sister's ashes—at least a teaspoon of them. I never did become an official Seelie royal, so I wouldn't get to see Adrianna in the Elysian Fields and tell her how sorry I was. She was Artemi, and I was still human. Keeping the stolen droplet of her animal gift wasn't enough to change what I was. I would never get to see her and apologize, to tell her that I had *finally* gotten them all back for what they did to her—every last one of them.

Especially him.

Just the thought of being in the same room as my father made me want to rip the flesh from someone's bones. It instantly sent the darkest of my thoughts to the front of my mind—the ones that told me I should end this all, burn the entire world to the ground, and piss on the ashes.

Frustrated beyond all measure, I walked back to my shadowy nook and crouched until my back rested against the rock and I could slide down to the ground. The fire was as full as it was going to get, and I needed to get some sleep as well. The boys said that they only needed a few hours and then they would be healed enough to continue. I hoped for the same magical healing that I had experienced before. I knew they healed fast, but even their estimate seemed like quite the feat that I wasn't sure would happen. Mendax had a hole in his shoulder, and Eli's face and legs were covered in huge gashes from the sickle.

I grabbed my leather pouch and pulled out the cloth-covered scroll that my father had sent me. It was unlike anything I had ever seen, and it somehow made me hate even more that something having to do with him gave me such a sense of wonder. It was some sort of glass that had the ability to be folded and rolled while still maintaining its glossy, cold texture. It was something my fact-based mind couldn't quite wrap itself around.

The words on the scroll were so familiar to me by now, I didn't even bother to skim them. At least a thousand times along this journey, I had scoured the scroll in the hopes of finding clues that might give me an advantage in Moirai once the time came. The note was cryptic, leaving me at a loss for what was actually going to happen once we got there.

Calypso Petranova,

Good day. You have been summoned before the Fates in requisition of Ties and Bonds with breach to laws 14.2 and 370.003.

Failure to appear before the Fates will result in the application of death to all parties forthwith.

Further instructions will be located in the Lake of Sheridon.

On behalf of the Fates,
Zef
a.k.a. Your Father

I rolled up the scroll again and replaced it in my bag before settling closer to the fire. I watched as the orange flames licked and tickled at the dead tree branches, coaxing and caressing the wood until it turned black. Exhaustion overpowered hunger, and soon I was asleep.

When I woke again, I shot up, nerves coursing through me, terrified that Eli and Mendax had left me. My heart pounded so hard, I swear I heard it clicking against my skull.

My neck and shoulders rolled as I took account of how I was feeling—still not normal but significantly better, surprisingly. Food would help, and I needed to get more wood for the fire.

Like little spiders crawling across the hair on the back of my neck, I felt the tickle of someone's attention. I turned to see Mendax sitting up against the cave wall, his sinister eyes fastened on me. How long had he been awake, watching me? Why was it his broodiness always seemed to evoke such a visceral reaction from me?

"You're awake—"

"I'll kill him for you. Your blade will be untouched by his blood." His steely eyes glanced in Eli's direction. Had his shadowed irises not glinted against the reflection of the fire, I wouldn't have known for sure that he watched me from where he was hidden in the shallow depths of the dark cave. The shadows welcomed him as their own, blurring the lines of his body.

"Who will you kill for me?" My voice was thick and raspy, as it so often was when I spoke to Mendax. Was he referring to my father or Eli?

"Everyone."

My shoulder blades trembled as a chill overtook me; awareness of his intensity dug between them like a knife. I knew from experience that he made no false threats and delivered on his words. He would kill everyone for me. Whether it was to hunt me down and find me or because he didn't like them looking at me, one by one, he would kill everyone who existed until it was only us if he wanted to—if *I* wanted him to.

Under his shadowed gaze, I felt like a rabbit that had just caught the notice of a wolf lying in wait with a watering mouth. "And if I said that I wanted you to *never* kill another soul, would you ever kill again?" I asked slowly. The crackle of energy was dark and sensual as it pushed between us and into the bond.

"Yes," he stated without a moment's hesitation. "I am not offering to kill for your ease or desire. I am *threatening* to kill for you. This effort is purely selfish, I assure you. Your wants sit far beneath my need to possess you."

I could almost feel him touching my skin, the tension of the bond was so explosive. "In Moirai, they will choose you to die. We both know they will decide to sever the bond that ties Zef's daughter to evil." I stood, so entranced with this man that I hardly registered the small pains in my body. It was like a live wire was connecting us. "Then what will you do?"

"You assume at the point we enter Moirai, there will be another man to choose from." One corner of his mouth lifted slightly, causing one dimple to appear in his cheek.

The blood drained from my face. "No matter what, promise me you will *not* kill E—" I started.

"No," he cut me off.

"Malum, *please*," I whispered. "Anyone but him. The rest of my life's happiness depends upon it. I'm begging you. Please."

Mendax clenched his jaw and turned toward the cave's darkly lit opening for a moment before his eyes returned to me. I could practically see the anger pouring from his irises. "And what makes you think I care at all about your life's happiness?" he questioned in his deep voice.

"Because I know how much you love me. You forget I can feel you through the bond as well," I replied. "The feelings you send aren't as threatening and dangerous as you would wish me and others to believe." I stared at the ground in front of my foot for a moment, searching for anything that would make him promise. "Please don't kill Aurelius. He saved my life, and now I will save his. Please?" I quietly pleaded.

For a moment, we watched each other in silence. A

40

thousand feelings pushed through the bond from each side in an emotion-filled torrent, each wave stronger than the last.

I broke eye contact first and added the last of our wood to the fire before I slowly took a step toward where Mendax sat with his back against the wall. His long, muscled legs stretched out leisurely in front of him, his hands laced behind his head, highlighting the smooth skin of his arms that peeked out of his black sleeves.

My feet slowly carried me to him. He was like a siren calling to a ship lost at sea—I was powerless against the pull.

I stood in front of him, heaviness pulling my mouth into something like a frown, though not as expressive. I stared and stared, waiting for it all to make sense, but it never would—or perhaps it already did. Mendax and I were cut from the same cloth. We had been spoon-fed our venom and malice from the same ladle. When our enemies tried to rip out our throats, we made certain they choked on it. We became our own demons, so we had nothing to fear.

I think Mendax would have stayed staring at me like that all day. But my eyes snagged on the hole in his shirt, where his wound was now closed with fresh pink skin. I wanted to turn my head and check on Eli, to see if he was awake yet, but my eyes couldn't seem to move from Mendax. My knees ground into the stone floor as I straddled him. When my skin touched his, my eyelids flickered like butterfly wings as I fought against the urge to weep. Instantly, his hands moved to my back, spreading across my tired muscles. A heavy sigh escaped me. I waited for him to grip my neck seductively or press against me and say something deliciously sensual, but he never did.

"I will help you kill your father," he whispered.

My fingertips ghosted along his smooth jawline, feeling the silky roughness of his skin. I pulled back slightly. "I don't need your help killing him. I want to be the one to do it," I said. *No one* would take this away from me.

He nodded in understanding. "You're cold." His eyebrows stitched together with concern while his hands wrapped

41

around me in something of a hug. "I can offer you nothing but coldness," he said and glanced to where Eli slept.

Already, the fake way I held myself together was unfolding from the tenderness of Mendax's hug.

The snow of the in-between did not feel as cold as human snow, but I remained cold and hungry, confused and at a loss for what would soon be happening in my life. I was guaranteed to lose the love of my life in one form or another, and his rough facsimile of a hug had just undone the last of the tired seams that held me together.

"I'm lost," I murmured into the crevice of his neck as a few stray tears welled and spilled over from my eyes. I didn't want to unravel like this, but every flutter of my stomach or touching word the men said left me questioning if it might be one of the last core memories I would have of them. But a large part of me refused to believe one of them was going to die at the end of this.

"Though it feels that way, I promise you'll never be lost ever again. I'll always be following you. No matter what." In that moment, Mendax's eyes looked like the softest cloud-filled blue sky. A sentiment I didn't understand him to be capable of poured through the bond.

I shifted my legs together and tucked myself as far into his chest as our flesh would let me, letting myself feel the comforting beat of his heart. No matter what, I wouldn't let them take either of these men away from me. There had to be another way.

He enveloped me, and for a minute, it almost felt like our skin melted together, we were so close. I felt the expansion of his chest as he inhaled more deeply than normal, then let it out. This could be really awkward if Eli woke to see this. I didn't want either of them to feel bad or be upset, but I didn't want to feel bad either, and this was the only thing my bruised soul cried for.

"How does it feel?" I asked as I grazed the skin around his freshly healed wound. I tipped my chin up so he could hear my whisper. My lips moved against the silky skin, just under the sharp line of his jaw. He let out the softest breath, something so faint, I likely wouldn't have heard it had my ear not been pressed against his throat.

"Our health will eventually regenerate. We will be fine. I am fine. How do you feel?" He moved his mouth so that his pink lips pressed against the space between the corner of my closed eyes and my ear. My pulse began to race.

"Why would you be asking how I feel?" I asked as I shifted myself slightly on his lap.

I was barely keeping my lustful thoughts at bay with our closeness, but when I felt him stiffen beneath me, my thoughts became dazed and filled with urgency. Being in the quiet, dark cave in the middle of a blizzard on what could possibly be our last night together made it disturbingly easy to forget what I should and shouldn't be doing while Eli lay asleep not so far away. I shifted in Mendax's lap again, trying to get control of myself. His strong hand pressed into the curve of my hip, stilling my movement. My head swirled with blurry, incoherent thoughts. I recalled what Eli had said earlier about smelling my arousal and wondered if Mendax had the same talent.

Mendax gripped my face, a gentle hand on each of my cheeks, and kissed me in the most tender, loving way conceivable. Emotions I could never have imagined either of us capable of feeling cascaded through it.

As I let myself fall into the kiss, it felt like a piece of my heart was crying. My eyes dampened as I pressed into him harder. I felt as if I was going to combust from the squall of emotions. Countless times, this fae had brought me to the point of exasperation with lust or anger, but this was different. This was within us, this acceptance that the two of us might not be alive together at the end of all this.

The tender exchange grew feverish. Mendax pulled the leather tie of my pants and tugged the lacing loose. I threw my leg over to straddle his lap again, and as I did so, he slipped his hand inside my pants and slid his palm across my center. As my body came down to rest on him, he pressed two of his thick fingers inside me. My arms wrapped around his neck as I sat on his lap, rolling my hips to feel the length of his fingers hungrily exploring me. My hips rolled harder against his lap while his fingers sped up. The feel of his erection added friction to where it was needed most as I squirmed and wriggled on his lap. The sounds of how wet I was were loud and crude as they swirled in the quiet cavern while he pulled his fingers out of me and ran them over my clit. He pulled the leather tie from the eyelets and continued to place kisses across every sensitive spot on my neck and chest. In the mix of tongues and panting, I felt the hot tip of his bare cock glide down my wetness, parting me only enough to moisten himself and let me feel how steely hard he was.

I lifted myself off him only enough to slide my pants off, and when I restraddled him, his length was free, rigid, and waiting for me. My arms wrapped around his neck, and I kissed him frantically. It felt like I might die if my lips parted from his. With greedy, panting movements, I moved myself over him until the head of his cock slid past the barrier and burrowed deep inside me with one movement. I didn't have the composure for anything less than this. His hungry kisses, still filled with sentiment, lit up my body with sparks that couldn't be doused. He thrust and ground against me with the same primitive, ferocious urgency that our lips clung to the other's with, parting only for bites and tongues. There was no emotion that could ever compare to what I felt in that moment.

Up until now, I had done my best to remain quiet. It had been somewhat easy, as we were so consumed by each other that sights and sounds blurred together in a flurry of ecstasy and need. But my ability to remain quiet quickly concluded as Mendax slowed the pace and pressed inside me as deep as possible.

"I love you," he said breathily.

My orgasm erupted. It felt like an internal explosion of happiness, love, and goodbyes swirled into one act. "I love you," I panted. His thrusting gained speed, and I knew he was close. Coming down from my own orgasm, my senses began to sharpen. Being away from the castle, I had been taking no contraceptive tea or herbs for this situation. Did it even matter? Especially if not all of us would probably be dead soon as it was. "You should pull out. I'm not taking anything," I said through moans as I canted my hips along with him, refusing to let a single second of this be wasted.

"No," he growled as he bit my earlobe.

I inhaled a sharp breath at the sting of pain. My nails dug into the flesh of his shoulders as he moved up and down.

"You are mine in *every* way."

He pulled down the neckline of my shirt and began to bite and suck on my nipple. A moan left my mouth and quickly began to build as another orgasm. Sensing it, Mendax bit just hard enough on my nipple to cause a shot of pain surging straight between my legs. I cried out.

"The second you tighten around my cock, I am going to push every drop of my release into you. You're going to look me in the eyes as your body pulls and works every bit of cum out of me and inside you."

His filthy words were my undoing. My head dropped back as the orgasm threw me over the edge and consumed me. Mendax gently gripped the sides of my face and pulled it back to look him in the eye.

"Yes—uhh," he moaned breathily as he held my face only an inch or so from his. One of his hands moved to my hip and grabbed it in a viselike grip while the other moved down to my neck as he fought to catch his breath with each thrust.

I gripped the wrist of the hand that held my neck and dug my nails in, knowing it would be the last thread before he, too, would be lost to the ecstasy.

"I will never leave you, Calypso, never. Stars—agh." His thrusting slowed, and I felt the throb of his pulsing cock release inside me.

"Oh my suns," I cried out, shocked with how strong this

orgasm was. "Yes—yes—" I bit at his neck and curled my face into his chest as both our climaxes slowed.

Mendax pulled his slick cock out of me but stopped me when I tried to get up. He licked his four fingers and moved them over my sensitive clit before gliding them to my entrance. Immediately, my body bucked at the intensity of his touch, but he stilled me with a firm grip on the hip again. I could feel some of his warm cum dripping out of me.

"You wanted me to pull out, pet?" he said huskily. "That's not ever going to happen again." His four fingers glided over me, and this time, he swiped his fingers over the drips of cum and pushed them back inside me with two fingers. "We are in this together, always. You are mine only, regardless of the Fates' decisions."

I swore and gripped his shoulders, losing my breath all over again at the unbelievably raunchy things he was doing. He knew exactly what parts of me to touch, what to say—everything that lit my body on fire with lust and need. I pushed against his fingers as a shiver took over my body.

"You think I don't want to put my offspring inside you? That I don't want to be tied to you in every way possible?" Another swipe of his fingers as he pushed his cum back, farther inside me. This time, he bit his lower lip and continued to move his fingers in and out, enjoying the close view of me. "Fuck, Caly..." he moaned. It almost seemed as if he was enjoying it as much as me. "You should see how red and wet your pussy is after it's been fucked. Yes, do it, come again for me." He pulled out of me and gave a wet slap to my pussy. Stinging pain gripped my body as every muscle clenched. Mendax made a primal moan and moved his hands to my ass. Within a second, he had me pulled up against his mouth while his palms smoothed and gripped my ass cheeks, working me over with his tongue. The hot, gliding sensation of his tongue was delicious as he nipped and licked my clit.

"Mendax!" I cried out.

He instantly pulled away. "Tell me you'll love me in every lifetime, and I will let you come," he said with a cold smirk.

I moaned breathily, my face felt numb and tingly, and I *needed* to come. It was the easiest command he had ever given me. "In every lifetime, in every realm, in *every* span of time, I will love you endlessly, Malum."

He descended on me like a starved man. Emotion wrecked me, and my eyes welled with tears as the most powerful and overwhelming climax took hold of me, reshaping every corner of my being.

I collapsed on top of him, completely spent and sated. We lay like this for a few moments, just holding each other and looking into each other's eyes before I eventually came back to reality and realized we were not alone and there was no possible way Eli hadn't heard us.

The second I thought of him, awareness filled me, and I knew something was wrong. I sat up to look at the place where Eli had been sleeping.

In Eli's place lay nothing but the crumpled-up shirts that I had covered him with.

He was gone.

CHAPTER 5

CALY

AFTER SCOURING THE LAND THAT SURROUNDED THE CAVE TO no avail, we came to the conclusion that Eli must have woken up and decided to go on ahead to Lake Sheridon. At least that was what Mendax continued to tell me to reassure me. How could I let that happen? How could I be so insensitive and careless to have done that right in front of Eli?

We left the cave after deciding that we would be smartest to meet him at Lake Sheridon, assuming that was where he went. Where else would he go? What must he be thinking right now? How awful that must have felt to wake up and find Mendax and me having sex. His best friend and supposed fiancée fucking his enemy *right* in front of him while he slept. It was bad enough he had already seen Mendax and I together once before, no thanks to faerie mead.

I would never want to hurt Eli in any capacity. I had worked tirelessly since we were little to make sure he never got hurt, and now I was the cause of it.

Loving them both was hard, but trying not to love each of them with harder. My only crumb of hope was in knowing that with the tie, Eli could feel some of what I felt and knew I was helpless in fighting those feelings. Everything with Mendax was that way. I seemed incapable of staying away from him. We were like magnets, and the farther apart you pulled us, the more we needed each other.

My love for Eli was not slight in comparison; on the contrary, *more* parts of me loved Eli. The parts of me that were calm and safe and reliable, they leaned on him. The parts of me that I trusted and that I knew were best for me, those were the parts that loved him. It was just a different kind of love: all-consuming in a comfortable way. I couldn't imagine a life without Eli in it, and I knew more than anything, I didn't want to. He had always been the only one who made me feel safe, the one I knew I could rely on no matter what.

Seeing his handsome and familiar face all grown up after we hadn't physically seen each other for all those years added a bit of attraction into the confusion. I'd always loved him, but after Mendax, I knew I didn't love him in the same way. But I still loved him in a way that I don't think many people ever get to experience.

The reality of what would take place today settled in like the last stage of poisoning: one of them would die tonight, in Moirai, because of me.

Mendax and I trudged on in silence, occasionally stopping to collect mushrooms or snowberries to eat. The snow was thick and silent. It seemed like the forest of the in-between went on forever, and in some aspect, I suppose it did. Several times, I had accidentally gone off course, and Mendax had to correct my direction. Apparently, as well as devastating good looks, fae also had a natural sense of direction that a human like me could only dream about.

Wintery stillness suffocated the icy air as we walked, so much so that a crisp breeze startled me. It lifted and carried a dusting of snow up and into the air and back onto my face. The snow brushed against my already chilled cheeks like bits of sandpaper. I wiped my face with my sleeve—well, Eli's sleeve. Subtle notes of happy citrus remained with me after I pulled the shirt from my nose. Worry filled me. What if he had stepped out of the cave and something had happened to him? What if he hadn't gone ahead?

He didn't deserve any of this—not from his mother, not from Mendax, and most assuredly not from me. He was the best person (besides my sister) that I'd ever met. My mom was wonderful as well, but she had secrets too. Now, more than ever, I was certain of that. Looking back, there were always little idiosyncrasies about her, things that I'd give anything to be able to go back in time and ask her about, like her chest tattoo—an ethereal-looking skeleton holding a ring full of old-fashioned keys. It had never seemed to fit her style, and she had never spoken about it. Of course, there was also the fact that she had two children with a near god and never spoke about him other than to tell us he had left us all behind. No stories, no explanations.

My eyes snagged on a small imprint on the snow.

"Wait!" I shouted at Mendax.

A rounded triangle and four little toe prints depressed in the snow. I nearly screamed with relief. It was no wonder we hadn't seen Eli's size-thirteen footprints breaking up the snow; he had shifted, which, without a shirt, was likely far more comfortable in this weather, even for him. I wrapped my arms around myself and felt the warm fabric of his shirt. He shouldn't have had to travel alone.

He deserved better.

"Eli's tracks," I said with a smile, pointing. "He must've—"

My thoughts were cut off when something moved in the crevice of one of the snowy toeprints.

There was no way that was what I thought it was.

My knees pressed into the snow as I dropped down to get a better look.

"I know your human tracking methods are mysterious, but if you lick that snow, Calypso—"

"It is—it's a glasswing!" I looked at Mendax in disbelief.

The fae's only reaction was to stiffen his jaw and stare at me.

I hadn't seen one of these since Adrianna was alive.

50

I carefully lay down on the snow to get a closer look at the magnificent winged creature. Cozy nostalgia blanketed me as I watched it move its little antennae before fluttering up into the air and away. I sat up and watched as its clear-as-a-windowpane wings carried it off into the snowy distance.

Mendax clasped my hand and pulled me back onto my feet before he helped dust some of the snow off my clothes. Thank god this snow and weather weren't as cold as human snow, or I would probably have frostbite by now. Was that how butterflies could survive in this weather? But wait—

"How can the glasswing butterfly survive in this weather, but the luna moth and monarchs can't?" I questioned Mendax.

He squinted as if I'd offended him. "How should I know? I've never seen one before, at least not that I recall. Also, it's small. My luna moths could easily destroy it."

I stared blankly at him after his masculine response. "The last time I saw one of those, I was with Adrianna, my sister."

"You miss her quite strongly for only seeing her as a child a long time ago," Mendax stated.

I opened my mouth to tear him apart but then stopped myself. Sometimes he was so caring and full of tenderness that I forgot he seemed to lack the ability to feel that way for everyone. "Yes," I replied simply.

"I miss Walter, and I miss my mother."

His confession surprised me. I don't know why. It had always been obvious Walter was a cherished friend, though a part of me doubted he even realized how much until after Walter had died.

"I miss Walter too," I added, reaching out and squeezing his hand. "And unfortunately, you will find you'll miss Walter more as time goes on, not the other way around." I nodded solemnly. "I suppose at least I am human. I will only miss them another forty years, if I'm lucky. You—you will miss them for the rest of your long preternatural life."

"Or perhaps only another few hours," he replied with a grin.

I didn't return it.

CHAPTER 6

CALY

S o Moirai is at Lake Sheridon?" It had been too quiet during our last stretch of forest, and I was asking just to hear Mendax's voice—or wanting the creepy forest to hear his voice. It didn't matter how much time I spent in these faerie realms, I would never get used to it. It was unlike anything in the human world. The magic that radiated made every single thing so full of energy that sometimes it was overwhelming just to be surrounded by all of it.

The farther we walked, the stranger the snowy forest felt. The idea of Eli being out here alone made my insides clench and cramp, though that may have been the snowberries I just ate. What if something happened to him along the way? How would we ever find him? He would have lost his mind if I had gone off on my own.

Awareness drifted to my feet temporarily. My boots were solid and strong, but they hadn't stopped the blisters from forming. My toes were completely numb, whether from trying to keep pace with a six-foot-five fae or from the freezing-cold weather, I wasn't sure.

I had been so much warmer when Eli had been here. His SunTamer magic meant he naturally radiated a significant amount of heat, but I was starting to wonder if something else was going on. Before Eli and Mendax had become injured fighting the sickle, I'd thought the snow hardly felt cold. On top of that, I hadn't had but the smallest ache in my body. Even in places I had been sore for months, I felt great. I would even go so far as to say healed. The bond and tie had been taking it out of me for a while before this journey. The boys had made it abundantly clear that because I was ninety-nine percent human, those magical links would take me out first— that I would begin to feel the effects of the bond and tie, and my health would begin to deteriorate. They had. My body was struggling to heal even the simplest cuts and had begun to break down and hurt. Of course I hadn't mentioned it to anyone though. Why would I?

Then, all of a sudden, one day, it stopped. I felt as healthy as an ox. Not even the normal pain in my leg that always hung around or typical things, like cramps, were gone. (First trick to making an awkward journey? Try to explain human menstruation to two male fae. Spoiler alert: female fae, along with *obnoxiously* good looks and perfect skin, also apparently didn't experience monthly courses.)

I didn't know if it was even possible, but I couldn't help but wonder if one of them had been doing something through our tie or bond somehow.

"Huh?" Mendax grunted, obviously thinking about something else far, far away.

"Moirai. You know, the place where the Fates are. Where the Ascended live with my father? Where you and I will both probably die?" I added sarcastically.

Mendax's blue eyes held mine in a threatening stare that of course made my thighs feel the need to clench. I cleared my throat and tried to hide a grin.

Suns, I was fucked up.

"Lake Sheridon is Lake Sheridon," he stated, sounding a little annoyed.

"The prince of smoke *and* prose, I see. Would you care

to elaborate, oh philosophical one?" I had to look away from him to keep a straight face. He wasn't as used to my sarcasm as Eli. I couldn't see it, but I most definitely felt his sexy, broody, dagger-like scowl on the back of my head.

"Moirai appears. At least that's what they say. Clearly they've not extended me an invitation prior to this, so I wouldn't know. It is an incredibly small group that goes and a significantly smaller one that returns. It is *always* by invitation only, and I've heard tales from the *very* few who have returned that it moves and relocates, appearing only by necessity so as to keep the Fates and the Ascended from harm."

He grabbed ahold of my hand casually as we walked.

Stunned by the simple gesture, my mouth gaped open like a trout as I watched the prince of death and darkness hold my hand like a fourteen-year-old trying out affection for the first time. It felt so...normal.

Mendax squeezed my hand in his, making certain it was in just the position that he wanted, and then continued on as if it was the most natural, common thing in the world.

And it was.

My fish mouth continued to suck in cold air as I stared at our casual connection of flesh. My barely mended heart swelled nearly painfully. I squeezed his palm back and was hit with a depressing wave of sadness. I would have given anything to get to feel this feeling years ago, when I could have relished and marinated in it for a lifetime. Now, I felt like I was counting the minutes we had left together.

I had to figure out a way to get Mendax out of Moirai alive—and Eli. I was the *only* one who should be killed. Others may not see the good in Mendax, but I did, and I would do anything to keep him alive and safe. No one else would die because of me. I wouldn't let that happen.

"Besides." Mendax interrupted my panicked thoughts, bringing me back to the cold, eerie forest. "Moirai isn't going to be at Lake Sheridon."

I pulled back and looked at him as a scowl creased my

forehead. "What do you mean? The scroll says in order to get to Moirai, we have to go to Lake Sheridon."

"It says further instructions will be located at Lake Sheridon." A few minutes later, he broke the silence again. "We should be close… There. See it?" He pointed to a spot just behind a snowy hill in front of us.

All I saw was a field of white with edges of greenish-blue fir trees that were cloaked in snow. I used to love snow, but after this, I doubted I'd ever be able to look at snow the same.

"There," he said again as he moved behind me to point my head in the right direction.

Past the tip of his finger, there was a black patch in the snow tucked into the far-off white mountains, nearly hidden by surrounding trees. It looked like a drowning pool where nightmares went to swim and breed.

"Do—do you think Eli's there?" I asked with a swallow. Why couldn't I have fucking controlled myself around Mendax? Had I stayed on my side of the cave, Eli never would have left. *Suns*, I bet he was so upset with me. Technically we were still engaged, not that it really mattered considering one or all of us may be dead in a few hours, not to mention things had seemed…different between he and I after being together so much on this journey. Not bad, just…different. Things didn't feel romantic, and I couldn't help but wonder—and, dare I say, hope?—that he felt the change too.

"He's there. I can sense his heart beating from here. It's going a mile a minute. There are a few others as well," Mendax said as he closed his eyes and tilted his head ever so slightly to the left.

Well, isn't that a creepy party trick.

"We need to hurry. What if something is happening?" I bellowed after I had taken off running. "Hurry! You can get to him faster than I can. I'll follow in your footprints," I called behind me. Despite my best efforts at being speedy, Mendax was still right behind me.

"No," he stated.

I struggled to keep in front of him, even in a run now. Damn his long legs.

"He is not my friend. I hope he dies," he grumbled.

I couldn't do this anymore.

My steps faltered, and I stared at the ground. Mendax's boot prints in the snow looked harsh and dirty next to the crisp untouched blanket of snow that surrounded them. "I don't care what the two of you have fought about. All because of your *mommies*. I am *so* sick of hearing the threats! The—the scars and threats! Every time I leave the room, you two try to kill each other. You. Can't. Kill. Him!"

"Not yet—" he growled after stopping a few feet ahead.

"Not ever," I snapped. The snow crunched beneath my feet as I took the remaining steps into him until the towering fae was nearly bent over looking at me. "I couldn't protect my mother or Adrianna. Eli is the only person I consider family left alive, and I will *not* fail at protecting him. Do you understand me?" Stubborn tears slid down my cheek, leaving a cold trail on my skin. "I *will* kill you if I have to, Malum, but you will *not* hurt Eli." My eyes pulsed with the threat of more tears, but the cold and bitter stare I kept secured on Mendax held them off.

The Unseelie prince blinked for a moment, processing my words.

The breath was ripped from my chest as his hand latched around my throat and I was shoved back until my back met with the bark of a tall pine tree. I didn't attempt to break the hold—I doubted I could, and frankly, I didn't want to. I enjoyed when Mendax gave me his anger. I understood it. It was something we both spoke fluently.

"You would kill me to keep him alive?" he questioned. The anger on his face creased his forehead and eyes. It was evident everywhere but his voice. His whisper was instead cut with something akin to pain. His grip lightened a fraction, so I broke his hold with my arm, shoving him a step away. He didn't fight it, which made the ache in my chest hurt even more.

"You could never understand," I shouted as I stiffened my

jaw. "I love you both in *very* different ways. I understand that now, but Eli might as well be blood."

My eyes picked out every detail of his handsome face as I waited for what his next reaction would be.

Mendax glanced at his feet for a moment of apparent thoughtfulness before he clenched his jaw and spoke. His words were flat, without hope or spirit—something I'd never picked up on in his voice until now when it was missing. "Well then, I suggest you hurry, because his heart rate implies your damsel is in distress."

"Malum, I—"

"Have you ever noticed you only call me that after you've set out to cut me in one form or another?" he said with a devilish purse of his mouth.

I rolled my eyes. "Come on!" I shouted at him as I took off running. I couldn't think about how much I'd just hurt Mendax right now. Eli needed my help.

The back of my boots slid on the snow with every step, threatening to take me down. It felt deeper and harder to maneuver through than it had minutes before I knew Eli was in trouble. Every simple movement became impossible and too slow. This wintery forest was not made for fast.

"Fuck!" I shouted, almost in tears realizing the short distance I'd reached after having made so much effort. My cold, rosy knuckles cracked when my fists clenched at my sides. I kicked the few inches of snow on the ground in front of me, which did nothing but force bits of snow to tuck into the top of my boot and make my ankle cold. In that second, it felt like the last piece of my will was finally going to break. Eli needed me, and I was failing him, just as I'd failed them. I fought the frustration down and carried on, promising myself it would go smoother if my pace was a tad slower this time.

I lifted my foot to stomp on the snowy forest floor, but instead, my head spun, and I watched the white landscape of snowy branches and ground bounce and sway through a haze of black smoke.

"What the—" I realized Mendax had thrown me over his shoulder, but we were moving way too fast to be walking… and why were we bouncing as we were?

I barely believed my eyes when I turned and looked.

Two giant, translucent beasts made of black smoke bounded through the snow in front of us. Their misty-looking front legs cut through the snow like water. Mendax's lupine creations snarled like demons. They had the features of a wolf but with the build of a horse. Hazy, black smoke shot out in clouds from their nostrils angrily. Mendax lifted two long, thick reins of smoke, cracking them down on the running beasts. The Unseelie prince was pulling us in a black sleigh of smoke.

The trees blurred when we sped past them. Flecks of cold snow kicked up and into my face where I hung down over Mendax's back. As I let my body relax into the dark fae who held me, everything changed. I felt the shift in Mendax and gasped, just as his grip on my body lightened and I fell out of his arms and into a mound of snow and fallen branches.

The creatures of smoke were gone, completely evaporated, as if they never existed at all. Mendax stood, brushing snow from his shoulders with a look that was filled with disappointment, and I knew.

"You're out—you didn't have enough magic to sustain them, did you?" I asked through heaving breath.

Mendax's eyes couldn't hide secrets from me anymore. Cold blue eyes looked through me, completely defeated, and his jaw dropped open as I stood up.

His jaw shifted as he ground his teeth. "I suppose that's why he's your hero, huh? Rescuing never was my thing," he said grimly.

It took a minute, but I managed to stomp through the piles of snow until I reached him. "You've been giving me your powers, haven't you? Through the bond?" I swore as all the pieces fell together. "And now look what you've done!" I shouted. "You've completely depleted yourself just before— suns only knows what! Why would you give me your power?"

Fear appeared like a prowler inside my head. "Am I that bad off? Have the bond and tie really done that much to destroy me already? That's why I have been in so much pain off and on."

"You are a hum—" he began.

"I fucking know!" I shrieked, having fully lost any remaining composure. "I fucking know!" I turned around in a circle, completely exasperated and unsure of what to do to fix this. "Has Eli been doing it too, through the tie?" I asked, thinking more about the little signs I had so obtusely missed.

"I'm fairly certain of it, though it's been unspoken between us," he said, his voice remaining stiff and as cold as the icicles in the pine branches.

For a moment, we stared at each other.

I felt the click of my jaw as it tightened. "It doesn't matter how good you are at rescuing, because I've never been one to want to be saved," I reminded him.

With a nod of silent acknowledgment, we pushed forward.

CHAPTER 7

CALY

F OGGY GRAY MIST ROSE FROM THE FROZEN BLACK WATER OF Lake Sheridon. It drifted up into the air like dead souls that'd finally escaped their confines.

The air around the lake loomed with ruination and an uncomfortable feeling of emptiness, just like the rest of the in-between. There was no wind to make a sound. It felt like even the trees were afraid of waking anything in this eerie, unwelcoming area.

My eyes easily found the only ray of sunshine in the vicinity—Eli sat on a fallen log on the lakeshore.

I had expected to find him in some type of wild battle, flanked by thousands of horrifying monsters, from the way Mendax had described the racing of Eli's heart.

Mendax must have thought so too, because we shared a look of confusion as we trudged closer to the blond fae. Something wasn't adding up, and it made the hairs on my arms rise.

Eli, no doubt having heard our heavy footfalls, turned around to face us. His eyes passed over Mendax and landed on me with a look of profound disappointment.

Immediately I recalled the reason Eli had left the cave, and I fought off a wave of embarrassment and shame. But all anxieties about anything else left my head when I saw what he held.

"What did you do?" I screamed before launching myself at him.

Eli's look of disappointment turned ashamed as he held his hands up in the air; the broken pieces of glass shifted in his palm with a tinkling noise that echoed through the large expanse.

"The scroll was broken when I got here."

"Now wait a just tick, sunshine. The post of lying, conniving bastard for this group has already been taken," Mendax stated. "You were pissed off when you woke up and found your—as *you* call her—fiancée wrapped around my cock like a cobweb. So you left, beat us to the next clue from Zef, and broke it like the *whiny*, jealous bitch that you are."

Eli glowered at Mendax, and a jolt of magic rippled through me. I could physically feel the hate from each of them clashing through the bond and the tie like an electric shock. I had to bite my cheek not to cry out.

I took note of all the lines under my friend's tired eyes. I trusted Eli. What reason would he have for sabotaging our journey into Moirai? He wanted the bond broken as much as Mendax wanted the tie between Eli and I severed.

"It—it just seems odd—" I tried to reason with him.

Eli took the last step that separated us and reached out to lightly brush a stray hair away from my face. His brows pinched together over his weary eyes. "I know it sounds like I'm lying, but I swear to you, Calypso. I found it shattered here on the ground."

I glanced around the area, listening for anything that might help me understand this situation. None of it made any sense though. Who would have broken it? No one was here but us.

"That falcon delivered us the scroll last time," I stated, trying to piece it all together. It seemed unlikely that they would just leave the scroll sitting out in the open for anyone to see or grab.

"I was just looking for the rest of the pieces when you guys arrived. If they are big enough, we'll be able to piece them together and still see what it says," Eli said softly.

I could see the hurt lacing his features this close. It always took me by surprise how different he looked when he wasn't smiling. It made me realize how infrequently that actually happened. His grin fit him more than anything else ever could. He was meant to be happy and smiling, and when he wasn't, his sunshiny demeanor and aura felt wrong, as if the world had split in two.

I knew he was telling me the truth. He could never lie to me without me knowing.

"Well, then—" I began but faltered as flashes of "Earl" and the forest in Michigan popped into my head. Eli had lied to me before, and I'd had no clue. Maybe I wouldn't know if he was lying? I cleared my throat and started again. "Well, then let's find the other pieces." My eyes caught on the glimmer of glass he'd missed next to his feet. I bent down and grabbed ahold of the pieces before he could step on them.

My breath hitched as the thin pieces cracked in my palm. These weren't shards of glass in my hand—they were frozen glasswing butterflies.

"Why would these be out here? They obviously aren't from here. They are all frozen and dead." My eyes darted between the two faeries. The luna moths and monarch butterflies that typically followed the two of them had withered away to nothing as we'd walked through the in-between. "This doesn't make any sense." I glanced back to Mendax. "These glasswings belong to something, and if Eli is telling the truth, then it seems as if that something is trying to stop us from getting into Moirai."

"He already knows where all the pieces are," Mendax accused.

My head snapped to Eli. "Well? Where are the rest of the pieces?"

My best friend's eyes fell, and I knew whatever he was going to say next was going to be bad.

He said no words and instead pointed his limp arm toward the black water of the lake.

There, on the ice, about a hundred feet from the bank, lay a limp black falcon and the other chunk of the glass scroll.

"Oh my suns," I whispered as my mouth fell open.

"Yes, I'd say somebody definitely does not want us in Moirai," Mendax added.

"But how? There have been no other tracks. We would have heard something between the three of us, right?" I asked, completely puzzled.

Mendax shrugged before walking to the edge of the lake to look out at the scene.

"I am the lightest. I'll go out and grab the rest of the scroll—" My words and footsteps onto the ice were abruptly halted when Eli whipped me away from the edge.

"No!" he scolded. "Watch." After setting me down, he turned to Mendax and held out his hand. "Give me your boot."

Mendax looked to his left and then behind himself. "Excuse me?"

"Give me your boot," Eli repeated, wiggling his fingers impatiently.

"I'm not giving you my boot," Mendax snapped.

"Fine. Then give me your chest plate," Eli said.

Mendax scrunched his face in a deep scowl as he took a few steps back. "Use *your* chest plate."

The cold stung my wool-covered toes as I shoved my boot into Eli's hand. It was his turn to scowl at me as he gently shoved the boot back at me. "What are you doing? You're going to get your foot all wet! Put your boot back on." Eli grimaced and turned back to poke Mendax roughly in the chest with an accusing finger. "You made her foot get wet. Stop fuckin' around, and give me your chest plate. You'll get it back in a minute."

"*She* made her foot get cold when *she* took her own shoe off." Mendax rolled his eyes but finally acquiesced and slid off his black chest plate from where it hung off the back of his belt and hurled it at a waiting Eli.

Eli walked to the edge of the lake, twisted his body, and

whipped the armor onto the frozen lake where it slid to a stop amid the flaky snow that dusted the top of the ice.

"You piece of shit," Mendax declared.

Eli held up his hand to silence the other fae as he stared out onto the still lake with a blank expression.

Mendax and I exchanged looks.

I was about to ask if Eli had fallen on his head when a grayish-white shape moved in the black water of the lake and slammed into the underside of the ice so hard, I felt the vibrations rise up my ankles where I stood on the bank.

Eli caught my eye with a soft nod, silently urging me to keep watching.

Several more slams sounded from underneath the ice, moving across the entire lake and rattling me even more. Apparently there were several things in the lake, and they sounded quite pissed off at the chest plate. How were we ever going to get the piece of scroll if we couldn't get across the ice?

"Kelpie?" Mendax asked Eli.

"I don't think so. I saw hands," he replied. "Being that we are in the in-between, there is no telling what that creature could be. It's more likely we've never even heard of its existence."

The lake fell quiet again as the creatures stilled and the murky forms moved out of our view.

"Oh my suns," I repeated.

"I tried to get the scroll already. I think they can smell our flesh or something. I was two steps out, and the ice started to creak like it was going to break. One of those things was trying to bite through the ice to get to me. I was trying to figure out how to get out there and get the rest of the scroll, but then you two showed up," Eli said.

"So you throw my chest piece to demonstrate?" Mendax glared at Eli.

"You thought I was going to let Cal go on that to get her boot? Get out there, and get that armor, Smoke-Show. Hey, while you're out there, why don't you go ahead and grab that piece of scroll?" Eli goaded. "I'd move fast if I were you."

"I'm the lightest—" I interjected, interrupting a staring contest between the two men.

"No," they said in unison.

I flinched. "Agh, stop doing that!"

"Save the day, hero. Fly your golden ass out there. Get the fucking scroll *and* my armor," Mendax growled.

A muscle flared in Eli's sharp jaw, and I think I heard a tooth crack.

"As you already know, I don't have enough power right now to fly. I need more time to heal." His gaze flickered to mine briefly.

"Because of me." My voice cracked.

Eli's eyes snapped up to mine. He began to shake his head to argue but stopped.

"You've been sending me enough through the tie to keep me from feeling any pain, enough to keep me healthy. Mendax has been doing the same through our bond."

Eli slammed his fist into Mendax's face before the dark prince even had a chance to flinch. "You son of a bitch!" the Seelie cursed.

Mendax grinned, eyes darkening as he wiped the black smudge of blood from his cheek.

"Knock it off!" I shouted, stepping between the two men.

"You've been sending powers through the bond, you piece of shit. And then you tell her? How do you think that makes her feel?" Eli tried to move me aside to get at Mendax again, but I blocked him in a weird hug-like move.

"I don't understand. Wouldn't it be more helpful if you both were sending me stuff through the bond? It would use less of each of your powers that way?" I asked.

Mendax chuckled under his breath behind me, and Eli's face heated, turning a shade of rosy pink.

"Just like you can't be bonded and tied to one person, you can't accept things from the bonds and ties from more than one person. It's too dangerous. He could have killed you," Eli snapped as he pushed around me and shoved Mendax hard in the chest.

"Stop!" I shouted.

Mendax smiled darkly. "You think she's going to die from too much healing in her mortal veins? I knew what I was doing."

"This is exactly what I'm talking about!" Eli shouted in Mendax's face. "You don't really care about her, or you wouldn't have even risked it. You didn't know how much power I was giving her! And fucking her in the cave? Had to do it so that I saw? That's exactly what you're after. Tell me, do you just sit around all day and come up with ways to hurt her and get back at me? You are going to die in Moirai, because you're the shittiest one out of all of us. The Fates know who truly cares about her. You won't be able to lie to them like you do her."

"You know *nothing* about what you speak of, Seelie. She was clearly on top, fucking me," Mendax replied with a devilish grin.

"That's it. I'm gonna kill him, Cal," returned Eli. "Cal?"

The ground trembled as the eerie thuds rang out, echoing around my feet on the frozen lake.

I barely heard Mendax's and Eli's cursing while I walked as fast as I could across the slippery ice, trying not to look down at the monsters that waited below. Both men were shouting at me, but I couldn't let myself listen. I needed to focus on the piece of scroll, glinting against the white dusting of snow scattered across the black lake like beacons.

"Fu—ah!" The hard slam under my feet caused me to slip. I caught myself before I fell, but my eyes made contact with the grayish-white thing beneath the ice.

It was ghastly looking. Its skin almost reminded me of the smooth texture and color of a beluga whale, except unlike the beluga whale, its upper body was similar in shape to a human with long arms and hands, but that was where the comparison ended. I couldn't really tell what was beneath its torso, as its

66

upper half was the only part visible as it pressed violently against the other side of the ice. Its pale-gray head pressed against the frozen water before pulling it back and slamming into the hard surface again. There was no face or hair, no ears—nothing on the smooth, murky face but a mouth full of long, spiral teeth.

I caught the scream in my mouth and moved a few steps, trying to get away from its hideous body. It was directly under me.

"Oh my, ooh my fuck." The terrifying thing sped under me again as I moved, rattling my senses. Another slam into the ice, then another. There were at least four around me. They had me surrounded under the water. "Okay," I said, trying to calm myself. "Only a few more feet. Then I'll have the key to Moirai. To killing my father." I let my eyes fall closed at the comforting thought, breathed out slowly, and continued walking. It was too slippery for me to move much faster, but I tried anyway, desperate to get the scroll and get off the lake.

Slam. I hit the ice with my face.

Immediately, one of the creature's faceless figures was under mine. All that separated us was a sheet of clear ice—probably not as thick as I'd like. This close, I could hear the muffled scream of the creature in the water. I scrambled to all fours, struggling to get my footing.

Slam. Slam.

They were hitting the ice together. They were working as a team now to break the ice.

A crunch sounded, and I looked to the right in horror. The ice was cracking about ten feet behind me. Panicked, I looked to the shoreline where Eli and Mendax were shouting, but my adrenaline was too loud, and I couldn't hear what they were saying with the sound of blood rushing in my ears.

I scrambled to my feet and took off at a shuffling run, barely lifting my feet off the ice. If I didn't hurry, they were going to shatter the ice. If I fell again, I could crack the ice and fall right through.

Eli. That meant he would die too.

With renewed fight, I slid as steadily as I was capable against the textured surface, occasionally pushing dustings of loose white snow. I could see the letters etched into the glass of the scroll, I was so close now. Mendax's black armor lay only a few feet to the right.

Slam. Slam. Slam.

The hits from under the ice were harder now. The ice behind me crackled and broke. Black water began to spill over the cracks and onto the surface as a clear triangular sheet broke apart and was swallowed by the black water.

My heart was beating painfully hard now. I was gasping for air. I clawed at the ice with my hands, pulling myself to the scroll and the dead falcon as I felt the shivers of breaking ice settle in my bones. Shimmers of light moved across the small area.

Glasswing butterflies littered the area, some still flapping their crystal-clear wings.

The outstretched tips of my fingers touched the broken glass of the scroll. It slid against the ice, now a few inches farther away. The black bird lay completely still in a lifeless heap of blue-black feathers.

Icy water sloshed behind me, leaching through the fabric of my pants as more ice broke behind me. I struggled forward, finally able to grip the scroll, trying not to break it any more than it already was in my panic.

A scream shot into the air, so shrill and grating to the senses that I dropped the glass scroll, my hands slapping over my ears, trying to block out the painful sound. Behind me, the ice had cracked, and a wave of murky, black water rocked and peaked behind me. I wouldn't be able to go back. I was trapped now and had no choice but to cross to the other side.

Another shrill scream from the open water shook me to my core, pushing out any other thought but the horrific vibration of that sound.

I reached down and grabbed the piece of glass. I wouldn't let these...these...*things* stop me from getting to my father.

"Calypso!" Deep shouts came from behind me.

Movement snagged my attention. My own shrill scream let loose at the sight of the faceless creature as I watched it pull itself up and onto the ice. Its sickly colored skin made my stomach twist as the scarce contents inside rose up my throat, but it was nothing in comparison to the sight of its twisted ivory teeth when it let out another scream. It stretched its long, humanlike arms and hands across the ice, digging its translucent claws in and pulling the rest of its disgusting body toward me, teeth flashing with each movement it made. Dents and rivets of bone and skeleton showed under its rubbery milky-gray skin with a creepy tail that hung like loose, dead flesh.

Another one leapt onto the ice behind it, and they both began sliding toward me, quickly gaining speed.

Suns! I would never be able to reach the other side in time.

I grabbed ahold of Mendax's armor and slid it on. The smell of him still clung to the hunk of smooth metal. I moved diagonally, seeing that more powdery snow covered the ice in that direction. It would give me more traction.

A scream tore from my lungs when I felt the inhuman pressure and muscles of the lake creature's hand wrap around my ankle and pull me down.

The stench of rotten, stagnant water laced with rotten meat and fruit, with undertones of decaying flesh, curled into my nose. I kicked at its face, but with no eyes or even a nose, my boot only slipped off its featureless flesh. It tugged roughly at my ankle and began dragging me back toward the opening in the ice. It was going to pull me in. I would be lost forever.

More screams cut through the air as the creatures' shrieks grew stronger and more frenzied with every crack in the ice. The lake vibrated beneath me as they went frantic, pounding the other side as their friend dragged me toward the black, sloshing hole of water.

The awful thing stiffened and froze just before the opening, suddenly dropping my ankle as it glided as fast as it could behind me. The other creature followed.

Slam. Slam. Slam! Slam! Slam!

Now the hits were coming from my left. More screams.

Still holding the piece of scroll, I glanced to see which side of the lake was still intact and the shortest distance to the shore when I saw the cause of their recent frenzy.

Eli was behind me on the ice, just in front of the bank, taunting the creatures, while Mendax was to my right, moving out toward me.

They were distracting them.

I needed to go diagonally, where none of them were. It was the longest route, but there were no cracks in that direction, and I had a chance at pulling the creatures away from the guys so they could get back to the shoreline safely. I would need to move quickly though—quicker than all of them, as two were still on the surface, headed straight for Eli.

I had an idea, but it was either going to be the dumbest thing I could do or the most efficient.

"Fuck me," I grunted as I tried to pick up speed while keeping my footing.

Ice is slippery because there is a thin layer of liquid on the surface. The pressure applied to the ice by the weight of someone standing on it lowers the melting point of the ice, making it *incredibly* slippery. I needed to find a way to increase my surface area so I could lower the applied pressure, therefore increasing the friction, which would in turn make the ice melt even more, making it even more slippery.

I held my breath and did a belly flop onto the snow, hoping I had been moving fast enough. My neck pinched and strained as I struggled to keep my head as far away from the ice as possible.

Slam! Slam! Slam!

It was working. The creatures sensed more mass in this direction, with my full body on the ice in comparison to the feet of the boys. Mendax's smooth chest plate worked as a sort of pseudo sled. I tucked my legs in tight to my body as I climbed on top of the giant fae's armor and had a bit of room to spare.

I slowed to a stop on the ice, still a good twenty feet from the snowy bank of safety.

Hideous, faceless heads cracked against the ice beneath me. There had to be at least fifteen. Trembling, I stood in a fluster and struggled to take steps as every muscle in my body was taut with panic that I would fall as the ice cracked, and I'd be lost to their long, sharp teeth. With so many under me and the ice already cracking, I had seconds before I was lost.

"Come on, sweetie. You've got this!"

Eli was moving onto the ice right in front of me. My blood turned as cold as the ice I stood upon.

"Go! Get back! You're too heavy!" I shouted. It didn't matter. I knew Eli would never let me die out here alone.

No matter what he had seen in the cave, Eli and I had something that ran deeper than any tie. We had been raised with it; it had grown in our bones deeper than any anger or magic ever could.

I sped up and repeated my belly flop, sliding across the expanse like a penguin until I was almost to Eli.

"Move! You have to move! Go to the bank, or it will be too much weight on the ice!" I shouted, though who knew what it sounded like with my neck strained as it was.

I needed to locate Mendax. He was bigger than Eli, and if he decided to move onto this section of ice, we would all be dead in the water.

"Come on! That's it," Eli calmly encouraged as he held out his arms.

I finally reached him. Now only a few feet left to go—

But instead of picking me up off the ice and running us off the lake, Eli put his foot onto the back edge of the armor and shoved me toward the bank.

"Wha—come on!" I yelled, unsure of what he was doing.

It was more than enough to propel me to the bank, where Mendax appeared out of nowhere with waiting arms to pull me up and away from the edge with a fervency that contradicted his stoic demeanor.

Panicked, my eyes shot to the ice. I looked out at my best friend—and yet again my hero—as he shuffled across the ice, his amber eyes full of determination and locked on me. Not an ounce of fear radiated through the tie as the ice trembled and cracked around him.

He really was a hero. In every sense of the word.

"Stay," Mendax ordered, squeezing my shoulders.

He walked to the ice, and my stomach flipped and plummeted. What the hell?!

The humungous fae took a few steps out onto the ice carefully and extended his hand to Eli. "Get the fuck off the ice, you golden sack of shit."

Well…at least he was still helping him.

Eli scowled, moving gracefully over the holes and cracks in the ice, reminding me of his fox. Even with his litheness, he was running out of places to leap that weren't littered with the snapping teeth and grabbing hands of the voracious lake creatures.

I'm not sure if Mendax grabbed Eli or the other way around, but when they made contact, Mendax flung him like a Frisbee off the ice and into a bank of snow, burying Eli's head completely in the white powder. I let out a stale lungful of breath and finally relaxed into the snow.

Mendax walked over to me and stopped, his dark figure looming over me as his eyes hooked to mine.

"Thank you," I whispered.

He continued to stare at me, a harsh look.

No one will ever take you from me in any form. That includes by dying on the other side of the tie. Don't mistake my actions, pet. Aurelius dies the minute the Fates sever the tie. Should they break our bond and kill me, I will gut Aurelius with pleasure, knowing you will accompany me to Tartarus.

I shivered, feeling Mendax's voice through the bond and inside me.

Even though it's against my wishes? I pushed back. *Do you really want a partner or a captive pet?*

A smirk darkened his features.

I want to crawl inside you and consume my way out, knowing that every part of you is forever a part of me. I crave command over every thought you've ever had, to feel every worthless surface that has ever touched your skin. I want your needs and cravings buried so inside my own flesh and bones, they become indistinguishable from my own. That's what I want, pet.

"Do you still have the scroll?" Eli interrupted as he moved to sit on the snowy ground next to me and put his arm around me.

Mendax let out a deep, chest-reverberating growl.

"Shut up," Eli snapped and squeezed me tight before leaning back to look me over. "Are you all right? Suns, you scared the piss out of me, Cal."

I nodded as I took in the contrasting appearances of the men in front of me. The realization of exactly how much they each meant to me stung my eyes. I doubt anyone in the world was lucky enough to have something so powerful and deep between themselves and even one soul, but to have it with two...

"We can't go to Moirai. I don't want to go anymore." I struggled to speak over the lump in my throat that seemed to be cutting off my oxygen as well. I grasped Adrianna's ashes as they dangled from my neck. The V-shaped scar on my thumb methodically ran back and forth over the metal vines on the pendant. Getting vengeance for my mother and sister—getting to Moirai and killing my father for what he had done to them— meant *everything* to me; it was all-consuming.

Until this exact moment.

The men shared a look before Eli turned my shoulders to face him and gently took Adrianna's pendant in his hand. He whispered a respectful "Feuhn kai greeyth" before dropping my pendant. "Cal...we don't have a choice. The strain of the bond and tie are killing all of us now—slowly but definitively." He brushed the hair behind my ear, ignoring Mendax's hum of disapproval. "It's already gone too far. Even if you decide not to kill Zef, which I don't think you should, it's inevitable. We have to go to trial in front of the Fates."

"No." I couldn't stand to hear him speak the words right now.

"At the end of this journey, Mendax or I will no longer exist." Eli looked away, trying to hide his own emotions.

"I personally can't wait to watch them kill you." Mendax's gravelly voice broke the gentle curtain of emotions that hung in the air. "Keep your paws to yourself, or I'll detach them." He collected the piece of glass, keeping an unsettling stare on Eli, before he started to walk to the other side of the lake, where the rest of the pieces of the scroll remained.

Eli moved to follow, but I grabbed his forearm, keeping him next to me. Mendax continued walking, a black drop of ink leaking across the pale snow.

"Cal, if this is about—"

"I'm so sorry." I cut him off. "The thought that I've hurt you—"

He put his hand on my thigh, and I swear I heard Mendax's protest in my head.

"*I'm* so sorry," he returned.

Any words I'd prepared to say dropped from my mind. My brows tugged together, not understanding why he apologized. I shook my head to stop his nonsense, but he continued.

"I—I just missed you so much, and I was so worried about you being in Seelie for the first time unprotected. It all happened so fast. Then my mother was pressuring us to marry, and I thought about it. I thought about how much I hated being away from you and how much I love you, how happy I would be to see you every single day, and, well, I guess I just didn't understand. You are beautiful, and I have never been that interested in another woman, so I just..." Eli rambled on.

"I missed you too. Eli, none of this is your fault. You saved my life and put yours in a constant state of risk by doing so. If anyone is sorry, it's me," I said. "I let a childhood crush get out of control."

"I'm sorry I didn't see you and Mendax for what you were before," he choked out.

"What—"

"He loves you," he stated as he turned and looked out at the dark figure across the lake. "In a way that I am incapable of."

Like a broken bobblehead doll, I just nodded, unable to figure out what it was I really wanted to say.

"You and I are not supposed to be together in that way. Be honest with me, Cal: we both feel it. What you and I have is a soul-tied friendship. We've been through things most family members don't go through together, and we are both insanely good-looking. Of course we were going to get a little confused after not seeing each other for so long," he said with one of his ridiculously charming winks.

I let out a soft sigh. It felt like a thousand pounds had been suddenly removed from my shoulders. "You're right," I mumbled, realizing just how much sense his words made. "We were destined to be together in some way. I guess neither one of us cared what shape our relationship was in as long as we were going to be together."

"Mendax will never ever experience the friendship you and I have...but we will never have what you and he do. When I woke up in the cave, I watched you two—"

"Eli, oh my suns," I said, feeling my face heat.

"No," he chuckled. "I left when clothes started coming off, but before that, I saw how he looked at you and, more importantly, how you looked at him. Through the tie, I *felt* what you feel for him. I saw the man I've fought a thousand times, the man I would consider worse than *any* monster alive, turn gentle and kind, even vulnerable, with you." He let out a soft chuckle as he looked at Mendax. "He's swearing at me right now for sitting so close to you. I can hear him from across the lake." He shook his head slowly as a smile pulled at the creases of his eyes. "What I'm trying to say, Cal, is you are family to me, and nothing and no one will *ever* change that. If I had the choice, I'd tie my life to yours all over again, but our life together is as friends. We both know that."

"Are you breaking up with me?" I snorted, unable to hide

the relief I felt. I had realized a lot of things when I was in the cave with Mendax. No one would ever compare to Eli in my eyes—*no one*. He was there for me more than my own parents were. He was my only ray of sunshine when my world was draped in gray skies and devastation. Even now, he was my beacon of light, the warm glow of the candle's flame that enveloped me in comfort and safety when bleak horrors threatened to suffocate me.

"No, because we never had anything to break, and what we do have is unbreakable." He smiled his usual warm, comforting smile. The one that made my insides feel cozy and at home.

"Feuhn kai greeyth," I whispered, and then with a laugh, "even though I am but a lowly human."

His shoulders relaxed at my words, and his eyes sparkled. "I dub thee with all my unofficial powers a true Seelie now, never again labeled as a lowly human," he laughed. "And it will always be true, Cal. Our love and friendship *are* eternal. No matter what. I need you to remember that, especially with everything we are walking into."

His serious words rattled me, bringing me back to the situation. It was amazing how comfortable he could make me feel sometimes.

"And *just* between you and I, Smoke-Show is starting to grow on me. I think you might be right about him. Maybe my dream of peace between the Seelie and Unseelie realms isn't so far away after all."

"Yeah, maybe," I replied, in awe of my friend's golden heart. "Except he's still planning to kill you as soon as the tie severs."

He rolled his eyes. "He won't admit it, but he's starting to like me too. Hey, do me a favor," he said as we stood to leave. "Don't tell Mendax we don't feel like *that* about each other. Not yet anyway."

The boyish, mischievous look in his warm amber eyes told me all I needed to know. He was about to mercilessly antagonize Mendax.

We walked to where Mendax was and saw that he had laid

out the glass pieces. Just as with the other scroll from my father, this one looked and felt exactly like normal glass with the exception of how malleable the material was, reminding me more of hot plastic except for the fact that it broke and cracked off when you manipulated it too quickly. As a scientist, I struggled to wrap my mind around it. Large chunks were missing, and it was impossible to read with all the cracks and chips.

"Mendax, show me the bottom of your boot," Eli said wearily.

"I'd be happy to," the dark fae growled menacingly.

Eli rolled his eyes so hard, they almost closed. "I need to see the track. Look at this," he said, pointing to a few odd-looking footprints.

Mendax lifted his boot alongside Eli's. The tracks were much smaller with no details in the steps other than the outline.

"Someone is definitely attempting to stop the three of us from finding Moirai," Mendax said with a laugh.

I didn't think it was funny at all.

"Who would be trying to stop us? How would anyone even know where we're going? How did we miss them following us?" I asked, growing more irritated by the minute.

"We didn't see them following us because I think we are following them," Mendax said.

"Who all did you tell that you were going to kill Zef? He is the Artemi Titan. I imagine he has somewhat of a rather powerful range of admirers," Eli said.

"Look," I said, pointing to the ground around the markings. "Glasswing butterflies—more of them. Whatever attracts these butterflies most definitely is who or what is trying to stop us. They were all over the falcon on the ice as well."

We moved away from the footprints, all a little more confused now than before.

I put handfuls of snow over the shards and chunks of the scroll and asked Eli to heat it up. I felt how hard it was for him to call even a small amount of power, but the water blurred the cracks and chips, making it a little easier to read.

Calypso Petranova,

Salutations and so on. Presumably, if you are reading this, you have made it past the benthyc of Lake Sheridon.

For further directions to Moirai, continue onward to the weathered. Coax her into initiating the flood, and further instructions will find you.

The Fates

CHAPTER 8

CALY

W E WON'T MAKE IT." MENDAX SPOKE SHARPLY AFTER WE HAD made our way to the first large slant of mountain. "Perhaps their plans of killing us are simply to cause us to expire through our attempts at finding this miserable place."

The Unseelie prince had been in a mood ever since we'd left Lake Sheridon. I couldn't say as I felt much different. Who would go through with all this? Why the macabre scavenger hunt before they murdered one of us?

"Can the Fates be killed?" I asked Mendax as we trudged through the sharp rocks.

"Calypso!" Eli gasped. "They are the deciders of everything. You do not want to piss them off. They know everything that is going to happen."

I rolled my eyes. "Then they already know I'm planning to rip out my father's throat, and now I'm thinking about how I could hang them with it."

Mendax let out a deep rumble of a laugh. My chest bloomed with sudden warmth. It felt so good being the one to cause his rare laugh.

Eli caught my not-so-discreet smile and rolled his eyes to the back of his head. "You two are so fucked up," he teased.

"How do we know how to get to the weathered?" I asked as my foot settled on the ledge of the rock. Eli had suggested we follow our instincts to get to the weathered since we had been given no directions. Somehow along the way, Eli had developed this all-encompassing faith in the Fates, speaking about them as though he trusted them with his life. I suppose for a fae, it must have been a big deal to get a letter from the Fates. They were more infamous than most of the gods.

"My feet are sopping wet and frigid, and my boots are blocks of ice," I complained. I was *so* tired of walking, and if I never saw another flake of fucking snow again, I'd be the happiest woman alive.

"How big is your foot?" Mendax asked.

Eli's head snapped to me as he pointed at the other fae, mouthing, *Likes ogre feet.*

I smiled and tried to stifle my snort as Mendax looked at us. It felt like a father suspecting his unruly children of stealing cookies.

"Why do you ask? Are you going to cobble me a new pair of boots atop the mountain, my love?" I nearly choked on my words, meaning them to be silly. I had not meant to say the last part.

Mendax smiled victoriously and looked at Eli. Why had I said that? I shrugged it away. I supposed the only reason for it to truly be inappropriate had already been settled with Eli back at the lake.

A soft breeze removed some of the snow that dusted our path, revealing more of the sparkling quartz of the mountain. It was unlike anything I had ever seen. The ice was almost indecipherable from chunks of clear crystal that stuck out from the granite of the mountain we traversed. Little bits of amethyst mixed in with the ice and quartz, sparkling in the small patches of sun that were visible through the dappling of snow that clung to the tight, winding ledge of the mountain. It was still nowhere near as cold as snow and winter were in the human realm, but it was cold nonetheless, and we had been out here for what felt like ages.

"No, my love," Mendax said. "I was going to offer you *Aurelius's* boots. They are no doubt smaller and daintier than mine. Much more likely to fit you."

"And then what would I wear?" Eli asked with a broad grin.

Mendax looked at Eli, his features blanketed with disgust. "I don't care if your feet freeze into stumps. I find it foolish that you think I care what happens to your feet at all."

Eli winked at him, and I pushed to the front, tired of hearing the two of them.

The boys had explained that "the weathered" was the keeper of—you guessed it—the weather.

"So this one person controls all the weather?" I asked.

"Not that much is known of the weathered other than that they are responsible for the weather in all the realms," said Eli.

"How much farther are we going to go?" I questioned. Every one of us was beginning to struggle more. Neither of the men had much power left, and I could see that it was physically starting to take a toll on each of them.

"How should I know? I've never been here," grumbled Eli. Even the good-tempered Seelie's attitude had begun to sour with fatigue.

"Then of all the excursions for us to attempt to find the weathered, why was a mountain the first?" I snapped but immediately felt bad for taking my exhaustion out on him.

The path we were on seemed to spiral around the mountain, gaining in altitude with each pass. We continued in silence. My own mind swirled with questions about how we would know we'd found the so-called weathered.

The higher up the mountain we trekked, the crisper and more pleasant the air was to breathe in. The skies had lost most of the gray, and the glittering mountain gave us a beautiful view of the forest and lake below—deceptively beautiful looking down on it, as opposed to being in it.

By now, Mendax had moved to the front of our little ensemble, as he had a tendency to do. His broad shoulders moved like a wall in front of me. Eli was behind me, giving me small nudges when I slowed down too much or stopped to look at the view for too long.

All the fresh air had gone straight to my head as my thoughts began to clear.

If one of us had to die, then it would be me.

They were likely going to kill me after I beheaded my father anyway. I deserved it the most. All these men had ever done to get in this position was love me, and there were already too many who had been punished for the same reason. They were both idiots if they thought I would ever let either one of them die for me—die without me. I'd spent a lifetime wishing I could have joined my mother and sister, praying to anyone who would listen to turn back time and place me in the car with them.

My hand found my sister's ashes, and I squeezed it tight, and for a single moment, I could practically feel the hug I would give to her when I saw her. I could be with Adrianna again. My pulse quickened—I could take care of her the way a big sister was supposed to.

I shook the senseless thoughts from my head. I was human with only a drop of Adrianna's powers. It wasn't enough to send me to the Elysian Fields to spend my afterlife with her. The only other way you got into the Elysian Fields was if you were an official Seelie royal—

Wait a minute.

I stopped in my tracks. Eli's hard chest shoved into my back at the unexpected stop. I waved him off, discretely gathered myself, and forged on. *Technically*, I had just been dubbed a Seelie royal by Eli when we were back at the lake. Of course he had been joking, but with both the Seelie king and queen dead, his statement was no longer powerless. As far as faerie laws were concerned, the highest-ranking member of the Seelie royal family had just given me a position among the court *and* the Elysian Fields. I had to bite my lips together to stop myself from squealing. Of course, Eli would have bestowed me the honor anyway, had I asked. But the fact of the matter now was that I didn't have to ask.

My skin tingled as it did when a plan began to come together in my mind. Excitement caused my heart rate to pick up yet again, and I silently swore when the men looked back, no doubt having clocked the uptick.

The plan was settled. I would wait until the perfect time, when all the dominoes were lined up perfectly, and then I would tip them over. When we got to Moirai, I would wait until my father was calm and relaxed around me. I would make certain that if Eli or I died while in Moirai, it just severed the tie and didn't kill the other, and then I would sever his head. Boom. Easy.

I debated a less gruesome and faster method, but I needed to be certain that his head was removed completely, and also, I didn't come all this way to fuck around. After I killed my father, I would turn the blade on myself. With me dead, the bond *and* the tie would be broken, and the Fates would be appeased and allow Mendax and Eli to live.

And I would finally get to hold my baby sister in the Elysian Fields.

"You okay, Cal?" Eli asked, making me jump.

Even after all my quiet excitement, just hearing his voice made my stomach knot and churn. How was I ever going to leave these two?

I nodded and smiled, continuing to walk as if nothing was wrong. My eyes found the back of Mendax's head and his handsome silhouette, and I silently cursed myself for my decision to leave. Leaving Eli gave me an unfamiliar warm feeling, like for once, I would be his hero and save his life. But when I imagined being separated from Mendax, all the warm feelings turned to cold emptiness. It would destroy him. He would turn shades of dark the world had never seen, but then his life would go on. The world didn't stop for heartbreak or devastation. That I knew.

CHAPTER 9

MENDAX

I WONDERED IF THE FATES WOULD TAKE PITY ON ME AND KEEP Calypso alive if I shoved the prince of sunshine off the ledge of this mountain. The trip had been quiet for a while now as we walked and walked. Caly had distanced herself from me the smallest amount. Nothing one would even notice unless they were obsessed with her—like I was.

Something was going on in that beautiful mind of hers, and whatever it was, she kept it and any feelings associated with it *far* away from the bond. I could feel her blocking something from me, and I loathed it.

Snorts and giggles from the two of them bubbled up the edge of rock and curled around my head. It stuck me in the gut like a harpoon. I wished more than anything I could evoke that same wild laugh from her lips.

It made complete sense to me why Aurelius was so full of cheer and happiness. Those two had spent a lifetime together. I had only known her existence for a speck of time, and she made my world shades lighter than I had ever known could exist. She'd provoked feelings and desires within me that I refused to believe existed before she conjured them. I'd probably be as jovial as him too if I'd had a lifetime of her.

When silence had filled the air again, I envisioned smashing the Seelie prince's head against the rough wall of rock to my left—repeatedly. I continued this daydream with every passing boulder, adding to the imaginary assault with every crackle of laughter I heard from her. I realized as we progressed up the mountain that something had changed between the two of them, and it worried me. Laughter and jokes flowed easily now. There seemed to have been guards up from one of them, if not both, that now, for whatever reason, had been torn away. Never had my patience been tested as it was while thinking about the chance of her loving him back.

Deep animallike snorts sounded behind me. I spun in my tracks to see the Seelie had lifted Caly up onto his back, her arms wrapped around his neck as she laughed so hard that noises escaped through her nose instead of her mouth. My eyes shot to his hands on the bottoms of her thighs, holding her up. My smoke fought and pulled as it tried to build inside me—unsuccessfully. No doubt fate had designed it that way, for in that moment, I didn't have the restraint not to kill him. It wasn't just the fact that he was touching her but how she was responding to him. She looked so…happy with him.

A lock released in the secret, buried compartment inside me, and for the first time, I questioned if maybe I should let her go.

I knew my many strengths, but I also knew that it was far beyond my capabilities to make her laugh and smile like Aurelius could. The sound of her passions was a drug to me. The sound of steel and fire when she wanted to burst forth in flames and fight. The sound of her screams when they bubbled up her lungs like a babbling brook before they ripped free. The breathy little intakes of air that whispered from her lips and made my cock as hard as forged iron. But unlike the other sounds she made, of which there were too many for me to properly give justice, her laughter and happiness seemed to pour into the broken box hidden in my chest, as smooth as faerie mead and as dangerous as poison. Her happy sounds had set up a little home in that box in my chest, and I found that I missed it, even felt frightened when it wasn't there…when I couldn't feel her happiness.

Aurelius took note that I was staring at his hands on her. His demeanor changed, but it wasn't unfriendly. He was so odd, that one.

"Finneas," he said as something mischievous danced in his eyes. Caly puckered her lips and raised her brow in confusion over his shoulder. The Seelie grinned. *He was always grinning.* "That's what we decided to name our firstborn child."

Before I realized I'd moved a muscle, I was on him. His windpipe vibrated against my palm as I squeezed it. I tossed my free arm around Caly's waist and yanked her off his back, holding her tightly to my side. With a hard and heavy hand, I slammed Aurelius into the mountainside just as I'd been imagining, reveling in the feel of his throat *finally* collapsing under my grip.

"Stop! Stop!" Caly cried against my side as she flailed.

The golden piss stain of a fae had the gall to grin—to grin still? To grin again? It didn't matter. All that mattered was he was *smiling* at me and what he'd said about Caly.

I moved to hurl him over the steep edge of the mountain.

He made a strangled sound as he attempted to say something, *still smiling.* I squeezed harder, looking to see the worried change in his eyes when he realized I wasn't going to stop this time.

"Mendax! Stop right now! You'll kill me too! You don't want that, right? Stop!" the vixen wailed frantically. She knew I was going to do it this time; she could feel it. I was going to crush his throat. Her heart rate slowed, stealing my attention and making me realize what was happening.

Fuck!

I let out some feral noise and reluctantly released my grip on his throat. He coughed and choked, still with a stupid grin plastered on his oddly symmetrical face.

Caly was angry and shouting at me, but the words were

muffled and lost in my mind. I squeezed her tightly around the waist and began to walk away with her in my possession.

Where she would remain—laughter or not.

"Ivy," Aurelius's grating voice called out, now a bit hoarser. I stopped in my tracks.

"If we have a daughter," he said.

I whipped around to descend on the fucker. If I couldn't kill him yet, then I would beat him to the point of unconsciousness so I didn't have to listen to him exist anymore.

The fae had balls though, I'd give him that.

Dare I say I could even begin to understand a little better why Caly gave him her time. Aurelius had always owned the heart of a warrior. On opposing sides, it was an easy task for me to tear his character to shreds. The things his mother had him battle for were foolish and greedy. Not respecting the man was getting a bit more difficult though when we fought for the same thing.

I moved for him again. I was most notably *not* the type to be taunted twice.

"Tell him, Eli!" Caly bellowed from under my arm.

"Tell him what?" Aurelius asked. "That you are already carrying my child?"

Another. Fucking. Smirk.

I dropped Caly to the ground and leapt at him, gripping two fistfuls of his shirt—the one that Caly had worn earlier in the journey. Smelling her on his shirt made me blind with lividness. With as much force as I could produce given my lack of powers, I hurled him to the rocky ground and began to unleash on his pretty face.

"Enough! Stop!" Caly screamed as she tried to push me away. When that didn't work, she shoved herself between my fists and the bastard's bloodied face.

I put my hand to her sternum and shoved her away from the ledge of the mountain, which had somehow gotten closer than it was only a few moments ago.

Aurelius's mask slipped, taking the stupid smirk with it.

The air between us shifted. "Don't you fucking push her," he seethed, landing a lucky hit to my left eye. Another strike, then another to my side, all of them catching me by surprise.

Tartarus! Had he fought me like this in one of our many battles, I think that I would be the one wearing the majority of the scars. Ironically though, it seemed that he only fought with this urgent passion and ferocity when it involved *her*.

Somehow he had gained control of the situation and had me pinned. Hits came from nowhere and everywhere all at once. Nothing rested beneath my head when it snapped back from another blow, and I realized it was because my head and neck were hanging over the ledge of the mountain.

He heaved and panted as dark-gold blood dripped down his battered face and onto me. Where had this wild, unpolished man been all this time? This was someone I wanted as a cohort!

He had bested me, and we both knew it. Over his shoulder, I scanned the mountain's wall on the other side of the trail, looking for Caly.

She stood a short distance behind him. Her beautiful round eyes were red with worry, but she remained standing tall and proud. The only tell that gave away her discomfort was that her arms were crossed as she hugged herself while watching with miserable eyes.

"Don't you ever, *ever* touch her like that again," Aurelius stated through clenched teeth. "Ever."

I had no words. Walter was the only one who *ever* got shots in on me like this.

The quick and swift image of my cousin in our sparring suits blurred, replaced with the image that provoked my nightmares: the image of the golden queen's blade—Aurelius's blade in the queen's hand—colliding with Walter's head. The amount of blood that spilled from the man who was like my brother onto Seelie soil was something I could never forget, and I would never let *any* Seelie near me forget.

Overcome with emotions, I made a move to flip Aurelius,

but once again, he shocked me with a firm block that pinned me to the edge of the mountain with even more force.

This fucker was going to kill me.

Nothing was stopping him.

Unlike their tie, Caly wouldn't die if I died. And I recognized the rabid look in his eyes.

All because I had pushed Caly.

I nodded somewhat to myself and stopped my attempts at moving him. A spider-sized amount of admiration for the man crawled in and stayed with me.

I locked eyes with Caly behind him. "Your fiancé seems to be under the misapprehension that you still can't handle yourself. Tell me, pet, have you not been so enamored with *him* that you have drawn a blade to put against his throat? I happen to know that's your favorite form of foreplay, my queen." I laughed coldly. "You try to rip me off him, but you stand by and hover as your apparent *lover* drops me from a mountain?" I yelled the last sentence, surprising myself. It all came out sounding different than I had wanted it too.

"I tried to pull you from him because *you* are prone to fits of violence, and I know I have a small amount of sway with you occasionally! I thought I could make you see straight and stop." She swallowed hard.

My eyes followed the movement of her throat. It was godly.

"Eli *hates* violence," she continued. "If you pushed him to that level, I know well enough there was no stopping him." She shook her head wildly with a feral laugh. "Both of you are foolish, but you've reminded me of something the two of you had made easy to forget: I don't need *anyone* to defend me. I don't need either of you. I am the only villain I truly fight, and I am the only hero I need to save. Fight each other to the death if you like, but don't look at me to rescue you. My hands are full."

If there had ever been a single, minuscule, unintelligible moment that I doubted or questioned my undying infatuation with this woman, this statement put it to rest. What had I become? I was close to salivating for her on the ledge of this shimmering mountain in the middle of nowhere. Had my hell-hound been wielding a knife, I think I would have come in my trousers like an inexperienced virgin.

Aurelius turned from Caly to smile down at me.

He leaned over and spoke so softly, I assumed I was the only one who could hear his words. "She doesn't need me to kill you. In fact, I don't doubt that the heathen would rather do the deed herself." He sat back on his heels a bit but shifted, blocking her, so I could see only his ugly, smiling face. "She is correct. She has never needed me to save her, but no matter how hard she fights it, I will. Always. Touch her like that again in my presence, and I will gut you before either one of you has even gathered a breath to protest it." Reluctantly, he lightened his grip on me.

A newfound respect and admiration for the man rested heavily in my bones. He leaned in once more.

"And you should know, I'm no longer competition to you. Calypso and I have and will always be the closest possible friends. Soul-tied friends, if you will. *Nothing* will ever come between us, no matter how hard anyone tries. You should know that romantically, there is nothing between us and never will be. Do not take what I say as a removal of my claim of her. Quite the opposite. Now that she and I have fully had a bit of calm to discover the true ingredients of our friendship, I will be watching you closer than ever, because no matter what, she is family to me. She's right—I dislike violence and strive for a peaceful realm, but do *not* think for one second that means I will not disembowel you for hurting her in any way."

He gave one final shove as if he needed to purge the last pulse of anger before he let the situation go. Then Aurelius rose, leaving me half-stunned on the ground.

What an absolute lovestruck fool he must have thought me, and he was right. The fucker had baited me with names—*names*. And I'd stepped right into it. Neither one of them felt romantically about the other? When had this occurred? The attachment had always seemed to be most prominent from

Aurelius's side. Had he just been spurred on by the jealousy of another man in her life?

That was what had changed between them, what caused the relaxation between them. It made sense now.

I stood, feeling the slightest tinge embarrassed by my weakness. I don't know why. I'd always known she would be my weak spot, the tender pocket of me that no armor could shield. Aurelius and I both knew that had I possessed my smoke, he would have been gone. Leastwise, that was what I continued to tell myself, even though, to be honest, I wasn't all that sure anymore. He was loyal and protective, I would give him that. I didn't hate the idea of someone with that type of fight protecting my woman, as long as he understood to whom she belonged.

"Are you all right? Did I hurt you?" I asked Caly. My fingertips coiled around her hip like a snake. I had to touch her.

She shook her head. Something was still off with her.

"Would you like me to?" I asked, bending down to run my mouth over her earlobe.

She softened slightly under my touch.

"Knock it off," Aurelius said.

"I thought there was nothing between the two of you?" I asked, pulling her closer.

"I still don't need to be the third wheel," he grumbled.

"What's the matter?" I asked Caly.

"Nothing. Let's hurry before you two spend the last of your energy fighting and I have to carry you," she said with a fake smile.

Aurelius appeared to have bought the expression, but I knew by the map of her eyes better than to believe the lie.

"By the way, I still like Finneas and Ivy. Aurelius has a nice ring to it also, should you ever be in search of the perfect baby name," he laughed, quickly back to his lighthearted self.

CHAPTER 10

CALY

"WHAT IF HE ISN'T AS BAD AS YOU THINK?" ELI PRODDED.
"Eli," I warned with a look.

"I'm just saying, think of all the people who stood up for my mother, and all the while, she was a monster. What if your father is the opposite? What if he had a reason for leaving you guys behind? Look, all I'm saying is you have a lot of questions about your family and things, right? Maybe you should talk to him before you kill him. My father always spoke highly of him."

He put his palms up to stop my argument before I could start it. He'd been intermittently hounding me with the same plea throughout the trip. At first, it made me annoyed and furious. I felt betrayed. He knew what had happened to me as a child. He knew everything that I had been through. How could he think it was all right that my father left me and my family? None of them would be dead had Zef stayed with us. The queen never would have targeted me. I wouldn't have been put through half the horrible things that had torn and sliced me into what I was now.

But as usual, Eli eventually got in my head.

At first, it started with tiny questions; he wondered if it was possible things somehow could've been worse had my father remained with us. To be honest, I had never even given such an idea a second thought.

From then on, throughout the quiet of the journey, little thoughts wafted into my mind, like, *What if he ascended thinking he could bring us with him later?* I hated admitting it, but after everything I'd learned about the Artemi, I could sort of understand some of his reasoning for hiding us in the human realm. From the sound of it, most of his enemies were unable to cross over to the human realm. Saracen had made it through though.

I'd never allowed myself a thought in his favor or even in any direction other than him being a greedy, selfish bastard who chose to kill his weak and gentle daughter when he designated and dumped all his powers onto her. Look at all that I was capable of. I didn't shy from pain; I enjoyed it. It let me know I was still alive. So why hadn't he chosen me and spared Adrianna?

Unacknowledged questions began to leak into my brain, pooling in the little nooks that had always been so easy to skip over when I focused only on my hatred of him.

How had he and my mother met? I knew what most of the other realms thought of humans, yet he had sired children with one. My mother never spoke about him. Was it simply that she never had a chance? Or was it out of pain? Hate? Were they even together? Or had it been some tryst that spawned my sister and me?

I was naturally a curious person, and now it seemed as though the dam that blocked the stream of questions had broken. I decided at last that I would find out some answers before I killed him—and myself. At least I could take some answers with me to tell Adrianna that way.

"This is stupid. How much longer are we going to circle around this mountain?" I asked. We hadn't been on the mountain for all that long, and I didn't blame them for thinking it might be home to a supposed weather goddess. The glittering mountain was beautiful and ominous. Even I—who had no trustworthy instincts compared to Eli and Mendax—looked to the mountain for what could be our next clue to Moirai.

It somehow felt a little more magical than the ground below it. Still, I couldn't help but worry that we were wasting all this energy in vain.

The trail was wide enough for the three of us to walk shoulder to shoulder, but that never ended up happening. It was like one of the men needed to be in front of the other.

"Guys," Eli said sternly from the back. The tone of his voice was serious and weary, catching both of our attention.

Mendax and I turned to find Eli cupping his hand, holding it out and staring at the contents. Weakly flapping in his palm were two glasswing butterflies.

Shit.

"I thought something touched my ear, and when I went to swat it away, I grabbed these." Eli's jaw clamped down. He shifted his gaze to Mendax. "We are being watched. Whatever sabotaged the second scroll is most likely trying to stop the third. Which means that we are on the right track."

We did the usual things, like backtrack to search for footprints or eyes in the sky, perhaps a stray bird that was feeding our whereabouts to its owner, but we came up with nothing, which somehow made it even creepier.

"Well, whatever's following us is either gone or significantly more skilled than us at hiding," said Mendax.

"What is it that we're supposed to do once we find this place?" The lack of food and energy was beginning to get to me. I was struggling to remember things that would typically be easy. I dug into my bag and pulled out the largest piece of the broken scroll, recalling what it said as I read it out loud to all of us. "Calypso Petranova, Salutations and so on. Presumably, if you are reading this, then you have made it past the benthyc of Lake Sheridon. For further directions to Moirai, continue onward to the weathered. Coax her into initiating the flood, and further instructions will find you. The Fates."

"I know nothing of the weathered. In Unseelie, we have few changes to the scenery or environment," Mendax added.

"I don't know much more than rumors that I've heard," said

Eli. "Like any of the old gods, the weathered are to be feared. They are old and wise and change the weather based on what she calculates will be the most beneficial to the highest number of fae."

"Is there more than one weathered? Or does just one control all the weather?" Sometimes it still felt like I was in a dream when all these fantastical and magical things were brought up. I think that was why a part of me got lost to science when I was younger. It was so solid, opposed to all the magic that had hurt me and Adrianna. It was solid and had easy answers.

Mendax opened his mouth to speak, but his words fell silent when we rounded the corner of the mountain.

My mouth quickly dropped open.

From the side of mountain we had just been on, the in-between was empty other than the trees. Eerie forests and silence took up the majority of what you could see—a blanket of white snow through a gray forest. Now I took another step, barely believing my eyes.

My stomach clenched and growled loudly as the smell of sweet and savory hotcakes was brought to me on the icy wind.

The entire mountainside was filled with small wood-and-stone houses. One of them had rich smoke swirling from the chimney. The houses were maintained, but none of them seemed to be the type of house a powerful, weather-controlling goddess would live in. As a matter of fact, none of them looked lived in. The mountainside town looked completely abandoned, save for the delicious scent and the houses not being in disrepair.

"The suns is this? I messed up," Eli said. "Maybe someone here—if anyone *is* here—will give us rest and point us in the direction of the weathered."

Mendax looked to Eli. "What makes you so sure the weathered isn't here? Why do you give your instincts so little trust?"

"Nobody lives here," Eli replied "Look around. Most of the houses are abandoned. The person we need is a goddess and clearly not here. We should look for a larger house on the top of the mountain."

"You've so obviously never been fooled by a tattered, muddy black dress and bloodstained hair," whispered Mendax as his sultry blue eyes landed on me.

"At this point, I don't care what's here other than whatever that smell is. I am so hungry, I could scream," I complained.

"Why didn't you say you were hungry? You promised you would be better at telling us when you needed nourishment," Mendax scolded.

"You told me three hours ago you had plenty of rations for yourself in your bag," Eli snapped.

"Sorry, mother," I bit out. The truth was I had run out of rations and snacks for myself days ago, but neither man needed to eat like I did, being fae, and I was fine going a few days without food, but we'd miscalculated and were supposed to be in Moirai by now.

"If I need to hand-feed you myself so you do not die from starvation, I will, but I will be sorely disappointed in your lack of self-preservation, pet." Mendax glared at me.

I bowed my head in defeat and promised to do better about letting them know when I was hungry. As annoying as it was, it was also nice to have someone care about me enough to worry. Having two someones worry felt too good to be real.

We moved down the path, weaving our way through the rows of houses until we came to the one with the smoking chimney. My hopes of getting a fabulous meal began to diminish the closer we got to the small house. It was apparent there were people inside, but the cracks in the windows and the tufts of roof led me to believe that even if they had a hot meal, it was not going to be enough to feed me and the two giant men beside me. Perhaps I could still get something small to tide me over while they pointed us in the right direction.

We all looked to one another to see who would knock on the tattered wooden door. Mendax and I immediately stepped back, leaving Eli closest to the door. He was the people-y one. Plus, everyone liked Eli...well, except Mendax, of course. Eli would be able to get answers out of them without threatening their lives.

Eli took the remaining steps until he stood just before the front door. He ran his fingers through his blond hair and then rapped the small bronze knocker in the middle of the door. A ruckus sounded on the other side of the door, and a gray-haired, elderly woman opened it, stepping into the doorframe. She looked tired and worn down but good-natured enough. The many lines of her face gave the impression of a wise and knowing woman. Her cool brown eyes stood out against the sunspots that covered her face. She didn't look surprised to see us in the least. She cooked a mean hotcake, I could tell.

"You must be here to see the weathered," she stated.

Surprised, we all exchanged wary glances. This was really not who we had expected to be the all-powerful weather goddess the Fates had talked about. Though upon further inspection, she *did* have the face of an astute and judicious woman. I supposed it wasn't all that far-fetched.

"Yes," I said, stepping up with a large smile in place. "Yes, I can't believe we found you."

She let out a little laugh. "Oh goodness, I'm not the weathered." She called into the dimly lit house, "Jamie, some people have come to see you. Do be nice."

The old woman retreated from the doorway and disappeared into the small house just as a young, raven-haired girl who looked no older than sixteen popped into the doorway, a hand on her hip.

"What do you want?" she said as she popped a piece of hotcake in her mouth.

CHAPTER 11

MENDAX

Caly and Aurelius stared blankly at the young girl in the doorway. Unsurprised, I craned my neck to get a better look inside. For a moment, no one said a word as they stood there in shock.

"*You're* the weathered?" Caly asked.

"Told you so," I mumbled under my breath in Aurelius's direction.

The puzzled fae scrunched up his tan face. "Told me what?"

So dumb. "That the weathered would be here," I said quietly.

"I'm the one who guided us here," he said, squinting at me.

The girl pushed the last piece of golden-brown breakfast in her mouth. "Fine, you can come in, but don't ask me to do anything, or I'll get really mad," the girl said, making sure each of her words dripped with as much attitude as she could infuse it with.

She rolled her eyes but stepped back and let us inside the small house. When I walked past her, I realized just how small she really was.

"How old are you?" I demanded as I stopped in front of her. Abnormally large, vibrant, blue eyes locked with mine, squinting at me. I remained still, waiting for her to answer before quickly realizing that had been her answer. I'd only met one or two other goddesses in my lifetime, and every one of them had been filled with attitude. There was no telling how old she really was.

She slammed the front door closed and moved to the front of our small group, huffing and rolling her eyes with every step, making certain we knew what an inconvenience this was for her. She wore a cream frock with a little lightning bolt embroidered on the front pocket.

As soon as we moved past the entryway, I realized what a strong glamour the dilapidated building had been under. It was still far from being a mansion, but the inside showed a significantly larger interior than the outside led one to believe. Inside, the home was nicely kept and tidy with a small number of children's toys scattered neatly on the ground in the front room. The old woman who had greeted us at the door sat in a chair watching over three younger-looking children.

The girl guided us to the back, into a modest-sized room with one window.

"Don't sit on my bed," she snapped.

Caly and Aurelius moved a stool and a chair near the bed to sit, while I remained standing. The room was plain with only a few small paintings and pieces of furniture that matched the dark wood of the small bed. Aside from the bed, there was a small wooden fold-down desk with a few stacks of books. I glanced at the books, curious to get a better idea of what exactly we were dealing with—almanacs and astrology.

"So the snow. We need you to stop it. Please, uh, Jamie." Caly sweetly spoke as she slumped down in her chair. I watched the lines of her long legs bend and stretch as she got comfortable. She was much more tired than she wanted us to know. And Aurelius and I were not regaining our magic as quickly as we needed to be to sustain us at this level.

The girl ignored Caly and instead made eye contact with me. In passing, she looked like a teenage human with her rounded ears, but the second you got closer or held the woman's gaze, you felt the power of a goddess wafting from her. "You know anything about the weather?" she asked me, completely ignoring the other two for the moment.

I didn't answer right away, for no particular reason other than I didn't want to. I wasn't in the habit of being pushed around by tiny weather goddesses. As eager as I was to get back to Unseelie and finally have Caly all to myself, I wasn't going to break my back for this goddess's games. I canted my head and wondered what weather would remain if you killed the weather maker.

A corner lifted on the girl's mouth, like she'd heard my thoughts.

"This is such a cozy space you've made here. Was that your mother that answered the door?" Aurelius's friendly voice filled the room, somehow spreading a bit of warmth into the chilly atmosphere. It was suffocating and felt pushy. I would let him attempt things his way but only for so long. Caly needed to get to Moirai.

"I asked if you know anything about weather?" The girl's wise eyes rested on me again. She looked sad and troublesome.

"I heard you," I stated, ignoring the eye daggers Caly shot at me.

The girl's demeanor was as cold as the ice itself. When she stopped looking at me, she turned to face Caly.

"Is this one your boyfriend?" she asked with a nod in my direction.

"Err…it's complicated, but…uh, I guess so?" Caly answered with a short laugh at the absurd question.

I wet my lips with my tongue and opened my mouth to ask Caly what was complicated about me being her king and owner—mostly because I wanted to hear all those things spill from her full mouth—but the girl began to talk again, cutting me off.

"I could tell. You both have the same dark air about you, but he's not trying to hide his. I'm good at things like that. Do *you* know anything about the weather?" she asked Caly.

The dark-haired girl, Jamie or whatever, moved from her bed to a wooden dresser and pulled open the middle drawer with a tug. She removed a crisp, white sweater from the drawer and pulled it over her slight frame. Her eyes flashed, looking more white than blue now.

"No, I'm sorry. I could lie and tell you otherwise, but my extent of weather knowledge is only from television in the human realm," Caly said with a smile.

Stars, she was beautiful. Standing a bit off in the corner like I was reminded me of watching her sleep in the Seelie castle. The way her skin smelled and tasted when she didn't know I was there. I had watched her for *hours* from the dark corners of her room. It was a game of will to see how long I could watch her sleep before I had to touch her skin. I couldn't wait to play with her more.

I watched Caly play the sweet, innocent girl, and it got my cock hard recalling how I'd been subject to the same act once. My fingers tightened around the wood of my chair in an effort not to walk over and lick every inch of her body. *Fuck*, even the way she anxiously bit at the flesh inside her cheek had me ready to make a scene.

"The human realm?" Jamie perked up. "Oh, that's Luna's doing. It's great, isn't it? I've seen her work before, really talented with the earthquakes. Did you see her tsunami in 1498? Volcano and everything."

"Really? Wow. I've heard a lot about her work, but no, I wasn't around to see that one…" Caly trailed off. The fire had sparked behind her eyes, just the slightest bit.

This was absurdly fascinating, watching her wheels and gears start to move as she formulated how to get what it was she wanted. She was not to be underestimated, and anyone who did underestimate her deserved what they got. She was magnificent in action.

"We are so sorry to intrude like this. You don't strike me as someone who has a lot of enjoyment chatting with three strangers, so we will speed this up," Aurelius said with an easy, kind voice.

"So that's what you think about me," the girl said as she crossed her arms.

Aurelius side-eyed Caly. "Is what what I think about you?" he questioned nervously.

The weathered moved to stand in front of a little wooden table with a square mirror leaning on the wall behind it. "You think I'm cold, that I think I'm something that I'm not? Is that it? That I don't have friends?" Her voice had escalated in pitch until I felt it grate the inside of my brain like claws.

Caly chuckled gently, standing to put her hand on the weathered's arm like they were old friends. "He didn't mean it like that at all. *I* can tell you have lots of friends. Can you tell me about all this snow? Is it hard to make so much of it?" she said, sounding like she had a genuine interest in it.

If I wasn't mistaken, the girl's eyes seemed to darken a little, making the white appear a bit more blue.

Interesting.

"I told you not to ask me for anything," she snapped at Caly.

My eye froze on the small window of the room. Snow had begun to fall outside. It seemed to be picking up speed somewhat rapidly.

I stilled, sensing a heartbeat on the other side of the wall.

"I'm so sorry. How annoying. Does that happen a lot, people requesting different weather for the in-between?" Caly picked up a silver brush from the vanity and began to brush Jamie's short, black hair as slowly and as cautiously as if she were grooming a nocturneye.

"Why are you grooming me? You are the one that needs a bath," the girl stated. "You think I don't know what you are doing? Leave, now. All of you."

A shadow cast over the corner of the window for a second before it vanished from sight. I saw the flutter of a clear butterfly landing on the windowpane for a moment before it was knocked down with the heavy wind and snow.

Someone was outside—the person who had been following us.

"Aurelius, Caly, step outside for a moment. I need a moment alone with…err…Jamie," I said as I adjusted my overcoat. I had insisted that Caly wear my chest plate after she had used it as a sled. She needed as many layers as possible in this weather, and I wasn't taking any more chances with her as she weakened.

My traveling companions looked horrified at each other before Caly shouted at me. "No! You absolutely cannot kill her!"

Apparently the in-between had caused my pet's discretion to falter.

"He can't kill me. No one can," the weathered grumbled.

"There are more glass butterflies outside this window, and they are alive at the moment," I said firmly, keeping my eyes on Aurelius. His hand absently reached for the long blade at his side, and I knew he understood my meaning.

Caly and Aurelius locked eyes before they fled the room, both eager to see who or what had been following us, as was I, but someone needed to get the weathered to cause a flood, and it was going to be me.

I noticed Jamie's face wrinkle in disappointment when the other two left the room. "Aren't you going too? You should hurry. The butterflies will leave when he does."

I wanted to ask what she'd seen, but I caught ahold of something that might be more helpful. She had the tiniest flicker in her voice, something barely noticeable, but still something I recognized.

"So you say *you* cannot be killed? But were *they* killed?" I sat down in the chair that Aurelius had been sitting in.

"Who?" she asked, sitting back down on the edge of her bed.

I waited and watched, choosing not to respond to her again. I was listening to the outside also but was having a hard time hearing through the strong glamour of the cottage.

"The person you are in love with."

Her cold blue eyes widened. "It's always the evil ones who are the best at reading people, isn't it? I don't care for your friend or your girlfriend. They are disingenuous and manipulative."

"Apologies. We are trying to find Moirai and are in a pinch with the time we have been given," I said flatly. "So can the person you are in love with die, as you say you cannot, or have they died already? It's why you are so frigid, isn't it?"

A crack of thunder outside confirmed my suspicions.

The girl squinted at me, overflowing with anger. "No, she hasn't died. Are you going to threaten to kill her too? You think that will get you whatever it is that you want?" she snapped. The volume of her voice rose with fury. Lightning cracked through the falling snow, sending a flash of light through the dim room.

"I'm going to get what I want no matter what." I moved around her room, picking up small objects that looked like they could be of importance. "I just happened to recognize the familiar sound of it in your voice."

"The sound of what?"

"The sound of loving someone you can't get to." I picked up a trinket with an unusual yellow flower frozen in a bubbled ball of glass.

"Don't touch that!" There was more feeling in those three words than I'd heard from her yet.

Perfect.

I moved to replace it on the small table but stopped just before it touched the wood, instead turning and handing it to her. She took it reluctantly in both hands. I said nothing but watched her face with interest.

"She—she gave me this to remember her while she was gone. It is a symbol of her love for me. She's the only one who can make this type of flowers." Jamie sat back on her bed, looking closely at the bubble of glass.

"So I have no grounds to entice you with an offer of her death to get what I want then?" I quirked an eyebrow, half expecting her to fly off the handle as she had done earlier with Caly.

Instead, the weathered smiled for a moment, and a flash of sunshine heated my shoulder through the window. It was gone as quickly as it had come. Her emotions were what controlled the weather. When she was icy, so was the weather. Anger created a small rumble of thunder that shook the walls, and it seemed happiness or fond memories caused the sun to peek through the dark clouds. How long had she held this snow? I'd heard my father, King Marco Thanes, speak of a snowy journey to the in-between ages ago.

The floorboards creaked and adjusted as the temperature turned unbearable. Thankfully, Caly was with Aurelius, and he would be sure to keep her warm for as long as this petulant goddess threw her icy tantrum, though from the sounds of it, the goddess rivaled me in obstinance.

"She cannot die. She cannot live. Flora is stuck...because of me," she said, repositioning the globe carefully on her empty nightstand.

"And why is that?" I looked out the window, feigning disinterest but also trying to get a bead on Caly. "Is she trapped in Tartarus? I have friends in low places. I'll have her out by tonight."

She rolled her eyes. "We are goddesses of the elements. When we expire, we simply reincarnate into whatever element the Fates wish. Besides, Tartarus is where the Unseelie and the worst of the Seelie go. Do you think I belong there instead of the Elysian Fields, where all the most exquisite of creations go to rest? You're definitely not as well versed in flattery as your friends."

"I care next to nothing about the in-between. In my realm, it is known only as a lost space where forgettable things go to slip from the minds of all other realms. No one remembers it even exists most of the time." I met her cold stare with bored, half-opened eyes.

She sucked in a deep breath, and her face flushed. I wanted to look out the window and see what weather this mood had brought with it, but I didn't dare show my interest.

"That's only because she's gone. Once, the in-between was quite memorable." The girl turned to face the back wall that butted up against the side of her simple bed. "It's awful and forgettable now because she can't return to me."

Fuck, this was so mind-numbingly boring. I should have left Aurelius in here and had a taste of Caly's little pink nipples in the snow instead.

I grunted. We would never get the next scroll if I left now. Both Caly and Aurelius were too good-natured for what needed to happen next.

"Flora is the goddess of the flowers and ferns. She's magnificent and beautiful and always brings out the best in me," the girl said with a soft smile as she looked down at her lap.

I didn't need to look out the window to see the sun creating long, demon-like shadows across the floor where I stood.

Shit. I don't want the fucking sun. I want rain—and a lot of it.

"What did you do to make her leave? Must've been bad." I chose my words—and how they cut—slowly and methodically, grating the blade against the surface...just enough to sting.

As expected, the shadows and sunlight left with her gasp.

She whipped around to face me, sadness brimming in her eyes. "It was bad. I miss her desperately. I am lost, hopelessly in love with her. Flora can only return when the lands are ripe and ready for flowers, insects buzzing and ready to pollinate. She...she cannot return until I bring the sun out."

Not quite yet...though closer...

"And you can only bring the sun out when you are happy." I filled in the blanks, awaiting confirmation. What was Caly doing right now? Was she warm enough? Also, could she swim?

"And I cannot possibly be happy without Flora here." Her voice quivered slightly, and I heard the distant tap of rain or hail on the thatched roof.

I moved closer until I was towering over her. Old goddess or not, I was gifted with the ability to induce fear in everyone. That was why I was the Unseelie prince.

Discomfort rolled from her little pores, and I felt the ground shake beneath my boots.

Son of a bitch!

Her trembling was causing an earthquake.

"I've seen those yellow flowers bloom through the frost before. She could come if she really wanted to," I stated softly. "It's obviously you she doesn't want. Why else would she stay away for an eternity?"

Closer.

Her eyes gleamed and shimmered with tears as she stood, frantically grabbing my forearm. "No, no! That's not it! You don't even know what you're talking about! It's my fault. I cannot bring her back."

There they were. Plump, steady tears began to roll down her deceptively youthful cheeks.

"Sure," I said with a nod before taking a few steps toward the open door. "How many visitors do you really get?"

She opened her mouth to answer and then closed it again.

"None," I said, answering for her. "If you do, it's only because they need you to perform a duty you are so clearly incapable of. I've never seen a more boring and forgettable goddess in all my life."

I could practically smell the ambrosia tang of her blood before I pushed the last bit of my metaphorical dagger in for the kill. I looked her over carefully and with a grimace walked to the front door, passing by the old woman and children still playing.

"Wait! I can help you! What is it that you needed? Something about the snow? I have a hard time listening. I just get so numb to everything. I want to do better. I know I can do better. Please don't leave yet." She clamored to block the open door as tears streamed down from both the sky and her face.

"You couldn't do it anyway. I'll go to the Seelie realm. Have you seen their sun?" I asked with a grin.

Her face fell before she answered, "No, but I've heard it's the brightest of all the realms. That's Kalista. She is the most powerful of us in that regard."

"My group will go to her. She is obviously the better choice," I said as I turned and stepped out the door and onto the small porch. I turned half-heartedly to face her as I scanned the area for Aurelius and Caly. "You certain those little yellow flowers from Flora are one of a kind? That only she can make them?" I asked. "There are absolute *fields* of them in Seelie. They are considered a weed, they grow so obnoxiously. Kalista must be a very talented weather goddess to have such pull over your love." I walked away, picking up pace when I spotted Caly's tired body sitting on an abandoned porch next door.

Thunder rolled with a loud crash as the rain came. The floodgates—so to speak—had been opened.

I didn't feel bad in the slightest, but there *was* a tinge of discomfort in knowing exactly how the goddess felt not being able to reach the love of her life. That had been me after Caly had left to go to Seelie. I had recognized the devastation in her voice because it was so familiar to me.

"We need to find something that floats, and quickly," I said.

CHAPTER 12

ELI

"THERE IS NOTHING HERE THAT WILL HOLD US!" CAL SHOUTED. I could hear the note of panic in her voice that she was attempting to mask from Mendax and me.

I hated to admit it, but Mendax had come through with the weathered.

Cal's hair was darker in the rain, hanging limply as it clung to her face, neck, and shoulders. I hated how much I worried about her in this weather. I wanted more than anything to take her back to the human realm and leave her in the safety of that world. Humans were kept out of the realms for a reason. It wasn't safe. Humans had no idea about all the magic that was only a fairy ring or tree hollow away. They kept their worries at bay and disguised and soothed their instincts with fables and fiction...or they believed it was all fiction.

The rain had come hard. As soon as Mendax had left the weathered's house, it began to pour from the murky gray sky, more lifeless and broken-looking than any rain I had ever taken note of. Maybe it was because I now knew it to be the tears of a weather goddess.

I hated the thought of any woman crying this hard.

I didn't know what Mendax had done to make her cry,

and I doubted I wanted to. What was worse was he'd probably loved every minute of it, the bastard. That was one thing I would never be able to understand: How could you want to hurt people?

I was in love with Cal, I always had been, but recently I had started to realize it was a different Cal that I was in love with.

When she had confessed to all the lies and deceit at my castle, my eyes began to open a little to who she really was. Every challenge and conversation along this journey to Moirai had only opened them more. I was desperately in love with the Cal who always seemed as sweet as honey and as kind and caring as Aether himself in the Elysian Fields. The Cal who wanted to be with the animals and in the forest because it made her happy. The Cal who was honest and wholesome and cared about helping people and animals was who I was in love with, and it had taken nearly this entire trip for me to realize that I was in love with a lie, with someone who wasn't quite her.

I had fought against her and Mendax being together tooth and nail, and at first, I assumed it was because I was more in love with her than I had thought. After all those years apart, I had started to notice small changes in the girl I thought I knew, and I had blamed the Unseelie prince's influence. I know now I was trying to keep the Cal I loved alive, to convince myself she still existed. The truth is I don't even know if the Cal I loved was ever real and not just a scheme. Cal had hidden so much darkness from me, I *still* didn't really know who she was.

I would never forgive her for killing my mother, even though I could understand it.

And I couldn't help but wonder if all the kindness and love I'd seen in her all those years ago had been the doing of her sister's drop of good-natured Artemi.

"I'm going back to the house to check on the weathered," I declared. My feet moved slowly and heavily through the water that slid down the mountainside.

Mendax stepped in front of me, blocking my path. "You will *not* return to that house. The scroll said to induce a flood in order to get the next clue, and that is what I have done. If you waltz in there and unload your bullshit empathy, this will all stop."

I tightened my jaw and stepped around him.

"Eli, stop! She will stop the flood, and then I will never get to Moirai!" Cal shouted.

Disappointment made my tongue heavy as I looked between the two of them. They really were perfect for each other. They had the same dark, selfish, uncaring scowl on their faces as they watched me.

"There were children in there. I don't know who or what kind of kids they are, but I'm not going to just assume any of them can get out before the house is overtaken by water," I snapped at her. How could she not care about the kids inside? Had she always been this way? "I will not stop the flood. You have my word." They both looked furious with me. My chest hurt, feeling a little emptier than it had only a few minutes before. I saw Cal's eyes recognize my disappointment. They flickered for a moment but then turned cold and steely. What was she thinking? If she were stronger, would she have tried to stop me? I thought she would have.

"They are not children, and you know it. Each is at least a millennia, I'm sure," Mendax offered.

"The rain is going to pick up quickly. Unless one of you has suddenly gained strength and can fly, I suggest you find something to hold all of us. We need to get to the top of the mountain." I didn't wait for a response as I turned and began to walk the path to the weathered's house with a tight jaw.

We were not that high up the mountain. The water would begin rising from below, and fae were notoriously bad swimmers, unless of course they were a water species. Mendax and I were too big to float. Realistically, I should have been carrying Cal up the mountain right now.

I banged on the door, and it rattled on the hinges.

"Please let me help. There is a flo—"

The door opened, and Jamie, the weather goddess, stood

on the other side with her dark hair mussed up. Tears poured down her red blotchy cheeks.

"I'm so sorry for whatever he did. Please let me take your mother and the children—and you—to safety." I couldn't help myself. She could still cry at the top of the mountain.

"I loved her so much!" she wailed almost incoherently.

I had no idea what she was talking about, but my heart broke as I watched her fall to the floor in a heap. She was sad and broken.

I swore under my breath before I stepped inside, out of the downpour, and closed the door behind me. I got down on the ground with the goddess, peeking around for the older woman and her children. I couldn't see anyone in the front rooms.

"Listen, I'm sure they loved you too," I said softly as I crossed my legs on the ground next to her.

"She never loved me! I've spent all this time waiting for her to return and hating myself for being the reason she couldn't come back to me." She heaved and gasped the words as she sobbed.

"I don't know what he said to you, but take it with a grain of salt. None of it may be true at all. I don't know the details, but if she was half as in love with you as you are with her, how could she possibly want to stay away?" I laid my hand on her shoulder and gently rubbed her back, feeling her bones shake with every wail. "Let's get out of here, okay?" I asked as I pulled her up to standing. "Where did they go? Your mom and the kids?"

"Mother Nature? She took the others to their realms and left. They are safe," she responded.

"Mother Nature." I smiled at the realization.

The weathered's tears came even faster.

"What? What is it?" I asked.

"Your smile—you're Seelie. You practically radiate sunshine. I bet *you* could have made Flora come back," she wailed, turning to wipe her nose on my soaked shirt.

"Wait, let's get you a—" *Gross!* "Oh, okay. So that's her

name, Flora? Like flowers?" I asked, starting to put the pieces together.

Jamie nodded.

"Oh! Well, that's perfect! You will see her soon then," I said, relieved.

She looked like she was about to punch me. "Flora can't come in the snow or rain. She can only return to me with sunshine," the girl grumbled with surprising ferocity.

I sighed and said a silent prayer to the Fates that I wouldn't regret what I was about to do. "Do you remember the first time you ever met Flora?" I asked her.

She snorted a sudden laugh, and tears flew onto my chest with her breath. The rain outside slowed.

Uh-oh.

"I do," she said with a soft blush.

I held my palms up to stop any details she was about to share with me. I needed to hurry. I wasn't getting my powers restored as I normally would have, and if I needed to use them in Moirai to help Cal or Zef, then this needed to happen quickly.

"You don't have to tell me about it. Just think about it. Do you think she still loved you when the two of you had to say goodbye?"

The goddess nodded, and a few tears fell from her closed eyes as the pitter-patter of rain returned on the roof. "I could see it in her eyes. I know she loved me. It was fate, her and I," she whispered, clearly picturing the sad moment in her mind.

"I truly believe the Fates make no mistakes and what is meant to happen will happen. Sometimes a shift in perspective is all that is needed. Trust me, I'm learning this myself right now," I replied. Was I ever.

"Why did you come back? Why are you helping me?" she said as she wiped her tears away with a sudden look of apprehension. "I know you needed weather from me, and I can only assume it was a flood. Your friend is a smart one. Evil and horrible, but smart."

I nodded and found myself thinking of my own situation

and what was going to happen in Moirai. "I came back because my fault is and will always be that I can't deny helping someone if it's something I am capable of, even to my own detriment. Cliché, I know," I chuckled. "I suppose it's the curse of being Seelie."

She shook her head. "Not all Seelie are like that. Initially, I had thought you were fake and manipulative. I see now that was not the case. You are a good man. Better than most."

My own cheeks heated slightly. "I don't know about that. I just came back to help. It's not that big of a thing."

"Okay, then help me bring Flora back," she challenged. Her voice cracked like a silent plea with each word.

"Okay, but you have to get to safety right after," I cautioned.

❦

"What did you do?" Cal asked with wide eyes as I approached. She and Mendax were busy wedging boards together from one of the old porches nearby.

The hazy sun that warmed my neck felt like the best medicine I'd ever been prescribed. Almost immediately, my mood and optimism about this situation increased leaps and bounds. Everything would be okay at the end of this.

I grinned so wide, my cheeks strained. "I just chose to help instead of hurt. We won't need this," I said, pointing to the makeshift raft.

"Every time I start to tolerate your company, you prove *exactly* why Seelie and Unseelie could never be peaceful with one another," Mendax grumbled as he stepped up to me.

The sun brightened for a second before the clouds veiled it. The little amount of sun had already done more for me than I could put into words, *including* restore a bit more of my power.

Mendax couldn't do shit to me right now.

The rain danced as it came from the sky, falling like happy tears to the sleeping ground.

"Look! A rainbow!" I nodded in the direction of the beautiful arch filled with vibrant colors. It was amazing. I turned to see if Cal saw it. Her eyes were on me. Her gaze was so intense, I broke first and looked away. "I just had her remember all the good moments she and Flora shared." I turned to face my friend. "I reminded her that even if what Mendax had implied *was* true and that Flora *had* chosen to be with someone else, it didn't mean the times the two of them had were any less special. I reminded her that Flora could still come to her in the in-between but that even if she didn't, there would be someone else better suited for her. I told her that if she truly loved Flora, then wouldn't she want her to be happy? That just because things hadn't gone as she'd hoped, it didn't mean their friendship or love had died. It had just changed."

Cal didn't say a word as she watched me.

"And that worked?" Mendax said gruffly.

"Feuhn kai greeyth." I smiled and closed my eyes, tilting my face up to the sky as the rain began to pour harder and harder. "Eternal love and friendship."

Caly smiled at me, and Mendax spat next to where I stood.

"Look! The water is rising!" Cal said as she looked at the land below the mountain. "You did it! We need to add more boards, quickly."

"No, we don't," I said with a smirk as I looked to Mendax and let my wings unfurl.

CHAPTER 13

MENDAX

N o," I snapped at Aurelius. "I'll climb the mountain before I resort to that."

Caly clapped me on the shoulder. "Well, you're going to have to climb pretty fast, because the water is going to be at our level in a few minutes. According to my calculations, I'd say no more than twenty-five minutes or so. It's already cleared Lake Sheridon." She scowled at me. "That means the benthyc, or whatever the Fates called those lake creatures in the letter, will be able to smell us and won't have a barrier to stop them—all of them—this time."

I know my expression must have been that of a pouting teenager. "Do you think so little of me, pet, that you think I can't handle them? Have you not witnessed me take down much larger—"

"That was when you had all your power. Now stop wasting time, and grab ahold of Eli," Caly scolded me, impatient.

"I am *not* hanging on to a Seelie unless I am tying his head to a branch," I harrumphed with finality.

Caly, the little minx, left her post by Aurelius and strutted over to where I stood. Even through the downpour, I could see the extra sway she infused in her hips with each step. Her shirt molded and clung to her perfect little breasts with the rain. She pressed against me and coiled her little fingers up around my neck.

My manipulative siren.

If she thought she was going to make me do things just by making me hard, she was mistaken. I was always hard around her, and no one, including her and her pretty pink bits, was going to make me do anything I didn't want to, and I *most certainly* didn't want to do this.

"Please," she whispered in my ear, biting the lobe. "I'll let you punish me later."

"You've evidently never been punished by me if you think it's something you'll *let* me do. You'll have to sweeten that temptation, my love." I tried to pull back upright, but the hellhound had a grip on my neck like a vise.

"I'll—I'll—" She released her hold on me as she struggled to think of something that would be tempting enough for me to accept. I could sense her absolute frustration as she toyed with the pendant around her neck.

"I'll owe you one," Aurelius said. "Whenever you need it. You have my word." The golden fae didn't blink as we assessed each other.

My brows perked with interest. "You'll owe me a favor, and the time and action are of my choosing?" I asked suspiciously.

"You have my promise," he said with a glance at Caly.

Fae *did not* barter favors lightly. He may as well have just signed his life away to me, and he knew it. The offer was made so quickly, it made me pause. Was this some sort of trick? He had seemed brighter since he returned from seeing the weathered on his own. Had something changed? I knew the sun shining had restored a modicum of his powers, but it was hardly enough for him to be offering me his death so easily— especially when we were on the way to a trial that would decide if he or I died. Surely, he wasn't so stupid. He was looking at Caly again. Was his confession all an act and he was going to fight for her love at the last second?

"Why?" I watched every line on his face for a tell.

Aurelius shrugged. "Because either you won't have enough time before they kill you to cash in on it, or I will be dead before you can ask more than what I'm willing to offer, and mostly because Caly won't come if you don't, and she's still my priority."

I nodded. That all made sense. "Fine. You owe me, Aurelius," I said with a grin.

He was a dead man walking—or flying.

Caly smiled and thanked her friend as she grabbed his side, keeping clear of the golden wings spread wide at his back.

Mine were still bigger.

"C'mon, Smokey, don't be shy. Snuggle up," the Seelie said as he grabbed me around the waist.

I pushed him away with both hands and was about to crack his freckled nose open when Caly's laughter slowed me. Her laughter pressed inside my skin and took me over with a spell.

Aurelius took the opportunity to grab me around the waist and take off up the mountain.

Unlike Caly, who he hugged closely to his body, I hung horizontally, loosely swaying in the wind as we gained height. Rain pelted my back, and I realized he could drop me at any time, the fucker. I was giving too much of my power to Caly to be able to fly and he knew it. I would have dropped him. The thought wouldn't have even lasted a second in my mind before I'd have let him drop had our roles been reversed. He was stupid not to. Even if Caly and he were only friends, if he didn't drop me before we got to Moirai, he could be the one to die. He would die even if they didn't choose him. I would make certain of that. I didn't believe he wasn't in love with Caly. There was no falling out of love with that woman, believe me. If it were possible, I already would have. Instead, I only fell deeper and deeper into the chasm that was Caly with every waking hour I existed.

I wasn't messy with my kills, and I didn't leave trouble behind to mess me up later. I prided myself on being thorough and strict when it came to those decisions, and Aurelius had been marked since the second he and his brother tried to take her away from me at Caly's second trial. Aurelius would soon pay the same price his brother had.

"What is that?" Caly shouted.

It was hard to hear with the sound of rain and wind beating against my ears in rhythm with the Seelie's feathered wings. One more reason why Smoke Slayers were superior to SunTamers in every way—Slayers moved in silence. I could shadow and fly without spooking a nervous sparrow because it wouldn't know I was there until it was too late.

"There! In the green!" she yelled as she pointed at the mountain top.

I was struggling to see anything with the wind and rain in my eyes, but it looked like a thin figure in green.

"It's a man," I shouted.

"It's the person who's been following us! They're trying to get the scroll and stop us again!" Caly screamed furiously.

Aurelius tried to hover above the soil and crystal ground at the top of the mountain, but the fae had already spent too much energy carrying all of us up, and he skidded to a stop before tumbling into the dirt so hard that he made a divot, thankfully already having dropped Caly and me a few feet back.

The Seelie rolled to a halt when he was only a few feet away from the figure. I could feel things coming from the man that I shouldn't—a power that felt ancient and didn't exist anymore. I brushed the goose bumps from the back of my neck before they could settle.

He was cloaked in a floor-length robe of forest green with no ornamentation or house markings. The rain slicked right off him, leaving his plain robe completely dry. A short gray and white beard and mustache were the only parts of his face that peeked out from the dark shadow of his oversized hood. A stern and tight-lipped mouth flashed out of the shadow and into view.

"Who the fuck—" Caly, ever the hellhound, went for the stranger.

I stepped in front of her, keeping her behind me as I held her tightly by the arm. I didn't want her anywhere near this stranger.

"No," I said over my shoulder as I watched the ominous man. Something in my voice must have given her pause, because she immediately stopped struggling against me and instead pressed into my back and peeked around my side.

I could feel how powerful this man was, and it rattled my bones in a way they hadn't been rattled in a long time—decades, to be exact. I hadn't even realized there was such a memorable, potent feeling attached to those battles until now.

Having been too young to have been in that specific war and thus having no idea what he was doing, Aurelius gathered himself and stood, towering over the stranger by at least a foot. Height didn't matter when you had power like this man though. My heart quickened. Even with our full power as a SunTamer and Smoke Slayer, we were easy work for this man's kind, so being near powerless was not going to bode well for either Aurelius or myself. Caly, bless her soul, wouldn't stand a chance in Tartarus against him except that I would die a bloody, lifeless shield in front of her practically human body if that was what it took to keep her safe.

We were fucked.

If, for whatever reason, this Artemi didn't want us in Moirai with the other Ascended, we were not going to get in.

The stranger stood confidently in front of Aurelius and spoke soft words that my ears couldn't pick up over the loud rain.

The weight of my body pressed into my heels as I prepared to fight with everything I had left.

Aurelius took a slow step back. He raised his arms up…and hugged the stranger.

"What the—"

"Fuck?" I finished Caly's question as we both stared.

The Seelie prince turned to face us with a wide smile, waving his floppy palms at us in a weak command to join them.

Caly and I joined the two of them, and Aurelius stepped to the side, giving me a clear view of the man's face from under the hood of the robe.

My eyes widened. I knew immediately who he was—not because I had ever seen him before but because that nose and those eyes were burned in my head. It was undeniable.

This man was Caly's father.

CHAPTER 14

CALY

Something was off, and I couldn't figure it out. Why was Mendax so wary of this stranger while Eli was so comfortable with him?

The air on the mountaintop felt different the closer Mendax and I got to them. As I stepped next to Eli, the man pushed back the hood of his robe to reveal his face. A few glasswing butterflies flew out from under the hood, only making it a few feet before the rain pummeled them into the dirt and rocks of the small landing at the peak of the mountain.

There was no denying it—the glasswing butterflies were the proof. This man had been sabotaging us from the beginning…and Eli was friendly enough with him to have given him a hug.

I peeled my eyes off the struggling, wet butterflies and saw a plain-looking older man with gray hair that was short on the sides and just a touch longer on the top. He had big blue eyes that made you feel seen, like he'd know if you lied or stole. Something about the way he carried himself—or perhaps it was the way the wrinkles near his eyes creased in a friendly sort of way—put me at ease. He had an air of superiority but a countenance that suggested the opposite.

"Cal, this is—"

"The man who's been following us," I interjected. Eli was a pushover, and unlike him, I wasn't going to let the kind eyes of *anyone* stop me from getting to my father. "Why are you doing this?" I demanded.

His eyes darted to Eli for a split second before they returned to me. He had the nerve to pretend he was surprised that we'd caught him. It was a good act but not quite good enough.

Eli moved toward me. "Cal, stop. You don't understand. This is—"

This time, the stranger was the one to cut off Eli's sentence, placing a quieting hand on his forearm. "I can tell it would take a lot more than words to convince someone as headstrong as yourself, but at this time, that is all I can offer you. On the contrary, I have not been following you, my dear, so much as I have been leading you," he said politely but somewhat stiffly.

"The glasswings," I said. Somehow it felt like I was losing footing with this conversation before it had even begun. "Are they your symbol? They must be if they follow you as they appear to. What are you?" Why was Mendax not doing something? It seemed so unlike him to be silent like this. I felt something from him in the bond too that I couldn't place.

The older man's eyes fell to my feet like I'd insulted him. I took the time to observe Eli. For some reason, his face also seemed to look a little uncomfortable.

"I am Artemi, Calypso. Forgive my surprise. I forget myself occasionally and fail to recall that no one around here sees Artemi anymore. Though we are unique in that each Artemi can have their own symbol, mine, as you've so aptly guessed, is the glasswing butterfly," the man said so softly, his voice almost didn't carry over the rain.

My head spun dangerously fast. How did he know my name? "You're Artemi…" It felt overwhelming to be in the presence of an Artemi again. I had never even seen one, aside from my sister. I gripped my pendant as if Adrianna herself would rise from the ashes inside it to save me. "How—how do you know my name?"

Eli grabbed my hand and squeezed. "This is your father, Cal."

I pulled my hand free, but no thoughts came that could tell me what to do beyond that. In a moment of pure panic, I looked to Mendax.

I'm here. I'll do whatever you want. Just tell me what it is you need from me.

What was it I wanted to do? I looked from Mendax back to...my father. Even thinking those words filled me with a blur of emotions that I couldn't begin to decipher. What was I doing just standing here? I should have been wringing his neck. If I killed him right now, I could leap from this mountain to my death and *finally* have completed all this; *every* plan and goal I'd made in my life would have been officially carried out. Mendax and Eli would remain alive, while I would be in the Elysian Fields with Adrianna, *finally*. It was the perfect ending.

So why was I just standing here? Why couldn't I move?

"Of course I would never expect you to call me anything of the sort. Please call me Zef, Calypso," stated the man with a gentle bow of his head.

Why wasn't I moving?! I couldn't even speak, yet I suddenly had so many questions, and not one of them involved asking what weapon he'd like to die by.

"You must be the slayer I've heard so much about. Smoke or shadow?" Zef asked, putting his hand out to Mendax. His voice was tighter and less friendly than when he had spoken to Eli and me.

Mendax casually let his eyes travel down to Zef's outstretched hand before they rose to his face again without taking the man's offered hand.

The Artemi pulled his hand back slowly, as if Mendax was a snake about to strike. "A bit odd, don't you think? Given our kind's history, I would have thought I'd be the one holding a grudge."

I caught Eli's eyes and, in typical best-friend fashion, silently asked him to somehow fill me in on what I was missing with a wide-eyed head tilt.

"I'm referencing the near-complete annihilation of our kind, Calypso," Zef said to me, eyes still on Mendax. "Your... boyfriend alone was responsible for a significant number of Artemi deaths during the Great War. That doesn't even include the destruction those of his lineage caused. He and his mother were two of the reasons I had to hide you and your sister in the human realm." The last sentence ripped away all composure he had, leaving in its place a rattled man filled with sadness and horrors of his own. It tugged at something in my chest.

It was something I'd never once considered—that he felt... well, anything about leaving us.

This was all wrong. This was not how my first meeting with him was supposed to go!

"I'm sorry to interrupt, but the water is rising fast. It will be here any moment," said Eli. "If you are taking us to Moirai, then we should do it soon."

Zef looked to Eli with a thankful pull of his lips and gave a nod. "Yes, forgive me, Calypso. This is not the time for a history lesson. We can discuss the Artemi struggles of your father and Adrianna's existence at a later time."

"Don't you *dare* speak her name." I glared at the man who so easily called himself my father. He wasn't my father—I had no such figure. "Dumping your seed in my mother never made you my father. It made you my sperm donor and *nothing* more." I palmed the dragon's claw concealed in my leather bag, fully ready to make him bleed.

But then something happened that surprised me to my core. I'm not sure why. Maybe because I had years to absently build the imaginary personality of my father and this was not at all what I had envisioned, but nonetheless, his reaction was unanticipated—and completely unexpected.

The man began to cry. Not a heaving mess or anything, but a few unrestrained tears. Truthfully, with the rain, I couldn't even see the tears, only the familiar expression of deep, in-your-bones sadness that leaks out when you least want it to. But that wasn't the part that surprised me. *My* reaction to it was.

My gut twisted and dropped. He was upset by my words, but not angry like I had expected or even hoped.

In that split second, in his face, I had seen the reflection of my pain *exactly* as I had in every bathroom mirror I'd ever broken down in front of. He was hurting too.

Was it possible he mourned the loss of them as I did?

Unexpectedly needing space from the group, I took a step back. I blinked away the zillion feelings that were attempting to overtake me and looked down to register that my feet were covered in water.

The flood had reached the top of the mountain—the tallest peak of the in-between that we knew of.

Again, I looked to Mendax. I don't know why. I wasn't some mindless woman without capabilities, but in these moments when there was too much clouding my thoughts, I knew he would make the decision closest to what my own would have been.

"I know that none of what is about to happen will make any sense to you right now, Calypso, but unfortunately, time is not my friend to explain further. I can live with you hating me, just as long as you live," Zef said softly.

"Sir," Eli said as he pointed to the now knee-level water.

How had it risen so fast? Whatever Eli had said to the weathered seemed to have made far more of an impact than what Mendax had attempted.

"Yes, yes," Zef replied somberly as he pulled up his hood to cover his head once again.

He waved his right arm, moving it in a long sweeping motion behind him, and a small wooden skiff slowly winked into existence in the exact spot he had waved. The empty boat swayed and rocked on top of the rising water.

Zef climbed into the oak skiff with the litheness of a teen-ager, waving us along as soon as he was in. Eli followed with a bit more of a struggle before he quickly stabilized and leaned over to help me in. Mendax lifted me up, his hands tight around my waist as he stopped midway to whisper in my ear, "You and I are in this together, no matter what." His cold blue eyes gave me every bit of strength I needed in that moment. He was right. We would be in this together until the very end—or until my end.

I nodded, and he continued lifting me into the boat, then climbed in behind me.

The perspective of the land was completely disorienting the higher the water rose, turning what a few hours ago had been an eerie mountain amid a snowy forest into a treeless expanse of blue-gray water. The sky still had a light sheen of sun poking through the clouds, but the farther up the mountain we rose, the closer the fluffy cumulus clouds got. Now, it appeared as if we were going to float right up into the clouds if the water didn't stop.

Scientifically, none of this made sense; it shouldn't have been happening, yet it was. I felt like I was in a fever dream of sorts when Zef held his palm straight and began to steer the boat with nothing more than a slight bend of his fingers. This type of magic was probably an everyday occurrence to Eli and Mendax, but to me, it still felt like I was imagining it all.

We continued this way for several minutes before Zef, at the front of the small boat, tuned to the three of us. "Oh my! Do forgive me!" he exclaimed before waving his hand at us and turning back around. The rain above our heads diverted itself as if there were an invisible bubble surrounding us—well, almost all of us.

Mendax remained next to me, still getting rained on.

Eli made a face at me, indicating how impressed he was. The silence was much louder now that the wind and rain had been redirected.

"He seems to be everything my father told me he was," said Eli, his voice filled with appreciation.

Of all the things to say to me right now. I leaned in close to his pointed ear. "Perhaps he'll visit your father in the Elysian Fields after I kill him," I whispered through clenched teeth.

Mendax rested his palm on my thigh and leaned in with a wink. "Say the word, pet, and there will be a mutiny at sea."

I squeezed his hand and laced my fingers with his.

"How much farther to Moirai, sir?" Eli asked.

"What a dick rider," Mendax sneered at Eli.

The water ahead of us seemed to have a lot more movement in it for some reason. The crisp, flat line of water in front was no longer flat; in fact, it looked almost beveled. The only reason for that would be—

"You son of a bitch!" I shouted at my father as I stood up from the small wood bench to see exactly what I knew I would.

We were headed straight toward the edge.

"What is it?" Mendax leapt up, causing the boat to rock so hard, it nearly tipped over.

"It's for the best," Zef muttered, facing away from us.

Mendax stepped to the front of the boat in a silent rage. As soon as his hand extended to wrap around the Artemi's throat, Zef's figure dissipated from sight.

Eli and Mendax began to shout at each other.

"Hold on!" I screamed. I barely had enough time to grip the board beneath me before we slowed to a stop, the skiff's bow hanging over the giant waterfall, teetering with nothing but air beneath the front half.

Whoosh! The boat tipped, nose-diving straight down.

All I could see was more and more water as I clung to the simple bench seat. My stomach tingled with the feeling of bottoming out from the sudden fall.

The boat's bottom dragged against the curtain of water, sending great sprays and splashes of water onto us. Suddenly, the cold water was pulling at my hair and throwing my body like a children's toy, yet somehow, I remained holding on to the bench.

Within a second, everything went dark. My body was submerged, but my head was still above the water's surface. I could feel it. My eyes opened in a panic to an overhead covering of wood. It took me a few seconds to realize the boat had flipped and I was under it, arms still looped around the bench.

I gasped for air and reluctantly moved one arm to swat around for Mendax and Eli with the hope that they would somehow be next to me. Panic set in when I felt nothing but the slow drag of cold water against my palm. They were too weak for this. What if one of them hit their head on the way down?

"Eli! Mendax!" My shrill voice echoed back into my face under the shell of the boat. I would need to flip it, but that would involve letting go of the bench completely.

The boat over my head flipped, and light burst into my vision, causing me to squint.

"Cal, are you all right? Are you hurt?" Eli grabbed ahold of my shoulders. His blond hair was slicked back, revealing more of his handsome face. "It's okay," he reassured me, encouraging me to let go of my bench so that he could put the boat in its upright position. "Mendax is up ahead. Let's get in, and the current will take us to him."

My head pounded, and my eyes stung. I felt like I had just been flushed down a toilet, both mentally and physically. I climbed into the boat, almost tipping it completely over again as Eli pushed me in before falling clumsily in after me.

Sure enough, the current wasted no time before dragging us down toward a dark figure I could only assume was Mendax. As we got closer, we began to pick up speed until we were barreling straight toward the wet fae treading water.

My eyes caught on movement at the edge of the stream. Along the sides stood tall, twisty trees with long, outstretched branches that seemed to be rattling with excitement as though they were watching our struggle.

"Mendax!" I shouted.

He rotated in the water, turning to face us head-on. As large as he was, I knew he had to be struggling to stay as still as he was in this current.

The small boat nearly took him out as it careened by, narrowly missing his shoulder. My stomach warmed with gratitude when Eli pulled him in the boat. I wouldn't have been able to get him out of the water had he left the task to me.

Mendax seemed to have taken the brunt of the fall in comparison to the rest of us. His face had small cuts that oozed onyx blood. Water dripped down like ink from his black hair. Somehow even after near waterboarding, he still looked like a god.

"Are you okay?" I croaked.

He was panting, so I was appeased by the rough nod that he was in fact fine.

"How are we going to get out of this stream? It's picking up speed as the channel narrows. Any idea of where we are?" Eli asked with a look to Mendax, who simply shook his head.

"What are those?" I asked as I pointed to the rough-looking trees along the water's edge. There had to be at least three rows of them back to back. It looked so dense. None of the branches had a single leaf on them, and I swore I saw faces on a few of them as they swayed and shivered. Horrible flashbacks of the forest bog tore through my mind and sent a cascade of goose bumps over my skin.

"It looks like the knots but older," Mendax said to Eli.

Eli said nothing, only relaying some side-eye to the other fae.

"Knots are a family of trees we have in most of the fae realms. They are as sentient as you and I are and live in the forest with other members of their family. A long, long time ago, a pair of fae brothers went into the forest to gather firewood for their family home. They accidentally cut down and murdered the knots' oldest living daughter while she was asleep. The knots turned aggressive and for centuries did not allow anyone to step foot into certain forests. Eventually, tree tamers came into play and everything got sorted out, but these knots seem a bit more…feral," said Eli as he glared at the trees.

"It's old, wherever we are. I can feel it," Mendax murmured.

The boat seemed to be slowing enough that I was sure between the three of us we could wade to the shore, but at the same time, I was hesitant to suggest it, because the knots along the edges seemed to be watching our struggle as though they were incredibly hard pressed for entertainment. I hated to think what untamed, feral trees would think was good entertainment if they could get ahold of us. I kept quiet and waited to see if perhaps we came across a better stopping point.

The stream ahead was almost completely out of view as it veered right so hard I feared we would be tossed to the shore and have no choice but to deal with the knots. Luckily we all three remained safely in the boat around the sharp turn.

Unluckily, we were headed straight at a wall of rock covered in vines.

Without a moment to spare, Eli jumped over the bench and hunkered down in front of me and Mendax. It was heroic, attempting to take the brunt of the crash, but unfortunately, with the speed we were going, if anything was going to happen to us, it was going to happen to *all* of us. There would be no avoiding injury.

Mendax rose to stand as we all clamored to find a way onto the sides before we smashed into the rock. The edge was too far away on either side, and wild knots lined the bank even if we found a way to get to it somehow. Their wild creaks and groans sang over the rushing water in a haunting melody.

"It's a cave!" I shouted as I gripped Mendax's forearm. "Behind the ivy, in the middle. Look! The water isn't splashing up. It's going through! There's a hole behind the ivy!" I shouted. I wasn't sure if that realization caused more excitement or terror. This felt like one of those awful water roller coasters in the human realm's theme parks, only no one had done any safety checks and there were trees that watched and cheered, hoping you'd drown.

A high-pitched scream left me. I gripped Eli's shoulders with one hand and Mendax's arm with the other. We were going too fast.

Our boat magically steered straight toward the black hole, which only served to open up another set of problems in my mind. Where did the hole go? If it went straight down—and I had a horrible feeling that it did—there was no way that this boat would be able to make it through a fall like that again.

Mendax squeezed my leg as we readied ourselves with one final look at each other.

The boat slammed into the wall of rock with a sound that will haunt me for the rest of my life—or at least it would have hit the wall of rock had the dark hole of the cave not moved. The bone-grinding sound was from the wall somehow moving until the opening was right in front of us.

Our boat sailed straight into chilly blackness.

"Oh my suns," Eli said with a heavy exhale.

I squeezed both my hands, seeking Mendax's and Eli's muscular comfort. I had no idea where we were going, but it somehow felt better knowing we would all be together.

We didn't stay in the darkness long before the boat picked up speed and the wind began to whip through my hair. The torrent of emotions around what was about to happen while not being able to see anything other than pitch-black was both horrifying and calming at once. It was like a part of my mind believed if I stayed in the dark, everything was a dream, and I didn't need to worry for another second. Of course, that wasn't true, and the other part of my mind wouldn't let me forget that.

Suddenly, the boat dropped. My hands fell away from both men as we plummeted. The nerves in my feet trembled as I kicked my feet into empty, black air, unsure of what or even *if* they were about to land on something. My hands clawed at the emptiness in a frantic effort to find something solid and unmoving, but they remained empty and untouched.

A bluish-gray light appeared from somewhere below me. Instinctively, I braced myself to land, tensing my body as the sensation of being dropped continued to tickle the inside of my belly. I heard two deep thuds accompanied by grunts that

I would recognize anywhere—the boys had just landed. My body remained tense and ready to hit the ground with them.

On and on and on I continued to fall until finally I saw what looked like a moonlit forest.

"Calypso!" Mendax shouted as he looked up at the stars and saw me plummeting toward him. He struggled to his feet and held his arms out—

—and I continued to fall past his outstretched arms.

I braced myself for the impact with the hard forest floor, but it never came. I continued to fall straight through it until I was tumbling through another sky, and then suddenly, I was lying on the damp forest floor.

My muscles ached as I lifted myself off the dirt. A bone in my back cracked, and I had a kink in my neck as if I'd been asleep on the floor for a year. Quickly, I stood, searching for Eli and Mendax.

"Eli! Mendax!" Even my voice cracked and scratched as if it hadn't been used for a long time. I could feel myself starting to unravel.

I quickly took note of my surroundings. The forest I was in was lush and beautiful. The trees looked like plain trees, not the kind that wanted to waterboard you, which I was very glad to see. The moss was green and spongy under my feet. It was beautiful, but I couldn't ignore the feeling as though everything had some kind of filter on it. It all just looked so…boring and lifeless. The air even felt different here, like I was seeing it in a photo but not *feeling* it. It didn't make any sense, but everything in this forest seemed like a decoration.

I heard soft sounds behind me, and I spun, expecting to see the boys.

Glasswing and monarch butterflies, at least twenty of them, fluttered slowly on a few trees behind me. A few sherbet-green luna moths were mixed in, along with a death's-head moth or two. Fireflies lit up the area. It looked like a fake display of butterflies.

"Wha—"

My eyes landed on the familiar circle of destroying angel mushrooms.

I was in the human realm—in the exact same portal I had used to get to Unseelie.

CHAPTER 15

CALY

S CREAMING WOULD DO NOTHING, I CONTINUED TO TELL myself.

A thousand times, I had stepped out of the fairy ring and back into it, and nothing had happened.

Calypso! Are you all right? Answer me, for fuck's sake!

The bond.

Mendax! The feeling of a thousand urgent, grasping hands surged from his end of the bond.

Are you hurt? It doesn't feel like it. You are in the human realm, aren't you? Are you safe? Aurelius and I can't get through the portal. We are in Seelie. We landed in a portal by a field of savage mini unicorns. One is attacking Aurelius right now. I like them a lot.

I sat down on the forest floor before I could fall. Being all alone, back in the human realm, felt like I had lost an appendage. It felt completely different to me after having spent so much time in the other realms.

What do I do? I pleaded through the bond. Of all the things I'd been through, the lies and secrets I had been required to keep, I couldn't remember ever feeling as alone as I did in this moment while sitting alone on the ground of the human forest.

Once, a long time ago, when my family had been taken

from me, I had wholeheartedly believed that I would never feel that kind of pain again, but in this moment, the same horrible feelings arose from within me.

What if I never got back into the faerie realms? What if I never saw Eli or Mendax again?

"No! No," I wailed. "You can't do this to me! You bastard!" I lay on my stomach and pressed the tops of my thighs and arms into the ground as hard as I could, willing the ground to absorb my flesh. Roots and dried leaves pressed into my skin, and my fingertips dug into the cool, damp dirt. I pushed my face into the earth with so much pressure, I saw sparkles behind my eyelids. But tears managed to get through, turning the crumbly soil into a muddy paint that stuck to my skin.

Mendax! Please, how do I get to you? Please!

I lay in the dirt sobbing for what felt like hours as I waited for an answer that never came.

Why would my father do this? It didn't make any sense. If he had wanted to be rid of me, he could have killed me quite easily, as powerful as he seemed. So he didn't want me dead, but...but he didn't want me in Moirai either. Hadn't he summoned me though?

On behalf of the Fates, I believe was how he had signed the first letter. Was it possible that he hadn't sent it? Was that why he had tried to steal—or rather break—the second scroll at Lake Sheridon? That letter had been from the Fates directly.

Was it possible that my father was doing all this because he didn't want to see me? Did he somehow know I was going to kill him? His track record with my sister and mother left nothing to be confused about. He only cared about himself.

I rolled over and sat up, feeling every minuscule bone and muscle in my body strain with the effort. I suspected that Eli and Mendax were unable to send any powers through the bond and tie to me, which was why I suddenly felt so terrible and weak. A part of me was glad they couldn't send me any powers. I was already enough of a burden on them both. I had never asked either one of them to bond or tie to me, but they had chosen me not knowing what a lie they had braided themselves into at the time.

Sitting here upset about the situation was doing me no good. Perhaps I could find another portal. I glanced around the wooded area. It was spring here, and though it paled in comparison to any of the fae forests, it was still a beautiful patch of woods. Fiddlehead ferns covered nearly half of the forest, and what wasn't covered by ferns or moss was decorated in beautiful yellow daffodils. A few common trilliums, with their three-petaled white blossoms, were scattered about, adding a bit of beauty to the deciduous forest floor. My eye caught on a small clump of particularly white trillium blossoms adjacent to a decent-sized ash tree.

I stepped out of the ring of mushrooms and took a few steps closer to the flowers. Were they…smiling at me? I knelt in front of the flowers, inspecting every corner of their petals, but had to sadly dismiss the little flowers as being ordinary. I looked over the bright daffodils next to the trilliums just in case, but like their neighbors, nothing was abnormal in their appearance.

I returned to my feet and began to turn away when the trillium blossom I had just been inspecting sneezed.

"Bless you—aaagghhh!" I jumped back, startled.

The little white flower giggled and tucked the two triangular petals on each side up against its little yellow…face? It opened its petal arms and slowly removed something from the little slit where its smile was. The trillium cupped the object in its petal and leaned toward me, bending its green stem as far as it could in my direction.

It was handing me something.

A common trillium flower, in what I thought was the human realm, was handing me a trinket. I snorted, unable to fight the absurdity before me. Had I hit my head?

I missed science. I missed how everything was reliable and measurable. I had gotten good at predicting and manipulating, though I had yet to discover gifting, sneezing flowers, so maybe I wasn't as good at predicting as I had thought.

My first thought was that it was somehow Adrianna's doing, that she was giving me some kind of token of hope or something that would get me back in the right direction so that I could still be with her.

"For me?" I stupidly asked the flower.

Of fucking course it was for me. Who else was out here? I rolled my eyes.

Even the flower giggled a little but courteously nodded its little flower body. Carefully, I reached out and picked up the small tan object it held out to me with my thumb and forefinger.

"Do you know how I can get back through the portal?" I asked hopefully.

The flower shook its head and shrugged its little petals.

"Thank you," I responded as I inspected the gift.

It was a tiny cream-colored scroll about an inch in size. I looked back down to the flower and thought about asking more questions, but it hadn't seemed to know much, and I felt silly talking to the flower as it was. It had laughed at me twice already.

As dexterously as was in my capabilities, I flattened out the tiny scroll, nearly throwing it to the ground in frustration when I saw the teeny-tiny cursive font scribbled on it.

"How the fuck am I supposed to read this?" I angrily shouted into the air. My eyes strained until all the words just blurred together. It took every ounce of strength I had left not to crinkle up the little note and give up. I couldn't though. What if this told me how to get back to Mendax and Eli? "Come on, Caly," I grumbled at myself, trying to think of how I could form a makeshift magnifying glass. If I recalled correctly, there was a small stream in the park a few miles over, but I would need a glass jar for the water, and I had no—

Glass!

I pulled the leather strap over my head and started to dig through my pouch, squealing excitedly when my fingers found the broken pieces of the glass scroll from the lake. It wasn't human glass, as it moved and bent obscurely, but being that it was crystal clear, there was a good chance it would still work.

I pulled the piece of scroll out and began to bend and cup the center of the small shard. It wasn't perfect, but I just needed to make a somewhat convex lens that was thicker in the middle. I bent the edges carefully so it curved out at the middle as best as it could. A convex shape would bend the light rays so they could converge together.

Water—I needed water.

Too impatient to try and find a stream or puddle, I pulled up my outer shirt and grabbed ahold of my still *very* wet undershirt. Nearly tripping over myself in my rush, I hurried to set the tiny scroll on the ground and then placed the bent piece of glass overtop. With both hands, I wrung my undershirt until my hands were red and raw. I untwisted the white cotton and glared at the small bit of water I had managed to get into the glass. It wasn't much, but it was all I had.

I looked down at the small scroll, and a sigh shook loose from my tight chest.

Calypso Petranova,

You have been returned to the place where you showed the most long-term happiness, Willow Springs, Michigan, in the human realm. Stay, and Cliff, Cecelia, and the rest of your small-town friends will welcome you with open arms, believing only that you were visiting relatives for a short week after your stay in the hospital.

Your tie to Prince Aurelius of the Seelie realm and your bond to Prince Mendax of the Unseelie realm will be severed under the stipulation that you never see them or any fae ever again. Both princes will be removed from the previously stated bond/tie with no penalty of death to either party.

Should you take the second option and enter the faerie ring that lays before you, it will take you to the Seelie realm with Mendax and Eli, where you will be met with a final letter containing the location of Moirai. The aforementioned bond and tie will remain in place, and the trial against you will commence, resulting in the death of one member of the arrangement.

All decisions/rulings shall remain in effect regardless of the life status of any related persons or relatives.

The Fates

I fell to the forest floor. Only when my chest squeezed painfully did I realize I was hyperventilating. I crawled until I could press my forehead onto the rough bark of the closest tree within reach. This decision would be easier if this was not an ordinary, boring human-realm tree but instead a knot that would kill me.

Eventually, my breathing slowed as it turned into ragged, coughing sobs. What was I going to do? If I stayed in the human realm, my problems with Eli and Mendax were solved—at least in the fact that neither of them would die because of me. Theoretically, I had been ready to take my own life after I killed my father, so I wouldn't have been able to spend more time with either of them. That was of course assuming everything went as planned. But that also meant that my father would still go on living his life without ever having to answer for what he had done to his own wife and child.

What was I going to do here? Settle down with a local and work at the parks forever?

For once in my life, everything could be…normal. I could get a job doing something with biology. I could live my life for me for the first time.

I was struck with a pleasant feeling of warmth in my gut at the completely mundane thought. How could that even sound nice to me after everything I'd done in the other realms? I'd spent my entire life working tirelessly to get to Seelie and destroy the Seelie queen before I went on to finish with my father, after which I would *finally* get to rest with my Adrianna, full of peace. I couldn't give up on things now…

Could I?

Eli had been joking when he'd dubbed me a Seelie royal. Even though fae laws were unusually true to phrase, what if it didn't hold true, and I didn't go to the Elysian Fields with Adrianna after I died? What if I went to hell with the rest of the mortals like me? Would I even be capable of killing my father? After seeing Mendax's reaction to my father and knowing what the Smoke Slayer was capable of, I was starting to doubt I'd even be able to kill him, and then what?

On top of all of it, I couldn't begin to imagine a world without Mendax in it. After everything we had been through recently, I hadn't given much thought to having a life without him somehow. It seemed like, even in death, we would find each other.

But not if I was in hell and he was in Tartarus.

Everything inside me, all the little voices of my subconscious, screamed at me to stay in the human realm, to let things go once and for all with my father and to be so filled with gratitude that both Mendax and Eli lived that I never even bothered to look back.

And perhaps that was what I would have chosen had I been a good, levelheaded person. But I was neither of those things. Not really.

I wanted retribution more than I wanted any kind of happiness for myself.

Especially after this.

My father couldn't stand the sight of me. He hadn't even met me, yet he was trying to sabotage us getting to Moirai just so he didn't have to look at me and be reminded of what he'd done and who he'd left behind.

I couldn't fucking wait to hurt him. I wanted to hurt him in ways I'd never hurt anyone. I wanted him to feel every little drop of pain that Adrianna and I had to.

An obscure thought suddenly occurred to me: maybe he had been right in choosing not to give me the Artemi powers. If I felt this destructive and ready to inflict pain as a human, I could scarcely imagine what it would have been like with the power of an Artemi.

I snorted to myself as tears fell down my cheeks. At some point, they had turned from tears of heartbreak to tears of fury. This realization hit me like a sack of bricks—that fucker had been right. He was right. Had he chosen to give me his powers, I would have massacred this entire realm right now. I wouldn't have hidden behind a veil. I would have waged a war on every single person who threatened me or my people. Everyone would have felt my wrath.

I sat back down, feeling weak again. Somehow this simple realization changed everything. My father had been right. Adrianna *was* and had always been the best one to take his powers. He…he had made the right choice.

After that, my choice was simple.

I read over the tiny scroll one last time before tucking it into my bag and stepping just outside the mushroom ring.

Feelings of guilt weighed me down for a moment before I pushed them aside. Sure, I could just stay here, and Eli, Mendax, and I would all remain alive. That in and of itself should have been enough for me to stay, but it wasn't.

Now more than ever, I needed answers. It was foolish to entertain thoughts that I would ever be capable of living a normal life in the human realm and be happy. I didn't even fully understand what happy was. That was not why I was in this world. I was here to avenge my family, and at this point, I didn't know what to think. I had so many questions running rampant in my head and only one person alive who could answer them.

He still deserved to die for what he did. Had he stayed and not left us, Mom and Adrianna would still be alive and with me. Had he stayed with us, maybe things wouldn't have been so hard for Adrianna when she got her powers. None of us knew how to help her but him, and he left us.

No, I would never be able to live a pretend life when all this took up my thoughts. I also desperately needed to say goodbye to Eli and Mendax before I left this life and went to rest with Adrianna once and for all.

I filled my lungs with air and stepped into the ring of destroying angel mushrooms.

CHAPTER 16

CALY

THE MOMENT I STEPPED INTO THE RING, I DROPPED. BEFORE I even had a chance to blink, I was falling, and for the first time, I welcomed the odd feeling in my stomach and the dizziness it caused.

I was going home one last time.

Knowing what was happening didn't make the fall any easier than when I had no idea what was going on or where I would end up.

"You better fucking find—ugh!" shouted a familiar, broody voice just before I smashed into something solid and landed on the warm, sunlit grass.

I opened my eyes and looked into the face of the most handsome man I'd ever laid eyes on. It felt like I was seeing him for the first time all over again but with fresh eyes that truly grasped how short our time together really was now.

"Calypso," he muttered. His voice felt like gravel and leather.

For the second time in my life, I had fallen on the Unseelie prince, only this time was much different from the first. Instead of looking at him with horror, as if he were a monster, I now stared at the darker flecks of blue in his cold eyes with complete and utter adoration and infatuation. Even though my life would be short, it had been filled with excitement, and Mendax would always be my favorite adventure of them all.

He rolled, pulling me into his lap in one smooth motion. He moved his head forward, and I wet my lips, preparing for a passionate kiss, but was surprised when he wrapped his arms around me and squeezed. Every crumb and morsel of doubt left my body in that moment, and I knew I had made the right decision.

"Please don't," Mendax whispered against my neck. "Don't leave me again. Ever."

The good feelings I had shattered and broke, and once again, my guilt returned. "I won't," I replied softly. The lie sat on my tongue as sour as a lemon. I would be leaving him again, only this time I wouldn't return. I'd like to think he would understand, but when it came to me, Mendax did a lot of things I couldn't understand.

The worst of it was if I was successful and arrived in the Elysian Fields to be with my sister, I was guaranteed to never see Mendax again. He was granted a resting place in Tartarus with the rest of the Unseelie royals. Even in the afterlife, we would never get another chance to be together.

"Stop hogging her," Eli shouted as he reached over and pulled me out of Mendax's grip. If I had thought the previous fae's hug was tight, I had been under a grievous misconception. My best friend squeezed me like a vise, spinning me around in a circle. He held me so tight, he almost pressed my broken pieces back together again. Everything had turned so complicated between him and me. It almost felt like this was the first time we were really seeing each other since we'd been separated for all those years. Before an engagement was pushed on us…and before I had killed his mother.

It felt like I had my best friend back.

Perspective is a messy bitch that knows no boundaries.

"Oh, Cal!" Eli exclaimed after setting me back down to the ground. "We couldn't get through the portal! I didn't know where you went. I'm so sorry. I had no idea Zef was going to be so…" He paused and looked at the sky while he thought of the word he wanted.

"Ouch!" I yelped, jumping a solid foot off the ground. Something had bitten me in the ass. Hard.

"Suns in the sky, this damn pony!" Eli exclaimed loudly.

I spun in time to realize that a floricorn had accosted me. It had a beautiful chestnut-brown coat with a pretty blond mane and big brown eyes below the most beautiful spiraled horn. The little unicorn pushed its stubby little body between Eli and I, putting her ears back and nipping at the other floricorn that stuck its nose near Eli. She snorted and pushed my hand until I rubbed her ear.

Immediately, I remembered the sassy creature from when she had been absolutely enamored with Eli during an earlier visit to the farm.

"Thimble!" I said happily as I rubbed the mare's ears.

"Thistle," Eli corrected me. When I gave him a questioning look, he replied, "I've thought about this beastly pollinator once or twice since we visited." He chuckled.

Mendax held out his hand and revealed a tightly rolled glass scroll that sat like a ticking bomb in his palm. He nodded, urging me to take it.

Reluctantly, I did. The smooth glass felt heavy in my grip. I looked to Eli for some sort of reassurance before I opened it. He watched while nervously petting his new friend.

"Talk with Zef before you decide to do anything." His voice was low and somber. He sounded so much more tired now than he had at the beginning of this journey.

"Okay," I replied with a nod. It was an easy response after my mental drawbridge of questions had been lowered. It was a clipped response, but I didn't want to get into it with him now. I was still furious he was siding with the man who tried locking me out of a realm just so he didn't have to see me and deal with the consequences.

I ran my thumb over the smooth glass. Prickly goose bumps

rolled down my back when I unrolled the scroll. Every time I did this, it was the same whimsical feeling. My human brain just *could not* understand manipulating glass with such ease.

Calypso Petranova,

1176 Arcanus Lane, the in-between
    The second room on the left. Hay is in the first room on the right.
    538 lilies

Attached to the very bottom of the letter was a small strip of ripped paper.

DIVIDE AND SWALLOW THIS TICKET FOR A SHORTCUT.

"It's the address! We have an address!" I squealed.

"Fucking finally," Mendax grumbled.

Eli let out a deep breath.

I handed the scroll to Mendax so he could inspect it and bounced over to Thistle and gave her a big kiss on the nose. She snorted at me but seemed to like the kiss.

"This isn't signed," Mendax noted. "All the other ones have been signed 'the Fates.'"

I froze. He was right.

"There's also that little note at the bottom. Since when have the Fates ever offered us a shortcut?" Eli interjected. "Nothing good ever comes from taking a shortcut."

"What's so weird about a note instructing you to eat it for a shortcut?" I asked.

Silence. The guys just stared at me.

I tossed my hands up in the air. "In the human realm, a flower pulled a teeny-tiny letter out of its mouth and laughed at me—not with me, *at* me. A mini uni—sorry, floricorn—is guarding you like a German shepherd. You can speak to me through an invisible bond tying our souls together, and *you* turn into a fox." I caught my breath. "So no, eating a piece of paper for a shortcut doesn't seem that weird to me here."

Another moment of silence passed as both men looked at each other thoughtfully.

"Ya know, she might have a point," murmured Eli as he refocused on petting Thistle.

"I don't like it. If something is too easy, it's about to make you experience something really difficult. I think we head back in the direction of the Inn Between. Someone over there can tell us where this street is, and then we can see if it's worth looking into," Mendax said.

"What? It will take days to get back to the inn. What if this street isn't even that way? We don't have enough strength between the three of us to do all that traveling," I argued.

"She's right," Eli said as he lifted the piece of torn paper up to the light.

"Mendax has a point though. All the other letters have been signed. What if this is another trick from my father to get rid of me?" I asked. Saying the words out loud made me furious all over again.

"Are you serious? He's doing this because he loves you. How can you not see that?" Eli asked.

I bit the inside of my cheek so hard, warm blood swirled on my tongue. "There's only one way to find out if this takes us to Arcanus Lane or not," I said as I snatched the strip of paper from Eli's hand. I ripped the paper into three pieces and moved to hand Mendax the scroll and his piece. His penetrating stare captured me as he refused to hold out his hand. "Here," I growled at him as I shoved the items into his chest. He didn't budge. "Fine," I said, setting the scroll on the ground with the remaining two pieces of the ticket promising a shortcut on top.

I moved a few steps away from the boys. I felt like a toddler who had disobeyed his parents and was being scolded.

"I'll see you at Arcanus Lane," I murmured.

"Cal, wait!" Eli moved toward me.

With reckless abandon, I stuffed the paper in my mouth. It tasted like glue and old books. The wetness of my tongue clung to the small paper, and I had a bit of a struggle moving the crumpled-up wad to the back of my throat, where I swallowed it.

My eyes darted between Mendax—still silent and broody—and Eli, who had begun to say my name in a falsetto while he lunged for me.

I blinked, and everything went black.

When I opened my eyes, I was standing at the end of a long, windy path made of bricks. My heart pounded at the realization that I had actually left the guys. My lungs filled with the crisp night air as I whipped my head around and tried to get my bearings.

Blue darkness claimed the upper half of my vision. The moon seemed abnormally large in the sky as it cast a silvery glow on the dew-tipped grass that lined either side of the brick road. There were no trees in sight, at least that I could see. A few clumps of fog floated in the lush grass, looking like faint clouds or ghosts. I was in the middle of nowhere and nothing.

Curiosity, ever my friend and enemy, urged me to continue up the brick path and see what lay in the shadows, out of my moonlit view. I listened for any animals that might tip me off to where I was or what was around me, but it was deathly quiet. Not even a mosquito dared to break the silence. I took a long breath, picking up on the scent of grass and something sweet and calming, like lavender…or maybe basil?

Something solid brushed against my shoulders.

Swallowing my scream, I turned and cracked my sharp elbow into whatever it was while I threw a low punch with the other hand. A cry ripped from my chest when my elbow cracked painfully against whatever was behind me as a strong forearm pulled me against a hard chest.

"Boo," Mendax's husky voice whispered into my ear.

My eyes fell shut with relief. I should have known he wouldn't let me go alone. "You came," I sighed. He adjusted his pressure on my neck, forcing me to turn around to face him. Eagerly, I wrapped my arms around his waist. "I think your armor broke my elbow," I whispered with a laugh.

"I think your elbow dented my chest plate," Mendax returned.

Laughter burst out of me. He had been so somber and reserved this entire trip, and it felt nice to see him lighten up a little. Embarrassed by my loud cackling, I looked up, expecting to see him with a scowl or another broody and stiff mask molded to his handsome face. He had never been the light-hearted, joke-making type, and for some reason, I thought he might be annoyed with my own humor, that maybe he would think I was letting my guard slip if I laughed or something. But when I sought out his eyes, nothing could have been further from the truth. Mendax's blue eyes looked two shades brighter as they glittered in the moon's glow. His mouth had dropped open in surprise, a hint of a smile lingering at the corners of his eyes and mouth.

He looked like he had just discovered he possessed magic.

In all my thoughts of Mendax, none had been of him appearing awestruck, but gods above, I hope it stayed. He looked so…so happy.

"What is it?" I chuckled. I shot a glance behind me to make sure there wasn't something else that was causing his expression.

"Nothing," he replied. His fingers laced into my hair at the back of my neck. His head lowered, and he pressed his soft lips against mine. Eagerly, my mouth parted, begging for more of him. His touch, no matter how threatening or gentle, sent sparks straight into my bloodstream. "I enjoy your laugh immensely." He deepened the kiss as he wrapped me tightly in his embrace. How was it possible one person was capable of making me feel this way? "I love you, Calypso. Stop leaving me though, or I will make you regret it, I promise."

My heartbeat doubled for a second. There was no way he could know that I planned to end my life after I killed my father, right? I hadn't said a word out loud. "I—"

The disgruntled whinny of a horse cut off my thoughts.

Appearing from nowhere, Thistle the floricorn stomped

her foot on the brick path just behind where Mendax and I stood. She put her ears back and took a step toward Mendax's butt.

"Do it and you'll be flower-scented adhesive." His low voice threatened the equine.

"Oh my suns! She must have eaten Eli's paper!" I clamped my hands over my mouth. "But if she ate his, that means he won't be able to—"

Eli suddenly appeared, almost on top of Thistle. "Fucking disgusting!" he exclaimed as he spit on the ground and rubbed his tongue feverishly with a swatch of his shirt.

Mendax and I made a face at each other and stepped apart.

"Oh no, don't stop your make-out session for me," Eli said sarcastically through bouts of spitting.

"Aurelius, why is that creature here?" Mendax grumbled.

"After you left, I went to grab my piece of paper, and this heifer"—he pointed to the chestnut unicorn—"ate my piece! I had to grab it out of her mouth, and I only got half—and it was wet!"

I grimaced. "You ate the piece after it was already in her mouth?"

Mendax burst out laughing. It sounded rough and new and wonderful.

"Did you want me to go to Moirai with you or not?" Eli huffed grumpily. Thistle proceeded to rub her head up and down against his thighs aggressively as he tried to shove her away but laughed and rubbed her head as she had wanted instead.

"She really loves you." I smiled at the two of them.

"All the better. I'm sure you were tired of being the third wheel by now," crooned Mendax.

"Look," I said, pointing to one of the bricks under our feet. Several of them had letters and words on the tops. One directly in front of my foot stuck out to me. "Arcanus Lane." The lettering was jagged and imperfect, reminding me of carving my name in clay as a child in school. "This says Arcanus Lane! Then the letter was real. It was a real shortcut."

Mendax looked to me, still wisely apprehensive of this being a setup of some kind. Eli was busy pulling grass from the side and trying to feed Thistle.

"Then I suppose we should continue up the pathway." I led the way with Mendax following closely behind me and Eli and Thistle bringing up the rear.

"Do you think we can stop to collect some grass before we get to Moirai?" Eli said, looking slightly bashful about asking. "I want to make sure Thistle has something to eat when we get there. I don't know if they have floricorns in Moirai," he said, completely serious.

"Oh my suns!" I stopped in my tracks and dug into my bag. "The scroll—the one we just got! It said something about hay!" I grabbed the scroll and read it out loud.

Calypso Petranova,

1176 Arcanus Lane, the in-between
 The second room on the left. Hay is in the first room on the right.
 538 lilies

"They knew this would all happen! They knew I would choose to return to you guys and that Thistle would end up eating some of the paper and coming. They put hay in Moirai, knowing all this would happen." My mouth hung open in pure befuddlement. I felt like a pawn.

"What do you think five hundred thirty-eight lilies means?" The golden prince absently combed his fingers through his new companion's mane as he looked around. The little pony leaned against him a little, watching him with loving brown eyes. I could feel how happy the mare was to be reunited with Eli.

"I don't have the slightest," I replied. If I didn't think he and this floricorn were so cute, I would have been jealous of my best-friend status being taken by a farm animal. Seeing how happy he looked made me realize how unhappy he had been before. I thought everything that had happened with his mother and the rest of Seelie weighed on him more than he would admit.

The silence of Arcanus Lane was the accompaniment to a noiseless chorus of finality. This was it. We would continue down this road to Moirai, where our lives would be forever changed.

With one final exchange of looks, Mendax led the way down the path that would end up being the cause of my sadness for years to come.

CHAPTER 17

ELI

I WATCHED CAL WALK BEHIND MENDAX. SHE WAS FAVORING HER right leg, obviously in more pain than I had realized. She never was one to complain about things like that. I thought of my father and how strong he had been, what a good person he was. There was no way he would have been as close as he was to Zef if Zef wasn't a good person. I knew it was foolish, especially after everything he had done, but I remembered Zef visiting with Father before he passed, and I knew Zef loved his family. I knew he loved Cal and Adrianna more than anything. He had to.

My mother had destroyed any chance Cal ever had at a loving, happy home life. Now that I couldn't be the one to give that to her, I had to be the one to make sure it happened for her. If that meant Mendax stayed bonded to her, then that was a sacrifice I needed to make. After everything my mother did to her, I owed that to Cal. I needed to convince her not to kill her father too. I knew her well enough to know she had something in the works in her brain—a backup plan that didn't involve help or actions from any of us. I supposed that was my family's fault too; she never felt like she could fully trust or rely on anyone, not even me.

I took a breath and made one last effort before we reached whatever lay waiting for us at the end of this path. She just needed to see that he wasn't as bad as she was making him out to be...I didn't think.

I knew in my gut I should leave things alone and not meddle, but Cal could miss out on having a real relationship with her father because she didn't bother to listen to his side. What if she didn't get to have her father in her life because she had an itchy trigger finger...or, I guess in her case, an itchy throat-severing finger and lost the chance to get to know him forever all because she was impatient and murdery. "Cal, Zef is—"

"An awful, horrible dead man walking?" she offered. Her quick response gave me a hunch that she had been thinking about him too.

My face puckered. "Awful? That's arguable. He put you in the human realm to keep you safe. I know it's not what you want to believe, but he cares deeply about you. I just know it."

"What?" She flinched. "Are you out of your mind, Aurelius?"

Fuck, the dreaded full name.

"He doesn't care about me at all. He put me in the human realm to keep me away. You think he would have purposefully stayed out of my life when I needed him so much because *he cared deeply* about me?"

"You know, this is just like you." I shook my head. "You *always* think the worst of everyone. Not every person is horrible and deserves to die. People make mistakes, Cal. It doesn't mean they should die for them. How will they ever get better and change if you won't let them?"

"Why do you care so much?" Mendax asked, stopping in front of me.

"I don't always think the worst of everyone, and you know what? You would be the same if you'd been through half the shit I have!" Cal yelled, stopping on the bricks.

"Oh really? I don't understand half the shit you've been

155

through? Like your friend murdering your mother? Or growing up with a mother who tried to leave you in a forest? Maybe your sister has been leading an entire army of Fallen fae—the same ones who have been trying to overthrow you and take over your castle because they have nowhere to go and blame you. Yeah, sorry to rain on your pity parade, but I *have* been through that!" I spun on my heels and took a few steps. This was not going how I had hoped, and who knew how much longer this road actually was?

"That's what this is about?" she snapped, taking a few steps toward me. "You told me you understood. Saracen killed my mother and sister and put me through hell! You think your mother deserved to live? That she could have *changed*?"

I knew I shouldn't, but the hinges of my mouth were loose with sadness. "Cal, what do you think the families of all those hits you did for my mother would say if they were asked that about you? Do you think *you* deserve to live? I know for a fucking *fact* you killed innocent people. Somewhere in your mind, you think it makes it okay if you kill because they have wronged you, but you're no better than them. You think they didn't have a vendetta? You think none of them had families? Sons like me?"

"Watch your mouth," Mendax growled at me.

Cal snapped her head around and shot him a look. She didn't need a fucking guard dog.

Thistle let out a hellish-sounding snort and pushed against me, letting me know she had my back.

"I don't give two shits what the families of the people I killed think or do, and do you know why?" she screamed. "Because the only people I care about are standing next to me right now or are dead! Don't act like you know more about my father than I do, Aurelius, just because a hundred years ago, he was best friends with your father. Look at who your father chose to marry. His judgment of people, much like your own, is not without flaws."

The sting of her words must have been written across my face.

156

"Yes," I said softly. "What kind of an *idiot* gets the wool pulled over his eyes for twenty years thinking a girl is sweet and kind when she's really a greedy, malicious, venomous monster filled with darkness who refuses to accept anyone could be a good person who simply made a mistake they regret."

It was her turn to feel the sting of harsh words.

The two of us glared at each other with clenched jaws.

"If you two ever decide to stop wasting time, we can get this journey over with." A few feet away, Mendax stood like a shadow, ready to evaporate into the dark landscape behind him.

Cal and I looked at each other again with mutual understanding. This was by no means the first time we had ever had a fight. That was another part of being so close to someone—you didn't always have the same views, but you loved them anyway, even when you didn't like them. This wasn't the time for us to be fighting.

"You could have stayed…" I trailed off. "You might have been happy in the human realm."

"Are you upset that I came back?" she snapped defensively.

"No, not at all. I just—I can't help but feel like this is about to have a horrible ending for me," I replied calmly.

"Mr. Positive, everyone," Cal announced sarcastically.

What a wiseass. "If you succeed in your attempt to kill Zef, they will kill you, and if they force you to choose between Mendax or I, you will choose him—you should choose him— so sorry for my lack of positivity."

"You don't know what you are talking about. It won't come to that, I promise. We will all get out alive," she offered.

"I know we will."

"No, we won't."

Our gazes both shot to Mendax, ever the contrarian.

"I don't think you realize what it will take to kill your father, Calypso. With the state you are in right now, he'd have to do it for you. What do you think is going to happen to us when you fail to kill him and instead only anger one of the most powerful Artemi that ever existed? I cannot protect you like this. There is *nothing* I can do to stop him if he goes for you, and I will likely die trying. None of us will leave Moirai alive if you attempt to kill Zef. It's as simple as that. I don't particularly care one way or the other, but Aurelius sure does seem set on living. I don't think you should kill him either. Not yet."

Mendax and I locked eyes. The large fae gave a slight nod in my direction.

How could Cal possibly not see how much people could change when she was in love with him?

CHAPTER 18

MENDAX

I F FELT NICE TO BE ENVELOPED IN THE DARKNESS OF ARCANUS Lane. I felt at home in the shadows and the unseen and had spent far too much time in the harsh sun during these travels. Not having my full powers made me feel weak and helpless, something I'd never experienced before. I didn't like it. Feeling the shadows lick at my darkness made me feel more myself than I had since I'd been in Unseelie.

I was ready for this to end. I was absolutely sick and tired of wandering around like a bunch of helpless sheep. It was not my idea of an enjoyable time watching my queen with another man. Though even I had to admit that it was quite obvious how much he cared for her—in a very nonromantic way. He'd seemed to have changed his intentions along the journey, and it was clear even to me that he really didn't have any thoughts past friendship with Caly. I wondered if that bothered her or if the timing of it all truly had been mutual. It didn't matter. I was still going to kill him.

I had been quiet on this journey, watching and waiting for when it would finally come to an end. I knew Caly better than both her and Aurelius combined. She was going to fall on the sword. Somewhere in her troubled mind, she thought that I would actually let her go, that I wouldn't know her duplicity. She had already shown me all her fiery, wicked little cards when she'd stabbed me in Unseelie the first time. Since then, I'd watched her closer than she could ever begin to imagine. I'd picked up every little tell she possessed. It was like she didn't even *want* to hide it from me. Every time she talked about one of us dying or what was going to happen when we were in front of the Fates, she touched the pendant on her neck with her sister's ashes. If she thought I would let her leave me again, she was grievously mistaken.

I happened to glance in her direction and watched her mouth move, unbeknownst to her, as she silently read all the bricks she could as she walked. I didn't believe her father was trying to get rid of her in the same way she thought it. He could have crushed all three of us like beetles on the boat had he wanted to. No, he loved her. I could see it on the ship when he wouldn't look at her—couldn't. I recognized that feeling from my own experience with her, though for much, much different reasons. He sent her to the human realm to keep her safe—from what, I had no idea. Perhaps he thought he was saving her from me, that sending her to the human realm would be better than being bonded or tied to the Unseelie or Seelie prince. No doubt he hated us, me in particular. My family was mostly responsible for their kind even having to go into hiding—*of course* he didn't want her with me. But much like Caly, he didn't have a choice either. She was mine.

We walked in silence, each observing the various words on the brick path. The soft clops of the floricorn's hooves on the path were like the ticking of a clock—or a bomb—counting down the seconds until our deaths. Aurelius fussed with the little pony like a fucking mother hen. It was a shame he hadn't had that thing with him this entire journey; it might have served him well to not have been so annoying.

The dark edges of the land seemed to move alongside us. Every stretch of path we walked expecting to see farther into the distance only proved us wrong, showing us nothing. Even I couldn't tell what, if anything, lay on the other side of the hazy darkness. It was all I could see. A moonlit sky, broad and silver, and a brick path that seemed to go on for an eternity, though I could see nothing around it and only a couple hundred feet in front of us.

This continued until eventually the darkness cleared enough to see a decent-sized house standing alone in the night. The bricks dead-ended right in front of the house, transitioning into a large gray stone walkway that led to a circular driveway of small rocks and stones with a tall, empty, and chipped three-tiered fountain in the middle of the circle. Iron gates were open on either side of the driveway. The house was black as night with ogival archways and pointed lancet windows. It was not particularly large but shockingly grand.

"Look." Caly pointed to several of the clear-winged butterflies we had seen before. They were a lot harder to see in the darkness, but their glassy wings reflected the cast of the moon, causing a glittering effect everywhere they fluttered.

"We must be in the right place," Aurelius said. "Look at all of them."

We had paused at the very end of the brick path to take in the surprising house. It was quiet inside, with no movement. It was obviously inhabited though, by the looks of the immaculate estate, not to mention the warm glow of yellow lights that shone through the windows.

"This isn't exactly what I had expected, though now that I think about it, I'm not exactly sure what I expected to be the headquarters of the gods and Ascended." Aurelius shrugged.

Caly sniffled. "No matter what happens inside, please never *ever* doubt how much I love each of you. You have both changed my life in so many ways that I'm not even capable of thanking you each properly." Caly began to tear up.

"Stop, Cal. This isn't goodbye. We will find a way to get out of this alive." Aurelius pulled Caly in for a hug, but Thistle neighed and moved between the two of them so only their upper bodies were able to hug. Thistle was growing on me fast.

"But what if…what if this *is* goodbye? We don't know what's going to happen once we get inside those doors," she said softly.

Son of a bitch. She was definitely going to take herself out when it was time. I could tell by the way she teared up. They were the kind she had when she was going through something really hard and couldn't share it with anyone. I had seen them before. Stars' sake, was she out of her mind? She wiped at her tears and wrapped her small hand around her sister's ashes.

I was so furious, I wanted to rip the necklace off and choke her with it. What the *fuck* was she thinking? No one was going to take her away from me but me!

"Okay, well, I guess no reason in getting upset quite yet, huh? Just know I love you both so much it almost hurts." She gave half of a fake smile and turned toward the door.

Aurelius and I locked eyes. He knew something was up too.

"We are following your lead," I stated. She had no idea how sincerely I meant that.

The blond hellhound turned back one last time before she got to the large black door and stepped up to me. She pulled my face down and kissed me so deeply and sincerely, I almost believed it was our last kiss. I felt the tear drop down her face and onto our lips. This was her goodbye.

I pulled her full lower lip into my mouth and bit, hard. She gasped and pulled back with flashing eyes. Mine had remained open, watching her. I must've looked angry as Kaohs. I was pissed off. Anyone that tried to hurt her was an enemy, and that included herself in this moment.

She pressed against me and kissed me again. Harder, needier. Her blood sang across my tongue, and I immediately felt my cock stiffen. I wanted to bury myself inside her and teach her a lesson in messing with what was mine.

"Go to the door before I take you on the front porch of your daddy's house," I ordered.

She pulled away, but her eyes were full of heat. She pressed her lip with her finger and turned to face the door, lifting her hand up to knock.

The door slowly opened with a deep creak.

CHAPTER 19

CALY

EVERY MUSCLE IN MY TIRED BODY TENSED AS THE DOOR creaked open. I held my breath as I waited for someone to come out from behind the large door and greet us.

Nothing.

I glanced back to Eli, puzzled. He looked slightly creeped out. His mouth turned down as he shrugged. My eyes landed on Mendax next. As I knew he would, he nodded for me to enter but began to step in front of me so he would enter the house first, keeping me safely tucked behind him. I cut him off and gave him a thankful look as I moved in through the door.

"Hello?" I called as I stepped inside.

The inside was beautiful, with a cozy, antiquated sort of appeal to it. A few wall sconces were lit with the familiar firefly-like lights I'd seen in Unseelie. They lent a warm glow that flickered just as a candle would.

"You can't bring that thing in here," Mendax grumbled at Eli.

"I'm not leaving her out there. Thistle's a part of the team now, huh, pretty girl?" Eli said as he rubbed the large brown ears of the squat mare.

Mendax rolled his eyes but didn't do anything more as the

clip-clop of the floricorn's hooves landed on the polished wood floor of the entryway.

"They said there was hay in here. They knew she would be coming with us," I added.

There was a large, formal dining room with a fully set long table to our left. To the right looked like some sort of a sitting room or something. It was hard to see much with the dim lighting. It really did give the impression of an old, haunted manor. It was even equipped with a winding, black staircase to the right that appeared to go up about two floors.

However, the most interesting part was the hallway in front of us. It was the most well-lit space in the house, leaving no question as to exactly where we were supposed to go. It wasn't very long; in fact, the inside of the house appeared modest in comparison to what I had expected.

I glanced to the guys before continuing to the hallway. It appeared to have three rooms that branched off from it, one on the right and two on the left. The door on the right was closed, leaving only the door at the end on the left open, with bright beams of amber light spilling into the hallway from inside.

"It said hay is in the first room on the right, but we are supposed to enter the second door on the right," I recalled.

I took a step forward, making room for Eli and Thistle. The old floor squeaked with the weight of my movements. Eli took a breath and then opened the door. Every one of us, including Thistle, braced ourselves, ready for something to leap out and attack us.

The plain black door glided open, and Eli gasped, making both Mendax and I grab our weapons.

"Okay, this is kind of freaky," Eli said, stepping inside and turning to us with a grin.

He and Thistle moved inside tentatively, and Mendax and I brought up the rear. The second we stepped inside the room, it was as if we were transported to a beautiful stable. A door inside was beautifully painted with vines and a small brown unicorn that said *Tack room and supplies*. Startled by my faltering steps, I looked down to see another brick floor, similar to the path we had followed to get here.

"Holy shit, look," I said, pointing to the bricks at our feet.

THISTLE was carved into at least ten bricks that lay in a beautifully staggered pattern across the center of the floor. The sides of the room were lined with clean, darkly stained stalls that I couldn't help but notice were the perfect size for a small pony. It was as if this room had been made just for the little unicorn. As promised, there was a mound of hay at the back wall that was so tall, it touched the high ceiling. I stared and stared, trying to understand how this room could be so big when I knew that the rest of the house was so small and that there were at least two other floors above this one.

Thistle happily walked over to a metal bin filled with grain attached to the wrought-iron top of the stall closest to us.

"You okay to stay here while we check out the other room?" Eli whispered to the floricorn.

She didn't move her eyes away from the large bin of food.

"Okay then. I'm just down the hall if you need anything, okay?"

Her mane flicked as she moved her weight to her other feet and continued happily eating.

Eli shrugged with a smile as he turned back to us. "Okay then, I guess it's time to go face the music."

As we turned and walked to the door, I noticed a small iron hook on the other wall draped with a beautiful leather saddle emblazoned with small intricate suns. A beautifully knit orange blanket lay next to it. I squinted as the boys moved out the door in front of me.

My breath caught in my throat at what I read on the small gold label attached to the saddle.

"Cal, you coming?" Eli asked at the door.

I bit my cheek as I passed him and walked out the door, looking at him in a completely different light.

Eli said another goodbye to Thistle and closed the door. As we stepped into the dark hallway, I noticed that the second door on the right now had a light glowing from under the crack at the bottom.

Mendax took the lead this time, stepping up to the black door and turning the round brass handle. Warm light spilled into the hallway, illuminating the cozy space. Not a sound could be heard throughout the old house other than the shuffle of our steps and the creak of wood.

Mendax stepped inside, and I followed close behind, once again ready should we need to fight.

The familiar smell hit me like a brick to the head, confusing me in more ways than I ever could have thought possible—the slightly dusty smell of old books.

We were in a library, and not just a medium-sized house library like I would have expected of a home of this size but a *humungous* library, with rows upon rows of leather-bound tomes. A modest fire burned at one end with two dark, wing-backed chairs positioned cozily in front. I noticed an ornate gold frame with an older-looking painting of a harpist, another with what looked to be a nicely suited man.

In school, I had spent many evenings in a library studying. It was one of the only places that gave me an escape from what was happening when I was at home. Our local library looked scant in comparison to the many volumes in this room. Just like Thistle's room, this one was shockingly large. There had to be at least four hundred thousand books in this room alone, and none of them looked newer than a hundred years, with many of them falling apart at the bindings.

"Well, what do we do now? This definitely isn't the secret lair of Moirai," Eli said.

I shrugged and began down one of the many aisles of books. The shelves were a beautiful dark wood that were lined up in a similar style to my local bookstore, except much grander with a gold wall sconce and painting on the end cap of every row. I moved down the aisle, scanning the book spines for some type of a clue. Most of the titles were in a language I didn't know; some didn't even have a title. I picked a random book from the shelf and flicked through the thick parchment pages of the deep red book, looking for some type of a clue.

It was completely blank.

I returned it and grabbed another. This one had a story about a girl and a wishing well. It looked fascinating, and for a split second, I thought about taking it with me, having completely forgotten where I was.

"Well?" Mendax asked.

"I haven't a clue." I shrugged. "Some are blank, while others have long, detailed stories. I haven't found anything significantly telling though. What do you think?" The fire in the back of the room sent a warm glow that backlit the enormous man, giving him even more of the appearance of a shadow than normal.

"I think this was some sort of a way to throw us off track by your father. No one is in this house besides us. I would be able to sense their heartbeat. Whatever this is, it isn't Moirai," he stated.

"But the bricks outside and Thistle's room? This is the address," I whispered. I don't know why I was whispering, other than out of habitual library etiquette.

"I don't know," he said, shaking his head. He looked so exhausted. Even his cheeks had begun to look sallow and sunken.

"Wait," Eli interjected as he joined us. "Five hundred thirty-eight lilies. What if that's a book?"

Holy shit.

"He's right. We need to check the books," I said, feeling my heart begin to speed up. It was so obvious. Almost too obvious.

"Check all these books? Are you mad?" Mendax sneered.

"I don't know." I shrugged defensively. "What else could it mean? We are in a library. I think that makes the most sense."

"And what if this is all just a ruse to waste our time?" He put his hands on his hips. The small action instantly made him look twice as intimidating—and sexy.

"Do you have any other ideas?" I was so aggravated. We all were.

He was silent for a moment. "Then I suggest we spread out

and hurry." He walked past us to the end of the aisle and turned sharply, heading to the next one over.

"He's not gonna make it much longer," Eli whispered.

"What?" I drew back in surprise.

"Mendax. He's doing worse than he's letting on—worse than us. If we don't get to Moirai and in front of the Fates soon, he's going to be the first to go."

"What do you mean he's going to be the first to go? He's fine," I stammered, knowing it was a lie.

Eli shook his head. "That's what he wants you to think. He's been passing you his powers since long before I was, but you obviously knew that."

My mouth fell open. "What do you mean? How would I know that?"

He tilted his tanned face and squinted. "The smoking— you only started doing it after you left Mendax in Unseelie, right? When you were injured?"

I couldn't find words.

"I think he's been sending you some of his powers through the bond since you left Unseelie and were injured in the last trial," he said.

"There's no way. That's a part of the bond, or it's because of my sister's Artemi powers. They took some of Mendax's powers," I whispered in complete shock.

"I don't think so, Cal. I think he wanted to protect you even when he wasn't around." His mouth turned down in a deep frown. "Except I think it's going to kill him, and soon."

"Oh my suns! What do I do? Can I give him some back? How can we help him?" I was going to snap.

"I think we just need to find this book, if that's what it even is, and get to the Fates as quickly as possible," he said as he took a few steps back. "I'll start at the end. Five hundred thirty-eight lilies."

He went to look, and I was left alone with my thoughts. Hot tears filled my eyes, and I had to grab the shelf in front of me to steady myself. Of course, Mendax had done all that for

169

me and never even let me know. He was going to die keeping me alive, and I couldn't do anything to stop him.

My chest tightened as I sobbed against the shelf, doing everything I could to keep my cries silent. How could I have let this go on for so long? Was that why he'd been so quiet? Because he was dying? He was right. How were we going to find one book out of all these?

My chest heaved, and I was forced to cover my mouth to silence the sounds.

I couldn't let this happen; he couldn't do this. Tears rolled down my cheeks as I turned the corner. My pace picked up as I began to run, checking each aisle for Mendax. I turned down the row he was in, and he looked up, surprised.

"What's happened?" he asked. His face turned menacing as he strode toward me.

My teeth ground together as the tears picked up upon seeing him. As soon as I was within reach, I swung at his face, quickly following with the other arm after he grabbed my wrist, stopping it before it could connect.

"You prick!"

He pulled me against him as he held my wrists. His thick black brows wrinkled with concern.

"You were going to let yourself die giving me your power!" I struggled against him, trying to hit him again. The tears somehow flowed faster when he let go of my wrists and held my waist against him instead.

"And?" he said calmly.

"What was the point of all this if you were just going to die before we even made it to the Fates?" I shouted.

"I should ask you the same question," he rumbled.

"What?" I wiped at my cheeks.

"You were going to die before we made it to the Fates. Am I wrong, pet? You were planning to remove yourself so that Aurelius and I could live. You would be at peace with"—he grabbed my pendant—"your sister. Am I wrong? Tell me I'm wrong, Calypso."

I opened my mouth to argue, but I was still shocked that he had figured all that out. "How did you know?"

"In your weariness, you've grown forgetful about blocking me from parts of your mind, love," he said harshly. "I forbid you from leaving me, and that includes via death."

I squinted. "You can't *forbid* me from dying," I barked.

He moved his face in front of mine and pushed my back into the bookshelves behind me. His eyes slowly trailed up my body. "I can do anything I want to you, and that includes forbidding your death." His statuesque body towered over mine.

"Then—then I forbid your death," I snarled back.

Even in the barely lit aisle, I could see his dimple when the corner of his beautiful mouth lifted. "Do you now?" He pressed his thumb against my lower lip, pulling it down as he continued to run his thumb down my chin, then my neck. He stopped below my clavicle and latched his hard, draconic eyes onto mine before he continued pressing his thumb down until it reached the top of my cleavage. Goose bumps riddled my skin.

"I do," I said huskily, suddenly aware of the pounding ache between my legs.

He grinned his wicked, lopsided smile, and I thought then and there that I could die completely happy. His thumb slowly moved from my cleavage, and before I knew it, his large palm covered my breast while he pressed his body against me. A ragged breath left my mouth. My head, suddenly too heavy to hold upright, fell back against the bookshelf.

"Say it again," his deep voice breathed against my collarbone. His left arm framed me in against the shelf while his other skimmed down my chest and abdomen until he was running his palm across my throbbing parts.

I nearly choked on a breath when my body reacted so atomically to his touch. It was electrifying. Heat seared through me, so full of want and need it was almost unbearable.

"Say what again?" I rasped as my hands moved to his shoulders and then into his thick black hair. I needed to feel his silky hair and touch his body.

"I do. Say it," he commanded.

I could feel his long length pressing against me. "Why?"

His fingers dipped in my waistband, causing me to suck in an empty mouthful of air.

"Because I told you to," he whispered sternly. Something about his almost terrifying demeanor always got me hot and bothered, and this was no different.

His eyes challenged me as he slowly moved his hand down the front of my pants. His cool, rough skin sent a chill over me as it moved across my warm skin and underwear.

"I do," I breathed the words into his ear as I bit the lobe. I was rewarded with his finger tracing the line of me over my panties, dipping just enough to feel my wetness transfer onto the fabric. I breathed out heavily and dug my nails into his shoulder.

"Oh, Caly," he sighed. His mouth found mine and quickly parted my lips, pushing his tongue into my mouth.

Neither one of us was able to taste enough of the other fast enough. Moans and breathy panting filled the aisle as we both struggled to be consumed by the other. His hand dipped into the front of my panties, parting me with his finger.

"Mendax," I gasped softly.

He breathed out, heavy and frustrated as he removed his hand from my panties. His hand went under my armpits and abruptly lifted me a few feet onto the edge of one of the bookshelves. My arms went around his neck as he pushed his lips to mine hungrily and gripped the waistband of my pants on either side, pulling them off torturously slowly. I lifted my hips to help.

As I sat on the shelf, his body parted my legs to either side of him.

"Say it again," he commanded, pulling only a breath away from my mouth. His forehead still pressed against mine.

"Why—" His hand pressed against my sensitive flesh again, and I let out a moan. "I do," I panted.

"Again." He pressed three fingers inside me, rubbing against my clit with every delicious motion.

I cried out. "I do, oh fuck, I do." I moaned.

He was breathing fast. His cock felt hard enough to break something as it pressed against the inside of my thigh. I pulled at the few pieces of armor he wore impatiently. He took a small step back and removed his chest plate, tossing it to the ground before reaching over his head and pulling his shirt off and returning to me. Greedily, my hands ran over his warm skin. I pulled his face down to mine and kissed him, biting his lower lip so hard I drew blood.

He pulled back with his eyes still closed and licked his lip. He looked absolutely euphoric. When his eyes opened, there was a dangerously intense spark to them. He held my waist with one hand and held the other out in front of him as his wicked eyes locked with mine. He spit into his hand and rubbed it against me. I dug my nails into his shoulder until I was certain he had to have been dripping with blood. My other hand gripped a clump of his hair as I ground myself against his hand furiously.

His moan sounded feral as he dropped to his knees and covered my throbbing body with his warm mouth. Books fell to the ground from the shelf next to me as my hand struggled to grip ahold of something, anything. I panted and moaned, but no sound came out. His magical tongue flicked and sucked as it pressed inside me and tasted my most sensitive spots. I gripped his hair with both hands and pressed and pushed until I thought I might suffocate him. I stopped worrying about it when every shove urging his mouth deeper caused him to let out a deep moan as he continued to feast like he needed my pleasure to survive.

I was close to climax when he pulled away and cold air hit me with a disappointed gust.

Mendax stood to his full height and wiped his wet face on his arm before undoing his pants with one hand and dropping them to his ankles. He stepped up to me and pressed his mouth to mine. The taste of myself and his smokiness danced on my tongue. I felt him rub the head of his cock along my slick center. Tingles burst over my body, and I was nearly ready to come from the quick action. He wasn't even inside me.

"Marry me, Caly." He pressed the first inch of his cock inside me.

I inhaled sharply and wrapped my legs around his waist. My body and heart tingled with emotion.

"You are proposing"—a moan slipped through my words—"while you fuck me? When one of us is almost guaranteed to die." The words evaporated as he slid another inch of his thick, solid cock inside me. I grabbed his arm that pushed against the bookshelf next to my head.

"Yes, pet, I am," he whispered into my neck with a bite. "Tell me again what you're going to call out when they marry us." He pushed his full length into me in one fluid movement.

I had to shove my face into his shoulder to muffle my cries of pleasure. He rocked back and forth slightly, adjusting himself to my tightness, sending waves of sensual tingles across my body.

"That's not it," he whispered huskily as he pulled himself almost completely out of me.

The sharp edge of the bookshelf dug painfully into the lower part of my butt and my back. "Mendax," I begged, growing impatient and angry that he wasn't fully inside me.

He leaned his upper body away slightly, and the lighting caught the dips and ridges of his chest and abdomen, highlighting the features of his warrior body like a painting. I opened my mouth to protest, suddenly afraid he was going to pull out and away because I hadn't said the words he'd wanted to hear. Instead, he reached above my head and pulled free a cream-colored, cloth-bound book.

"It may sound like I'm asking you to marry me, hellhound, but I'm not." He absently flipped through the book before he pressed the book's fore edge against my chest. "Marriage is simply a formality needed alongside the bond for us to return as king and queen of Unseelie."

He pressed the corner of the book into my skin and dragged

it slowly down my chest and over the top of the sensitive skin of my breast. It was sharp, and the pain coursed like waves that crashed into my lust. Mendax knew how to play my body like an instrument, easily getting the reaction from me he sought.

"I don't need a marriage ceremony to follow you." He thrust himself inside me, dragging the book's sharp corner over my hardened nipple.

My body clenched around him.

"You feel so fucking good," he said, sucking in a breath through his teeth. His eyes had closed.

For a moment, I thought he'd lost complete control as he pulled out and slammed into me so hard the books on the shelf moved. He caught himself quickly though, and when his eyes opened again, the pupils were blown out under heavy lids. He looked absolutely vicious like this. Anyone else would be petrified for their safety. It made me an absolute horny mess. I couldn't get enough.

"You're mine, pet."

He used his thumb to fan the edge of the pages against my nipple. The sensation felt like he was tickling and blowing on my skin times a thousand. I gasped at the multiple sensations when he began thrusting into me again, so deep it felt like I was folding around him.

"You will never escape me." He closed the book on my nipple and squeezed it together, pinching my nipple like a clamp.

I squealed in pain and moved to shove the book off my nipple. He slapped his hand over my wrist and pressed it against the shelf above my head, holding it there with force. I felt my mouth curl into a devious smile. My pleas were swallowed by his lips as he kissed me roughly. It wasn't a romantic or even a loving kiss. It was the selfish kind that burned inside you, turning you into a savage. He clamped the book together harder until tears prickled at my eyes and it was close to being too much.

"Whether I live or die, you possess me, Calypso," he whispered. "Your happiness is *annoyingly* important to me now. Tell me you will marry me after this is all over and you will rule Unseelie at my side forever."

The pain was starting to make me aggressive, so I dug my nails into his shoulder with my free hand. His eyes flickered shut, and his pace quickened. Still he held my nipple prisoner in the pages of the book.

It wasn't a real plan he wanted me to agree to, I knew that. It was a hope-filled dream that we could pretend we'd get to experience before we entered this mess. I would never be the same if Eli died because of me, but I could never move on without Mendax. If he had heard all my thoughts through the bond, then I was going to have to find a new way to take myself out so I could be with Adrianna.

Still, this wasn't a real plan—it didn't get to be. It was a fantasy that a dying man was telling himself to feel in control when he had none. It was the dream a girl who had to die would gleefully agree to.

"Yes. I will marry you if we leave Moirai—"

"When we leave Moirai," he corrected as he dropped the book to the ground and licked my nipple.

"Yes, oh gods, yes," I cried out as I bucked my hips against him.

He dropped his hold on my wrist to wrap his hands around me, lifting my butt off the shelf and cupping my cheeks as he plowed into me, pulling me off his cock and then slamming back into me. He was in complete and total control of my body as he pounded into me at the perfect speed. My eyes rolled back in my head at how deep his cock was and what it was doing to me. Never in all my life had I been fucked so good. He manipulated my body over his cock, and I just limply floated in euphoria, being controlled.

He spun, turning so his back was now against the row of bookshelves. My arms tightened around his neck as he let go of my body to grab my ankles and set each foot on a shelf at his back. I settled my weight in my toes as he grabbed my hips and slid me up and down on his cock. His head fell back into the shelf, and I realized what he'd done. I grabbed the shelf behind his head and one by one moved my feet up one shelf higher. I pushed off the shelf and used my leverage to bounce up and down on his hard-as-steel cock. He kept his palms on my hips and ass, but this time, *I* was the one in control.

"Finish me, Caly. Do you want to feel me when I lose it? I want you to feel everything. I want you to fuck me until you can't take it for another second. If I die today, I want that pussy tender and raw as a reminder of how I'll fucking haunt you even if I'm gone," he panted.

"Shut—the—fuck—up," I moaned as I rode him. He bit at my neck with a feral growl. "Maybe I'll be the one doing the haunting," I said through clenched teeth.

"Like Tartarus you will," he said as he lifted me up and spun me again.

My back hit the bookshelf as Mendax thrust into me. I had no way to talk or argue through the pleasure and pain that my body was feeling. All I could do was hold on and enjoy it. He was right. I wasn't going to be able to sit for days after him. Somehow the thought made me even wetter, and I felt tension coil in my lower belly like nothing I'd ever felt. My orgasm erupted, and all the tension turned to bliss as I started to come. Mendax's thrusts deepened and slowed with shallow grunts. He was about to come too. He stuck his thumb inside his mouth and ran it over his tongue, then pressed and rubbed it against my clit. I came and I came and I came.

"Oh fuck, you're coming so hard," he said, pulling out at the peak of my orgasm while he continued to rub me with his thumb.

He kneeled down and began lapping at my clit.

It felt like ten barrels of pleasure poured over me, and I felt my lower body clench.

Mendax moaned as he sucked and ravaged me with his mouth.

I felt liquid pour from me, and this time he completely lost it, sucking and swallowing against me.

"I would die happy if this was the last thing I tasted," he groaned. "Your cum has the taste of my salvation."

I blinked, and he was standing again, pushing inside me. I was about to protest, feeling the hot burn of being completely raw, but the instant my body filled with him, I felt another orgasm start.

"I can't," I whined. "Another one will kill me."

"Good. That's the only way you should go. Now, beautiful, at the same time as me," he whispered as he moved slowly in and out.

We clung to each other as we climaxed in unison.

"I love you, Caly. I love you like you'll never understand."

"I love you," I returned with tears in my eyes. "I love you."

We held each other for a moment in a ludicrously tender embrace before a shout broke through the quiet of the library.

"If you two are done fucking, then come to the last aisle. I think I might have found something," Eli yelled from across the room.

Mendax and I looked at each other with smiles playing on our lips. We kissed one final unhurried time and began to dress.

CHAPTER 20

CALY

D ID YOU TWO ENJOY YOURSELF?" ELI ASKED WITH A WIDE
grin.

Mendax and I were still adjusting our clothes and armor
when we entered the aisle Eli had called from.

"Sorry," I said, suddenly realizing how selfish that was of
us. Eli must have heard everything.

Eli's eyes sparkled. "Don't be. You both deserve a nice
moment together before…well, before whatever else happens
tonight."

"What did you find, Seelie?" Mendax interjected.

Eli smiled wider as if the fact that he annoyed Mendax
made him happier. "Look." He pointed to a shelf at the very
top, and my eyes grazed a random spine.

538 Lilies

"You found it!" I squealed as I flung my arms around Eli's
neck excitedly.

"I would have found it," Mendax grumbled quietly. "I had
my hands full." He winked in my direction.

"Ugh, you stink of sex." Eli grimaced.

I released him and let out a sigh. We had found it. This
was it.

"So how do we get it down?" I asked the question I knew we all were thinking. It seemed impossibly high. "Neither of you can fly, can you?"

Both fae looked dejected as they shook their heads.

"Well, I have an idea, but I don't think either of you are going to like it," I said.

"You're not going to climb up there. We don't know how secure these bookshelves are," said Eli.

Mendax chuckled. "They are pretty secure, but no, Calypso, you can't climb up there."

I curled my lip in disgust. "Well, that wasn't what I was going to say, but now I have the sudden urge to do a whole lot of whatever the fuck I want," I bit out. Who did they think they were? "I appreciate you both looking out for me, but I suggest you stop telling me what to do. It has been *far* too long since I've killed anyone, and I'd hate to fall out of practice." I grinned.

Eli looked hurt but put his palms up as if in surrender. "Fine, break your independent little neck."

"I wholeheartedly agree," said Mendax, looking off in the distance.

"You think I should break my little neck too?" I snapped.

"No, pet, it's been far too long since I've killed as well. Climb up that bookshelf, and *I* will break your pretty neck myself," he stated.

Eli frowned. "What was your idea, Cal?"

"Well, it's simple really. Mendax is the largest." I rolled my eyes as he positively beamed. "So he should go on the bottom with Eli sitting on his shoulders."

Mendax's smile fell to a disgusted frown.

I continued. "Then I'll go on Eli's shoulders. It will make me tall enough to reach the book safely."

Mendax looked ready to walk out the door, and Eli burst out laughing.

"I don't know why you're laughing. You are the one who has to sit on my shoulders like a little child," Mendax said.

"I'm laughing because my junk is gonna be wrapped around your head, tough guy." Eli burst into a fit of laughter.

Mendax lunged for him, but Eli dodged it and smiled.

"Children," I scolded. "Let's hurry up."

The dark prince of the Unseelie realm crossed his arms. "Okay, get on then."

Eli raised his arms up and let them drop, looking to me and then back to Mendax. "'Get on then'? What am I, a cloud leaper? How am I supposed to get on your shoulders while you are standing? You're six-foot-five!"

"I don't care how you get your sunshine ass up there, but do it and hurry before I toss you into the books," Mendax answered curtly.

"Yeah?" Eli questioned. "You're gonna toss me into those bookshelves? You probably don't even have enough power to carry me, let alone throw me."

"Let's try it, shall we?" Mendax took a large step toward Eli.

"I could have already climbed up there by now," I replied as I jumped in front of Mendax before he could get to Eli. "Just get down on one knee, and he'll climb on, then lift him up," I instructed Mendax.

The Unseelie prince looked like he was thinking about murdering me for a moment. Reluctantly, he bent down on one knee, glaring at me the entire way down.

"Wait, then how are you going to get on my shoulders up here?" asked Eli.

"I don't know. I guess I am going to climb up the bookshelf a tiny bit and then onto your shoulders. It's not that far up, before either of you say anything stupid," I snapped.

Eli's grin faded as he moved to get onto Mendax's shoulders. Suddenly, the jokester looked a lot more serious.

"Come on!" Mendax snarled.

"I know you're anxious for me to teabag your head, but calm down," Eli returned. He put one leg over Mendax's shoulder, and the dark prince sent me a look that should have burned me alive.

"Stupid fucking idea," he mumbled under his breath.

"Hold still! Quit moving around," sang Eli.

"Why is your crotch so warm?" Mendax asked with a grimace as he stepped back and knocked Eli's head into the bookcase behind them.

"Ouch!" yelled Eli as he grabbed his head and then squeezed his thighs tightly around Mendax's head in retaliation.

"Oh my suns," I mumbled.

Mendax slammed Eli into the shelf again, and Eli fell off Mendax's shoulders and landed in a pile on the ground.

"What the fuck?" shouted Eli. "You were supposed to hold my legs, you dick."

"I'm not holding your legs," Mendax stated with squinted eyes.

"Caly, I'm not going to be able to hold you or stay on top of Shadow Breath if he doesn't hold my legs," Eli huffed.

"Mendax," I said as I shut my eyes in frustration and let out a deep breath. "Just hold his fucking legs."

Mendax clenched his jaw and bent down again. Eli struggled to get on Mendax's shoulders but eventually succeeded.

"Stop grabbing my head," growled Mendax.

"Then grab my legs!" yelled Eli.

Eventually, they balanced enough that I began to climb the bookshelves like a ladder. Mendax moved close enough to the shelves that I was able to support myself on him and Eli when I needed to.

"Okay, are you ready?" I asked. It looked a lot higher up than I had envisioned, and I secretly wished I had just climbed up by myself and didn't have to worry about the two men dropping me. "Please don't drop me. That means, Mendax, you can't drop Eli."

"I'm not going to drop you. Just hurry up," Mendax grumbled from below.

I looked up at the green cloth-bound book titled *538 Lilies*. It wasn't that far away from me. This was going to work. The question was what was going to happen after we had the book.

"Okay, go nice and slow. I've got you," said Eli as I threw a leg over his shoulder while I held on tight to the bookshelf. I held on so tightly, my fingers began to cramp.

"Okay, I'm on." I let out a deep breath and held on to Eli's shoulder, gripping his shirt in my fist as my other hand reached up and my fingertips stretched toward the green book.

"You're so close. You got it yet?" asked Eli.

"Almost. I just need up a bit higher," I said. My arm had begun to shake as I stretched it as far as possible. "Mendax, can you get us up any higher? I can't quite reach it."

"What would you like me to do? Lift you both up?" grunted Mendax.

My fingertips brushed the textured cloth of the book, and my confidence grew. I leaned forward just enough so that the tip of my pointer finger brushed the edge of the book and I was able to grab it.

"I got it!" I shouted.

"Oh, thank suns," said Eli.

"Hey!" I tugged his hair playfully.

"No, not because of you. I'm tired of Smoke-Show wearing me like a necklace." Eli shifted on top of Mendax, and I nearly lost my balance and almost dropped the book.

"Knock it off! I'm going to fall!" My grip on the book faltered again, and I began to fall forward. The book slipped from my fingers as I grabbed ahold of Eli's face with my hands.

"Fuck! I can't see," Eli mumbled, swaying even more, which in turn caused Mendax to try and make up for the lack of balance by staggering. At this point, we were too far away from the bookshelves for me to grab them and climb off, so I just held on to Eli's face.

"You have to move closer to the bookshelf. I can't get off until you do," I shouted.

"I'm trying. Believe me, I'm trying," Mendax bit out.

We moved forward, and all of us scrambled to grab a bookshelf as Eli and I toppled over. My fingers gripped tightly to the edge of the wood as I looked down and saw Mendax looking up at me with no one on his shoulders. My heartbeat sped up as I looked to the ground, expecting to see Eli. I heard a deep grunt and turned to look on my other side where Eli had just leapt down from the shelf he had been holding on to.

Shit.

I was stuck.

"Go ahead and drop, Cal. I'll catch you," encouraged Eli.

"You're not going to catch anything but a fat lip if you don't get the fuck out of the way," argued Mendax.

My fingers were slipping, and I was up too high to land on my feet. If I fell, there was no doubt I would break my legs, if not something worse. Both fae looked up, each handsome and charming in their own way. My fingers were slipping, and I didn't have much time to choose. If I didn't pick between them, there was a good chance I would fall in the middle and break my back. A few months ago, I would've been stupid enough to try and land on my own, but I couldn't think that way now. I was too close to being done with all this, too close to seeing my family again and being able to tell them that I fixed it all for them. That I made it right while I couldn't be with them.

My fingers slid off the wood, and I fell backward. I closed my eyes and clenched every muscle until I felt the hard grab of someone's hands and body, softening my fall. Whoever it was held me tight, taking the brunt of our fall as we landed on the floor just in front of the other bookshelf. For one single moment, while my eyes were still shut and I remained held in an invisible cocoon of safety, I could pretend I belonged to both my best friend and my soul mate and that everything was okay. But as I had already learned many times in life, you can't close your eyes and make all the bad things go away, no matter how badly you wish you could.

"Are you all right?" I asked as I began to open my eyes.

"I'm fine. Are you hurt?"

Eli gently lifted me up and set me on my feet. Had I intentionally fallen to his side? Or had I just slipped off without deciding? My eyes were wide with wonder as I got my balance and tried not to read too deeply into it. I felt Mendax's stare, and I knew I wasn't the only one wondering if I'd chosen Eli intentionally.

Silently, I shook my head at the Unseelie prince and opened my mouth to explain.

"Get the fucking book." He turned and walked out of the aisle, stepping over the fallen green book.

"Thanks," Eli added softly. "Your trust means a lot to me, and I would never take it lightly."

I didn't know what to say. "It—you guys are thinking too much into it. I just fell. You caught me," I stammered. "Thank you, by the way."

"I'll always be there to catch you, Cal. Feuhn kai greeyth," he said. "Let's open this thing by the fire." He scooped up the book and walked out of the aisle.

My eyes followed his easy, confident gait for a moment before I moved to follow. Every step I took was filled with excitement and fear and hope and terror.

What was this book about to do to our lives?

I met the other two as they stood solemnly in front of the mahogany fireplace. The library seemed suddenly full of tension, like it, too, waited to see what was going to happen next.

All three of us looked at one another, gauging the others' reactions and seeing if anyone had any last-minute ideas. I had noticed it was something the three of us did frequently now, like we really were a team.

When no one said anything, I let out a heavy breath and gave a nod to Eli. His throat bobbed with a swallow as he held out the book. When I clasped the book, I held my breath as if it were going to shock me. What would happen now? Would this end up being another trick from my father? Had this all been for nothing? What if I opened this book and was immediately killed? If the Fates truly knew everything, as they were touted to, then wouldn't they already know my plans to kill my father? It didn't seem that far-fetched that they would try to kill me.

My hand trembled the faintest amount. Mendax's hand covered mine, holding it steady.

"I don't have an ancient saying to tell you, and I don't offer friendship, but know that you will see me eternally regardless of what happens tonight." He gently squeezed the top of my hand.

"I love you both immeasurably. Eli, you as a friend and family member, and, Mendax, you as my soul mate. Whatever happens, know that I never wanted either of you involved in any of this. This was between my father, Queen Saracen, my mother, and my sister. I'm truly sorry that either of you got wrapped into this all." My breath stuttered, and I had to stop.

"We're not," said Eli with a look to Mendax. "We love you, and sometimes love isn't exactly like you think it should be. Sometimes love is walking into a world where you have no idea what will happen, but you're happy to do it because you know you are together."

"If you don't open that book, I'm going to make the next person who speaks bleed." Mendax's words were full of threat, but his eyes were laced with a softness that was rarely evident.

My thumb found the edge of the cover and opened the book.

CHAPTER 21

CALY

I OPENED THE BOOK TO AN ANCIENT-LOOKING TITLE PAGE THAT said *538 Lilies*. Underneath and to the right, there was an embossed mark from the library of the Fates. It was just a normal book.

I didn't understand. Was there supposed to be another set of instructions in here? Were we supposed to put the book on another shelf and the entire wall would open to a hidden lair? How was this book supposed to be the end of our journey?

I turned the page in utter bewilderment, and the pages began to flip on their own, slowly at first, then picking up speed, until they were whirring to the other side. I tried to read the text, but I couldn't see it with the speed of the pages. The middle began to glow brightly. Thousands of tiny speckles of light, almost like dust, flowed from the pages and into the air, covering us.

"Listen!" Eli said, now glowing himself. "There's music coming from it."

Another few seconds passed, and then I heard it. It washed over me in a calming wave. Beautiful harp music played from the book, slowly growing louder as the light grew brighter and brighter. It would have felt almost angelic had it not also intertwined an air of danger and mystery with each note of music.

The opacity of the pages began to lighten, and a glossy sheen covered them. The pages slowed, and suddenly glass-wing butterflies—at least a thousand—burst from the pages, each wing covered with text as they flowed out, fluttering in different directions. The last butterfly remained on the opened page, the words of its wings the only text left.

How
Does
It Feel?
To know
That I
Love you
And

My heart beat so hard, I was certain I felt the scar on my heart rub against my ribs.

Those were words I would never forget. Mendax had spoken them to me at the Unseelie castle. It was the first time he ever told me that he was in love with me. Why had they been written in this book?

Slowly, I moved my pointer finger in front of the butterfly's forelegs in an attempt to get it onto my finger. The small butterfly lifted off the glowing page, taking flight in the direction of its friends, who were now busy flying around the library. My finger disappeared into the blank page, now textured like parchment instead of glass. Eli gasped, startling me as I removed my finger. It hadn't hurt, but I had felt a drastic change in temperature through the page. I pressed my fingertips into the glowing blank page and watched my flesh disappear. I removed my hand and set the open book on the floor at my feet and began to press the toe of my boot in.

"Wait! Thistle!" Eli said in alarm. "I can't just leave her here." The whites of his eyes rimmed the beautiful amber in alarm. His loyalty was unmatched, even to a floricorn.

"It's fine. Just go get her and bring her in, but hurry. I don't know how long this will stay a passage," I said calmly, even though I felt anything but calm.

Eli ran out of the library.

"Let me go first, and before you protest, it is a request this time, not a demand," Mendax said, his voice surprisingly soft.

I eyed him wearily. Nothing about that sounded like Mendax.

"What?" he snapped with a wrinkle of his black brows.

"Nothing," I replied. "It's just you've never been the requesting kind, is all."

He pressed a soft kiss to my lips. "I've watched you with Aurelius. He *is* a good friend to you. He makes you laugh and is much kinder than I will ever be. I will attempt to do better after I kill him. As my queen and wife, you deserve the highest level of respect, and I will slaughter any man or woman who speaks or treats you in any manner that Aurelius would have disliked...aside from myself, of course," he whispered before taking a step back and into the open book on the floor.

"Wha—wait! You can't kill him!" I shouted as I moved to grab him, but it was too late. Mendax disappeared into the book as if it were quicksand. It pulled the wide parts of him in, morphing him a little as he disappeared. The glow flickered slightly as he passed through but remained bright.

He was gone.

I looked around the library in complete panic. I wasn't sure what I was expecting to see. It wasn't like Mendax was just going to pop up next to me.

"She's gone! Thistle is gone!" Eli yelled as he ran into the library.

"She...what? How?" I said.

"I don't know. I went in to get her, and the room was completely empty. There's nothing inside it now, including her. Where's Mendax?" Eli was flustered and disheveled. It was obvious how much he cared about that little mare.

"I'm sure she's fine. They probably just moved her," I

reassured him. "Mendax went first. Come on. We need to go before this book stops doing whatever it is that it's doing."

I lifted my foot and stepped onto the book—except there was no stepping to be had as my foot touched nothing and continued to pass through. As soon as I lifted the other foot, I fell completely into the book.

In my experience of falling through the abyss, I usually got sick, disoriented, or all of the above. Something or someone hard generally stopped my fall, but this time was different. The fall felt calm and peaceful, less like I was falling and more like I was floating.

At least until I hit the water.

My body hit with a gentle splash. It felt like there was a basket or something behind me, softening my landing. I gasped and gulped as tepid water engulfed my body. My head remained above the water, and the rest of me likely would have as well, but the surprising feel of water caused me to panic and flail like a newborn. I had yet to come across anything friendly in fae waters.

Before my eyes even had a chance to open, the scent of crisp, clean air went straight to my head. It smelled like I was standing on the top of a mountain again, breathing in the freshest air possible. My fluttering eyelids calmed as I inhaled, now almost unwilling to open. I waded in the water, feeling the drag of my now-heavy clothes with every circle my legs or arms made. The soft hint of crisp evergreen and sweet, light, floral pineapple wafted under my nose next. Almost reluctantly, I opened my eyes to beautiful, blue-tinted water. I tipped my head up, and my face was doused in warm sunlight. Large lily pads covered the water in big groups of waxy green leaves and stunning white flowers. That must have been what softened my fall.

Sure enough, I pushed the water and turned to see a cluster of giant lily pads behind me, each with at least three or four large, white, multi-petaled lilies that poked out above the water. I scanned the pond. There were so many. There had to be at least—

Five hundred thirty-eight beautiful white lilies.

I rolled myself onto one of the larger green leaves and sat with my knees up, balancing on my hands as I looked around. It was like I had fallen inside a painting—except I'd never even seen a painting that could possibly do this place justice. Gray, moss-covered boulders lined part of the pond. The sound of gentle flowing water caught my attention. There was a small waterfall that poured into the pond from what looked like a shallow water garden above. Beautiful purple and gold flowers bloomed among the rocks before the water poured gently over the rocks and into the pond filled with water lilies. Full weeping willows touched the edge of the pond, their long, sweeping branches grazing the surface like toes dipping in the water.

The giggle of a woman and a splash snapped me out of my daydream. I looked in the direction of the giggle, but it seemed to be coming from around a bend that was blocked from view by several lush, green grasslike bushes. I didn't entertain the thought of going to check. I didn't know a lot of fae rules, but I knew a lot of their tricks, and that was a fae trap if I'd ever heard one. Ignoring more giggles, I looked to the landscaped area around the pond and attempted to figure out the best way of getting to it. The feminine giggles returned, now sounding oddly seductive, and I knew I needed off the water. It was my experience that the more beautiful something was, the more lethal, just like—

Mendax!

I nearly fell off the giant green pad. I'd been so enamored with the beauty of this place, I hadn't even looked for Mendax. Did he not land in the same place I had?

A scream shot out from behind the foliage where the giggles had been, and the figure of a blond half woman, half fish was flung into the water with a splash that sent a wave rocking all the lily pads.

Like a black water snake, Malum Mendax emerged, walking toward me with water up to his waist. His slow strides moved the water with each step; his wet hair looked as black as glistening ink. The absence of his armor revealed the wet fabric plastered over his broad chest and shoulders. He looked so dark and out of place in the serene atmosphere. I watched his eyes land on me. I should have yelled or asked if he was okay, but instead I watched, captivated with the way water rippled over the muscles of his biceps and forearms.

He sank lower with each step as his eyes targeted me. Eventually all I could see in the water was the top of his nose and the harsh blue of his eyes as he swam to me like a crocodile about to get an easy meal.

He deftly moved onto the giant lily pad next to me and removed his shirt, reaching over his head and pulling the wet fabric off.

If he was a crocodile, I was a fish with the gaping mouth of a carp, ogling him.

"Mermaid," he offered.

"Huh?" I eloquently asked as I watched him push back his onyx hair. It was like I'd never seen him in the light like this before. Every ounce of him was built like a god.

"Mermaid," he repeated.

"Mermaid," I mimicked as my wandering eyes roamed over the fabric clinging to a massive bulge between his legs. What had he said?

He grinned so wide that dimples dented both cheeks.

Had his soaking wet, half-naked body not been enough to cause any and all thoughts to leave my brain, the smile he gave just now would have easily done the trick. I felt my cheeks heat.

What the fuck was wrong with me? Between my legs was still sore from having him fuck the life out of me not hours ago, and here I was blushing at his smile?

"The mermaid was getting a tad handsy for my liking. Some kind of welcoming committee they have here," he said with a scowl.

"Have you seen Eli yet? Wait, what? It was a mermaid. *Wait,* did she touch you?" I said as I began to put all the pieces together.

"What if she did, pet?" Mendax asked without a trace of humor in his smooth, granitelike features.

Fury poured through me like molten lava, and I felt my face turn red, now for another reason entirely. "*If she did*, then I'm going to fucking fillet her," I bit out, immediately scanning the pond for her. "I've never seen a mermaid before. How do you kill them? I know many aquatic fae regrow their heads—" I stopped when I heard the sound of his low laughter. He had quite possibly the biggest smile I'd ever seen him wear, and I had never heard him laugh so heartily. The mermaid had already been forgotten.

"I told her I already had one pet and wasn't interested in fish keeping. Then I threw her to the other side of the pond for good measure. If you like, I can bring her to you?" The darkness danced in his eyes. "I think I might really enjoy watching you kill her for touching me. How will you do it?" he whispered seductively with that dangerous smile still in place.

He reached over to my lily pad and tugged me onto his with a slosh of water. He lay back and pulled my arm until I was lying on top of him. My needy hand moved to claim him, brushing over the wet ridges of his stomach before stopping for a quick second to run the side of my finger along the deep ridges near his hips and following them to his groin, where I palmed his stiff cock. His smile faltered but was replaced with a look of happy pleasure. I was hypnotized.

"First, I would remove her hands," I whispered before I moved to kiss the side of his neck. "For touching what belongs to *me*." He sucked in a sharp breath when my hand cupped his balls. Immediately, I was drunk on the power of his reaction. I reached in his clingy wet pants and wrapped my hand around his shaft. His skin was slightly chilled from the pond water. My eyes flickered shut as my sore pussy throbbed and clenched with needy desire. "Then, I would take the blunt end of your dagger—" I squeezed tightly as I jerked my fist over his cock.

"You would use *my* blade, would you?" His voice was thick and slow.

I moved my hand faster, occasionally grazing my thumb over his tip. "I would. You see I only have a dragon's claw for a weapon."

He panted as he moved to grip my wrist and take control, but I gave him a threatening look that urged him to put his hand back down at his side.

"That will be remedied. You need a better weapon," he breathed. "Then what would you do to her, my hellhound?"

"As I was saying," I said, removing my hand completely from his length, knowing I'd just taken all his pleasure with me.

He looked angry.

"I would take the blunt edge of your blade and descale her pretty tail. I've never really seen the anatomy of a mermaid before, but if she possessed any fins, I would cut those off next." I pulled my pants down to the middle of my thighs, high on power. I firmly gripped him again and began working his length. The noise that came from him made me grin. While I continued to fuck him with my hand, I grabbed one of his own hands and lifted it until it cupped over my water-soaked underwear. He tried to move his hand over me, and I released his cock, shaking my head no. His hand went limp again as I held it, and I used it to move my panties to the side. "Do you feel this?" I whispered as I pressed his fingers against my slick and sore pussy. "You've done this."

"Oh my gods, Calypso," he muttered.

"Can you feel how my body needs you?" I lifted his hand and pushed his fingers into his mouth and pulled my wet underwear back up. "It's because of *you* that I feel this way, and if anyone ever came between me and that feeling, I would kill the both of you."

"You are fucking *perfect*," he groaned, latching onto my eyes with a menacing stare and slowly licking me off each of his fingers.

He was still able to talk too easily, so I pumped his cock harder, using my other hand to work the top half of his cock, squeezing over the tip. I was so turned on, I could barely take it. I peeled back his underwear and spat on his cock as I made eye contact with him.

"Then I would insert the point of my blade just behind her head, with the flat side resting on her dorsal fin." The breath of my words dusted across his skin. "I would listen to her apologies as I cut along her back, from her pretty head down to her lustful tail."

I bobbed my head over him, sucking and humming. He was so close to coming. He groaned as though he were in pain and grabbed a fistful of my hair. He slammed his cock to the back of my throat, causing me to gag. My eyes watered as I made eye contact with him.

I let him continue this for a moment before I bit him.

He cried out and went to knock my head off him, but I had already lifted my head out of the way. I calmly lifted my pointer finger and waved it.

"I am the one in control now, and you're going to have to be *a lot* faster than that if you want to take it from me," I stated.

His dark eyes ignited as a small grin turned up one corner of his beautiful mouth. He understood my words and made a dramatic show of putting his hands behind his back.

Slowly—so slowly—I lowered my mouth back onto his cock. The second my hot mouth covered him, he let out a moan. He wasn't going to last another minute. I sucked and bobbed, running the tip of him over my tongue as my hand worked the rest of his cock. He moaned louder and lifted his hips. I felt his cock twitch as he filled my mouth with warm, smoky liquid. I tightened my lips around him and removed my mouth, making sure I got every last drop.

I sat up, still maintaining eye contact with him, and spit my mouthful of his cum into the blue pond, wiping the corner of my mouth with my pointer finger.

"Thought I'd let the bitch know, I got the job done," I growled.

Mendax stared. "You murderous little wench. Where have you been all my life?"

I giggled and moved to lie beside him when something big moved under the water in front of us.

I knew it had been too good to last.

Mendax fixed his pants and pulled his weapon free. I followed suit, moving to grab mine, but my fingers landed on the fabric of my shirt at my shoulder and not my bag.

"My bag." I'd left it at the library. "It has my weapon, the scrolls, everything."

Large bubbles rose up from the water in front of us. It swam under the lily pad and rammed into it. Water poured onto the sides of the large green leaf. Suns only knew what lurked in these waters. Had this been a setup? Had my father sent us on a wild-goose chase for a book that would send us into the pond of a horrible water monster that was sure to devour us? I knew he hated me, but this seemed excessive, even for a monster like him.

More and more bubbles popped at the surface as the shadowy figure rose toward us. Mendax kneeled at the edge with his blade poised at the ready.

Blond hair parted like a mop as it cleared the water, and Eli's face came into view. "Surprise!" he laughed.

Mendax swung at him, and I had *just* enough time to kick out at his forearm to stop him from taking Eli's head off. Mendax's hand opened under the pressure of my kick, and the weapon fell into the water, sinking quickly to the bottom.

Mendax turned to me with furious eyes. There was a good possibility that had I not just given him head, he would have tried to kill me right then. I grimaced dramatically. That now made two of us without a weapon.

"Hey!" Eli shouted at Mendax. "You saw it was me before you swung!"

"Oops," said Mendax flatly.

My mouth fell open in realization of how close he'd just been to killing us both. "You know, he and I are still tied. That means you just tried to kill me," I snapped.

Mendax rolled his eyes. "Don't be so dramatic. I wasn't going to kill him. I was just going to give that pretty face a few new scars to match his chest."

"Ha-ha-ha. Funny guy." I rolled my eyes. "Did you land underwater?" I asked Eli.

He grinned a boyish, charming grin. "There's a nice—uh—mermaid that direction that"—he coughed to clear his throat—"was very excited about my arrival."

I snorted out a laugh, and Eli smiled wide, flashing his straight white teeth. No, I didn't worry about him finding another woman to pine over. He had the charming, charismatic, confident, polished look that made most women fall over themselves. He could have been a complete asshole with the way he looked though, and women would still fall over him. It made it even harder for them to forget about him once they realized what a good person he was, not to mention one of the most amusing and affable.

"I left my bag in the library. It had my weapon and the scrolls in it," I confessed to Eli.

Always positive and optimistic, he frowned for a quick second before shrugging it off. "We are already here. I don't know why we would need the scrolls." A wide smile suddenly graced his face. "And I think it was fate that you don't have a weapon on our arrival. It means you can't kill Zef without talking to him first."

"Calypso once made a bomb from cabinet knobs and blew up my bathroom. You are a fool if you think she is somehow less dangerous without a weapon," Mendax declared with a hint of pride.

"Have you seen Thistle?" I asked Eli.

He shook his head. "No, but I'm sure she's supposed to be wherever she is. It will be okay," he stated, apparently having restored his faith in the Fates.

Mendax rolled his eyes. "I'm getting out of the water before I drown Eli," he growled.

Eli and I shared a look.

"You called me Eli," the Seelie prince gloated. "I knew you couldn't hate me for so long."

Mendax's upper lip curled. "Believe me, I can hate you forever. It was a slip of the tongue and nothing more."

Eli waded away from the lily pads toward the grassy edge. "I don't know," he called over his shoulder. "Sounds a lot like you might be starting to like me. This is the beginning of the Seelie and Unseelie faes' reconciliation, I can feel it."

Mendax dove into the water and swam toward Eli like a shark.

"Look, Cal, he wants to play in the pool with his new bestie," Eli sang with a laugh.

I couldn't help but laugh. "Need I remind you that he tried to lop your head off about five minutes ago?"

Eli chuckled and let out a high-pitched scream as Mendax moved closer. The lighthearted fae swam faster to the bank and climbed out in a humorous panic.

I pushed myself off the lily pad, feeling the water warm against my skin after my brief absence from it. I stepped into the squishy mud before the bank and had one foot on the grass when the other foot pulled free, leaving my mud-lodged boot in place.

"Shit! My boot." When I tried to step back to put my foot back into it, my foot squished into mud, and I fell in as water rushed over my head. Mendax returned to the water and attempted to help me out, but instead I took him down with me. Eli's laughter from land rang out like bells as Mendax and I struggled to find my boot. Now laughing myself, I took off the only boot in my possession and hurled it at Eli in the grass. "Stop laughing! You're not helping," I called out.

Mendax erupted from the water so coated in brown, watery mud, he was unrecognizable.

I fell into the water laughing. Hearty belly laughs pushed out of me until I was accidentally gulping so much water, Mendax had to help me out of the pond. My stomach hurt from laughing so hard as I lay on my back on the soft grass, completely covered in mud with one sock on and a missing boot. Every time I looked at Mendax, I lost it all over again. Even he was having a hard time not laughing at this point. Never in my years had I felt as light and as free as I did right then. Be it my denial about losing one of them for good or the feeling of accomplishment at being within striking distance of my end goal, I had no idea, but whatever it was, I never wanted it to end.

"Oh my. I take it you've just arrived?" came a snooty male voice.

Our laughter died as we looked up at an old man with a gold-rimmed monocle and long crimson robes, similar in style to that which my father had worn on the boat with us.

"Ugh, yes. We are here to see—" Eli politely began to respond.

"Have you checked in yet?" The gray-haired man interrupted.

"No. Where would one go to do that, sir?" Eli asked.

The man made a face, obviously completely put out by our existence. "Come along. I'll take you. Hurry along, would you? I have a game of chess I'm terribly late for." He tossed his red robes behind him as he took off, urging us to follow.

CHAPTER 22

CALY

I HAD NEVER BEEN A BAD STUDENT. SCHOOL AND LEARNING HAD always been an escape for me, a place that could muffle out the darkness that lay waiting for me at home with Commander Von or, when he was no longer there, the demons of my own mind. I knew though that had I ever been sent to the principal's office, it would have been eerily similar to my current endeavor.

The squish and slap of our wet feet was impossibly comical against the soft harp music filtering through the air as we followed the man with the monocle. I thought he moved shockingly fast for a man of his age, which reminded me that he was most likely somewhat ageless if he was in Moirai. He could be a god for all I knew, though the similar robe style led me to believe he was more likely another Ascended Artemi, like my father.

I desperately wished we had been going slower so I could have looked around at my own pace. It was like nothing I could have ever imagined. Everywhere I looked, lush plants and trees filled my vision. On the short walk, I'd seen more species of fauna and flora than I'd seen in my entire life, and I had studied it for years. Several times, Eli or Mendax had to grab my sopping-wet shirt or my hand and tug me along after I had stopped to examine one of the many species of butter-flies or praying mantis–like creatures. It was a nature paradise. Small bunnies and little fluffy creatures I had never seen before seemed to pour out to greet me, and as always, every time I gave my attention to one of the animals, my heart danced, thinking of Adrianna.

We continued along the flagstone path as it wound and curved through various landscapes until the rough-edged rocks of the path became flat, iridescent bricks of glass with tiny white flowers that carpeted the nooks and crannies in between each stone. I could see the worms and larvae in the rich brown soil under the glass. Hummingbirds or something that looked to be in the same genus whizzed by our heads, stopping to drink in nearby flowers.

Struggling to pay attention, I didn't notice the large glass structure in front of us until we were only a few hundred feet away from a tall door with welded iron edges in the shape of spread butterfly wings.

"Through these doors and into the front entrance," the man stated, looking slowly over Mendax and me in all our muddy glory. "No doubt they are expecting you." He gave a weak bow and turned back the way we had come, vanishing from sight.

The building in front of us was peculiar and beautiful all at once. At first glance, it gave the appearance of a somewhat traditional stone castle with walls of heavy irregular tones in various shades of cool gray, but upon further inspection, I saw at least every sixth stone or so was made of glass. Large glass sculptures of various animals decorated the various corners of the roof like gargoyles with matching clear statues scattered among the elaborate landscape. The building was large but sig-nificantly smaller than either of the Seelie or Unseelie castles. This seemed somehow cozy, if one could ever really call a castle cozy. Not at all what I had expected.

The iridescent glass of the butterfly wings shimmered as Eli opened the door and held it for me. Shards of opalescent light leapt across the walls of the entryway. There was picture-frame molding in the same sage-green color as the walls, a cascading banister of light-colored wood following beautiful stairs up several floors, and a vaulted ceiling high in the center. My bare feet felt dirty and slippery against the glossy white floor with sparkling grout. Flowing white curtains paired with the gentle walls of sage gave the interior a serene feeling.

A wooden podium stood at the center of the entryway with a small rubbed-bronze plaque on the front labeled *Registration*. A short, brown-haired woman with her nose pressed inside an open book scribbled away with an obnoxiously tall, fluffy cream quill that shimmied and swayed with each passionate movement she made.

The three of us shared a look. There was no possible way she hadn't heard our entry of sloshing, stomping feet. Eli, the obvious people person and cleanest of our obscure group, took the lead and stepped up to the podium where he cleared his throat dramatically.

The woman continued her frenzied writing. "Welcome to Moirai. I'm Anastasia. I'll be—Oh my Fates, it's you," she said once she looked up and slowly set the quill down, looking past Eli to me. Her awestruck eyes felt probing and invasive as she looked me over, mouth hanging wide.

I didn't know what to say, so I just stared back at her.

When I had pictured myself finally stepping foot in Moirai to end my father, there was never a receptionist or the most stunning array of plants and creatures I had ever seen. In my mind, Moirai had been dirty and sooty, with iron bars and spikes, something *substantially* more prisonlike than this. In my daydreams, my father fought me the second my feet hit Moirai soil, and I stabbed him like a stuck pig while I made him confess his mistakes in giving his powers to sweet Adrianna. I always spoke calmly and full of wit in these fantasies. I'd have him begging for mercy, and just before I slit his throat and removed his head, he would tell me something like, *You are a monster, and both your mother and Adrianna deserved their untimely deaths.*

Then I'd saw his head from his neck before going to be with my family once and for all.

Not once in any of those daydreams had I shown up covered in mud, with no shoes or weapons, making requests to a receptionist.

"Tell Zef he needs to come to the front immediately," the woman said, looking off to the right.

I looked around to see who she was speaking to and saw nothing.

"It's through here," she whispered, tapping her temple and giving me a wink, as if she were letting me in on a trade secret.

I nodded, still at a loss for words.

"You don't happen to know anything about a chestnut-brown floricorn, do you?" Eli asked under his breath.

"A floricorn? Yes, I believe one was just sent to Tartarus," she replied with a friendly voice.

"What? Tartarus! You sent her to Tartarus? Why?" Eli's voice cracked.

"I'm sorry. I think it was actually to the Elysian Fields," she said thoughtfully.

"What? Why?" he asked, obviously upset.

"I really don't know the details," she replied with a smile.

A loud bang sounded to the right like heavy doors slamming shut. It was followed by the echoes of heavy footsteps. My stomach flipped as I listened to them getting closer.

My father turned the corner and stopped in his tracks when his eyes landed on me. The familiar face with the neatly trimmed gray beard instantly fell, then turned tight and angry. His blue eyes hardened when they looked to Eli and Mendax.

"You're here." His voice dripped with disappointment so heavy, my eyes shot to Eli in a told-you-so scowl. Zef glared at me for a moment before shaking his head. "I did *everything* in my power to stop you from coming here, but alas, fate guides those who accompany it and manhandles those who resist." He let out a defeated sigh before scrunching his face at the long streaks of brown mud and footprints we had smeared across the white floor. "And you're somehow covered in filth already."

"You did summon me here," I bit out, finally finding my voice.

"No, my dear, I most definitely did not. I'm afraid that was all the Fates' doing. I didn't want you anywhere near here, believe me." His fists clenched at the sides of his forest-green robes.

Mendax cracked his knuckles and stepped so close behind me, I was able to feel the firmness of his stomach graze my back as he breathed in. It felt nice to know he had my back—literally and figuratively. It gave me the boost of confidence I needed.

"Don't call me 'dear' again. I'm not dear to you. You left me—left us," I corrected. This wasn't about me. I felt my blood warm with hate and anger. How had I let Eli convince me for a second that this man cared about me? His disdain for me was so pungent it pulsed from his features.

Zef nodded slowly and turned to the woman behind the podium. "Yes, well then, it's too late now. Let's find you rooms and fresh clothes. Anastasia, please get them situated. Calypso, please be decent in an hour, and meet me in the gardens." He looked at Mendax and Eli, slowly appraising each of them briefly before looking back at me with a disappointed shake of the head and leaving the way he had entered.

I was so overcome with anger, I could hardly see straight.

I wanted to hit something so bad, I felt like my head might cave in if I didn't. My arms trembled with fury that had nowhere to go. Not yet at least. He would get his soon enough.

"That was intense. Are you okay?" Eli asked, moving to stand in front of me. "I'm sorry. I—I guess you're right. I didn't know him at all. I still can't help but think there's more to it." The lines next to his eyes, the ones that normally lifted with creases of happiness, looked so out of place not wrinkled up. His big amber eyes made him look like a puppy that had been kicked and left in a ditch.

I hated seeing him like that. It somehow made me even

more mad that my father had made him sad. He was the Seelie prince! He was sunshine and freckles, laughter and dancing, yet here my father was, making him sad like me. I was always secretly afraid I would somehow ruin his sunshine, and moments like this confirmed my fears.

"I'm fine!" I snapped at him. "Don't I look fine?" I held my arms out dramatically to display my muddy clothes and bare feet.

"Just take it easy," he said, placing a hand on my arm. He had known me a *long time*, but I never let him see all the cracks or the darkness that hid behind them. By now he knew it existed, had even seen flashes of it, like when I'd killed his mother, but he still hadn't experienced it, not really. If he had, he would know that touching me wasn't a good idea right now. I didn't want to hide any of me anymore.

I shoved his hand away, turning my glare on him.

"Cal, there has to be more to it. You know I'm always right about these things. It's like I have a sixth sense or something. I'm telling you, he cares about you." He reached out to caress my arm but thought better and dropped his hand.

I squeezed my eyes shut and tried calming myself down. Seeing my father—being mere feet away from him in Moirai—was so much heavier on my mind and heart than I had ever thought it could be.

"Stop trying to make everything rainbows and sunshine, Aurelius!" My sudden shout echoed throughout the entrance. I reached for my weapon, and with none to grab, I clenched my fists until they went numb. I softened my voice, eventually whispering, "If you were *truly* my best friend, then you would be helping me and my sister right now. You would help Adrianna by killing him!"

"This isn't helping Adrianna!" Eli shouted back as he gently grabbed ahold of my shoulder and looked deep into my eyes. "This doesn't do anything for your sister or your mother! This does *nothing* but end another life!"

I knocked his hands away and glanced over my shoulder

to see if the woman was listening before turning back on my friend. I was frantic now. "You never met Adrianna! You wouldn't know how to help her or me unless your mother told you what to do!" The words were out of my mouth before I could mash them down into the box of forbidden phrases they came from.

Eli stilled. "I know you don't mean that." He looked to the floor and then the glass door. "You're angry and you're hurt, and you're taking it out on me, because you know you could never say anything that would change how much I care about you. You're right. I never did get to meet Adrianna, but even having *never* met her, I know she wouldn't want you to end your life to be with her. No sister would want that, and if she was even *half* as gentle and kind as you paint her to be, she wouldn't want you to kill her father either. You aren't doing this for your family, Calypso. You are doing this for you!" His chest rose and fell heavily as he waited for my response.

I moved to hit him and stopped myself. My steps faltered back, slapping against the cool tile as I ran to the large butterfly doors behind me.

"Cal, wait!" Eli called after me as I slammed through the doors and back into the plant-strewn paradise.

I couldn't hear his voice right now. There was too much happening, and I was going to do something I would regret.

I couldn't sort out my thoughts, and my emotions were flowing unrestrained. Why was my father so wretched? I knew all along why he had left. It was always because of me, and this had affirmed it. He had probably seen what a monster I was as a child and decided to sever ties then. How strongly must you hate someone to completely abandon them? And even more if you'd just given powers to another one of your kids.

I had barely made it out of the doors when my legs threatened to give out. Crippling pain knocked me to the ground. I gasped desperately for air as I struggled to get up again. Anger throbbed behind the veil of agony. Footsteps clapped over the pathway behind me. I felt like a lion with an injured foot that couldn't get away. The footsteps stopped behind me. A tan hand came into view with an offering of help.

"Sometimes help isn't always grand and showy, Calypso. If someone truly wants to help you, it isn't done for accolades or a pat on the back. It's done because they care about that person and want the best for them, irrespective of what they might think." Eli shoved his hand closer to me. His eyes flickered slightly, and my pain was suddenly gone save for a small, nagging ache in my legs and chest that always stayed.

I took his hand and rose from the ground.

"You've made your point, Aurelius. Feuhn kai greeyth! Feuhn kai greeyth! I get it." My voice softened. "Thank you for keeping me alive and pain-free with the tie that I didn't ask for." It didn't sound like it right then, but I really was thankful for everything Eli had done, including keeping me pain-free, but I was still so angry.

"I'm not talking about me, Cal. I'm talking about your father, and don't throw our words around like that. You only say them when you mean them with every fiber of your being," he stated, gruffer than I'd heard for a long time. "Otherwise, don't say them."

Rage poured through me until it felt like I might burst into flames. He had no idea what I was feeling!

"I think you're both fools," came a deep voice from the doorway. Mendax sloshed a few steps in front of me. "People only help another with selfish intentions. They help in the knowledge that their time and energy will be returned with benefit."

My rage turned on him. "So that is why you help *me* then?" I challenged.

He looked around slowly, as if I must be the only one who didn't understand. "Yes, most definitely. I am not here because I didn't want you to feel alone. I'm not on this seemingly *never-ending* endeavor with you because I want to be at your side in support while you work out your babyhood traumas, pet. I am here purely for selfish reasons, and I will continue to remain at your side for all of eternity for *entirely* uncharitable and selfish motives, I promise you."

"Let's get you to your rooms. I'm sure a fresh change of clothing could help everyone." The brown-haired woman popped her head into our little group.

I bit my tongue until it bled as we followed Anastasia and her crimson robes down another stunning path. I was upset with my father and needed to get a grip. Keep it to the side until I needed it. I wasn't mad at Eli or Mendax. I was hurt and petrified of losing them.

I had lived my life with a plan. The moment my mother and sister had left me, my plans for retribution kept me company. I had nothing but the thoughts of getting even. Somewhere along the line, those same plans blossomed into my only friend. Of course, they would disappear whenever Eli visited me in the human realm before reappearing with a jealous flare whenever he left. Most of the appeal of having the witch separate my heart had been in the hope that maybe, just maybe, I wouldn't feel as much after it was gone. Of course, it helped in my plan to convince Saracen that I was Artemi, but I had hoped that maybe it would also help me to have thoughts other than the incessant daydreams of killing Saracen and my father day in and day out.

It hadn't.

Since Mom and Adrianna left me, I'd not lived an hour of my life that had not revolved around thoughts of this very moment, yet I had already failed what I'd taken a lifetime to plan.

My father should have been gurgling out blood by now.

"Aurelius and Mendax, you'll be here. You will find an attendant inside that will help you with anything you should need. Calypso, please follow me," the woman said.

I jolted from my thoughts to look up from the beautiful path of creeping thyme. Two small cottages, tucked into a large hill of what looked to be various types of succulents and cacti that covered each mound. The buildings looked as if the hill had begun to swallow them whole and stopped at the arched wood door of each.

"Why is Cal not staying here as well?" Eli asked.

"These villas will suit you both best. Calypso's rooms will be a little farther ahead," she stated politely with a hint of annoyance.

Mendax and Eli exchanged a look.

"I assure you both that she will be safe where I take her. Please be aware that as of"—she reached into her robe and pulled out a glass pocket watch that sprang open, and the blossom of a stunning purple lily appeared—"ten past midnight, your powers will be in the neutral state." The tiny flower receded as she closed the glass lid of the watch and returned it to her robe pocket.

"A neutral state? They are keeping us alive right now," Eli said, suddenly worried.

"You have arrived in Moirai. In about an hour, the Fates will sort out the business of keeping you all alive until they summon you. I expect it will be closer to tomorrow evening, so please get some rest before then. This way to your rooms, miss." She began walking.

I took a step to follow her and gave a small nod to the boys. "It's probably best if we all get some alone time to think anyway. Aurelius." I turned to the golden prince. "I apologize for earlier. It…" A heavy sigh bottomed out from my lungs. "It seems that this is a bit more complicated emotionally than I had prepared for. You, being my best friend, already know that I don't handle emotions of any sort very well, but *especially* not when they involve my family. I owe you both my life in so many ways. It's hard for me to imagine one of us not living through this." I shook my head. "I'm exhausted and confused and not making any sense. I will see you in the morning or whenever it is they collect us. I love you both." I moved to catch up with the woman.

"Call if you need anything. I will hear you," Eli said.

I nodded my thanks and hurried to catch up with the woman.

We walked in silence for several minutes. She took me through a small path that wound between various stumps covered in spongy green moss. The short, dense grass of the path tickled my feet, and I felt the edges of my anger and sadness begin to ebb. I wondered if she'd chosen this path knowing that would happen.

A high-pitched clicking noise sounded above us and nearly squealed.

"You have bats here." I paused to look into the darkening sky and watched them fly around us.

She smiled proudly. "I knew you'd like this section."

I tilted my head in confusion.

"The bats are one of Zef's favorite sections to go through at night."

I rolled my eyes.

"Moirai is where the children and grandchildren of the gods live. It's home to the Fates and the Artemi, both beacons and creators of nature." She held her arms out. "Everything here is created with that in mind." She smiled. "It's only natural that you would like it while you keep Adrianna's powers."

"How do you know so much about me?" I asked her.

"I know a lot about you. Can I ask you an honest question?"

"You can ask me anything you want. Whether or not I answer it…" I shrugged. What the fuck was happening? I didn't want to make a new friend with the receptionist. I just wanted to go to sleep.

"Eli seems…lost, don't you think?" she asked.

My feet stilled on the moss. Was this some kind of a trick? "Lost?" I asked.

She pointed up to the blue-black sky where another bat squeaked by. "Yeah. Like he doesn't know what his destiny is anymore or something."

I didn't like talking to her about him. It made the hair on the back of my neck rise. "Yeah, he has a lot going on," I replied vaguely, suddenly racking my brain for something else to talk about with this random stranger. "Your pocket watch," I said as we continued walking.

210

She looked up with a genuine smile. "Yes, you enjoy my pocket watch. You see, there is this tiny flower that—"

"Photonastic movement."

She looked at me with a friendly smile and quirked her eyebrow. I had a feeling she already knew the answer but was humoring me, knowing she'd pressed about things she should have left alone.

So I continued. "It's the plant's response to the onset of night and the temperature change controlled by the circadian clock. The flower closes when the bottom petals grow at a faster rate than the petals on top, forcing them shut. It's amazing," I said.

"It's nature's magic." She continued forward.

"It's science," I argued, moving beside her.

She stopped again. "Are they not the same thing?" She winked and continued forward.

"Are you close with my father?" I asked.

She smiled. "Yes. I am quite close with Zef."

We moved in silence, each a little more closed off with the other than we had been. I wondered if she was Zef's girlfriend or something. And had she overheard me talking about murdering him? That could be bad.

We passed through a cozy meadow filled with tiny white, bell-shaped flowers and a stream, stopping at the back of a small cottage with an old wooden picnic bench. Goose bumps covered every inch of my skin as the blood drained from my face.

"It this some kind of a fucking joke? Did you do this or him? This was his doing, wasn't it? He just cannot let me have one moment of peace!" I shouted.

The woman ignored my question. "You are obviously familiar with the garden near the front entrance, since that's where you landed. Your father wishes to see you there in"—the glass pocket watch glistened like crystal water against the silver moon above us—"forty-three minutes. Here, keep the watch," she said with a hint of sympathy as she placed the smooth watch in my palm. "You'll figure out how to read it. Don't be late to meet your father. Clothes and food are inside. The Fates thought it best not to risk leaving an attendant with you, as unstable as you are right now, but please call if there is anything you need."

"Unstable! You—" My words fell silent when I turned to realize she was completely gone. I spun around looking for her, but she was nowhere.

They left an attendant with Mendax, but *I* was too unstable for one?

My shoulders sagged in defeat as I reluctantly turned my attention back to the house—my childhood home. Even the air had the same fragrance of honeysuckle and fresh laundry from my past. I moved a few steps to touch the faded wood picnic table. I knew none of this was real, but even the knots in the table looked the same. I forced myself to look out into the field where it had all started. My fingers grazed over the V-shaped scar on my thumb as they always did when I thought about that day.

My eyes snagged on a painted terra-cotta pot next to the steps of the back door. Now I knew he was doing this to torture me.

Unable to look at the place for another second, I palmed the tiny gold vines of Adrianna's ashes and spun to leave. I didn't have to be here anymore. I didn't have to remember it. I would go and stay with the boys.

The tears fell, weakening me with every drop.

Better yet, I would go now and kill my father—or myself. Anything that I could to make these feelings stop.

I turned around. As badly as I wanted to be gone, I wanted to be back with some of the memories even more. My feet carried me back to the house, only allowing me to drop when I reached the small terra-cotta pot again. I fell to the ground and lifted the dirt-filled pot to my lap. Large sticks of mulch fell out onto my lap from the drainage hole at the bottom.

Best frendz was scribbled on the pot in a child's sloppy handwriting. Above it were two stick-figure girls with interlaced arms. Adrianna had been tasked with painting us, and I had been in charge of the words because I was older. My body curled around the pot as I melted into the ground with tears that felt as heavy as a river. I missed her more than should have been humanly possible. I wasn't me without her.

"Calypso! Leave the frogs alone, and come inside for dinner!"

I startled upright at the sound of my mom's voice. My heart lodged in my throat at the sight of her as she stood holding the back screen door open. She looked just how I remembered her with wild hair and tired, nervous eyes. Absently, she adjusted her neckline to cover the top of her skeleton tattoo as she always had. She chewed the side of her cheek a second before turning around.

"Mom! Mom, it's me! Mom!" I ran to her.

The door slammed closed with a creak as she went back into the house, completely unaware of me.

"Mom, please!" I called, following her. I needed her to look at me. "Please, Mom, look at me," I cried as I turned the corner into the kitchen.

"Adrianna, get out of your sister's room, and sit down. Dinner is ready," my mom called as she moved around the kitchen.

"Mom," I whispered. Nothing. It was as if I wasn't even there.

"Where's Cal?" came a little voice that was much too painful to hear.

I watched my little sister climb up to our old wood table.

It was too much to see her. My back hit the wall as I tried to leave. I slid to the floor, my eyes unable to leave her little body.

"It should have been me, Adrianna," I began to blubber incoherently. "Sor—sorry, I'm so sorry, Addy. It should've been me she killed, not you. I'm so sorry. I'll fix it—I'll fix it."

Like my mom, she didn't hear or see me. Instead, she continued to play with her fork.

I made my way to the back door and fell out of it, tripping

over my own feet. It was like every scarred wound of mine had been ripped open and was bleeding out at the same time. Memories and feelings I had shoved away reared their painful heads, and as always, anger beat them back down before they could consume me. I clenched my fists and let out a scream that rivaled any wild animal's. I was going to finish this. Once and for all, I would be done with this pain.

The tears wouldn't stop falling, even cushioned by anger. My clothes had started to dry, and the mud crackled off in little crumbs that followed me, making me furious. I needed a weapon and *now*. I turned back to enter the house and grab a knife from the kitchen before I left to go to him.

"Let's get this over with."

My muscles snapped to attention hearing my father's voice.

I turned to see him standing about ten feet away, holding out a long dagger in my direction. It was clear and icy-looking on the bottom with a cloudy, white center. It had a frosted white handle with an intricate butterfly design around the cross guard and pommel.

I was running at him before he had finished his sentence. The stupid old man tossed the blade to me before brandishing his own. It looked similar to the one I now held, but instead of a white handle, his was all black other than the gold vines.

Without a second thought, I lunged for his heart. I would remove his head once I got him down. He stepped to the right, dodging my haphazard attempt. I tried again and again, putting every ounce of my will and training into slamming the blade into any part of him that I could. Yet every time, no matter how close, my father would calmly step away. There was never an indication of which direction he would go either. His face remained passive, almost somber as he moved about gracefully. I hadn't so much as grazed him, and I felt like I was about to collapse.

This continued until I was so exhausted, both mentally and physically, that I couldn't lift the blade one more time. I fell to the ground in a heap.

"Fine! You win," I panted.

He stepped to where I was slumped and held out his hand to help me up.

Idiot.

I pressed the blade into his chest so quickly, my fist hit his chest. Or at least it would have had the blade not disappeared from my hand.

He smiled, grabbing my empty fist and pulling me to my feet. "Your mother would have been so damn proud of you."

"You mock me." I glowered. "Was this not enough?" I asked, waving my hands wide toward the house.

"I do not say it in mocking, Calypso. She would have been proud. Your mother was one of the smartest women to ever exist," he said as he looked toward the house. "You take after her more than you will ever know."

"You will not speak about her. Not within my earshot," I snarled.

He looked offended. "My child, I knew your mother far longer than you and have grieved deeper than you can possibly imagine. Do *not* tell me not to speak about her, you who haven't even grieved her death yet."

I hurled myself at him.

Just as before, he moved to the side as if it were a choreographed dance and he knew all my steps. I was more exhausted than I'd ever felt in my life, in *every* possible way. Anger and rage, the beasts that stood guard of my other emotions, were too tired to fight anything else. Tears that felt like they were directly attached to my heart dropped from my eyes, taking molecules of my wholeness with them.

"You have no idea how hard I've grieved my mother!" I shouted like a feral monster.

"I do. I know everything there is to possibly know about you, my dear, and I'll tell you something that will *really* piss you off." He leaned in closer to me. "I love you more than you could ever imagine."

I made contact with his shoulder. The tip of the blade I'd

swiped from his hand entered his skin, but it wasn't enough to do anything. I swore in defeat as he took a step back, taking the blades with him.

"Yes, she would be—she is—very proud of you," he said as he touched his finger to the minuscule cut on his shoulder. He huffed a small, nearly silent laugh. "This reminds me of what you pulled when you took down that fae from Rosenbecks," he said. "The one that took your blade so you had to use, oh, what was it?"

My every cell froze. "The pin from his hat," I muttered.

"Yes! The pin from his hat. He looked like a strawberry after you were finished with him." He smiled a closed-lip smile that faded quickly from his eyes and turned to something sad.

"How do you know that? Were you spying on me?" I accused, though it sounded too quiet and gentle to be considered any type of real accusation and not hopeful wonderment.

"I've watched everything, my dear." His face dropped, aging him another ten years as his blue eyes fell heavily. "Everything."

"What? Gross!" I snapped, immediately thinking about some of the lewd and lascivious things I'd done.

Zef immediately jerked back. "Oh my, no! I suppose I should be more specific. Nothing indecent, I assure you." He cringed.

That hardly calmed me. "Why? Why watch me? You didn't care enough to stay and help us, so what is the point? Is that how you enjoy your free time? Watching your daughter struggle?" I walked to the picnic table with trembling legs and sat down. Silently, I prayed sitting for a minute would give me enough strength to take action.

"Calypso, believe me, I never wanted to leave you. It wasn't my choice. I ascended, as all Artemi are meant to. It was my fate, just as it would have been your sister's. Just as what you are doing now is your fate." He sat on the opposite side of the table.

"Was it your fate to destroy your daughter? You say you watched everything, but did you listen as well? Could you hear the screams of pain from your daughter when her powers began to come in? The powers you gave her? She wasn't even able to stay alive long enough to get the rest of them," I shouted. Suns, why couldn't I be stronger?

"Believe me, I know it won't make any sense to you and will sound incredibly harsh, but everything that happened to you, no matter how unfortunate it was, was what has led you to where you are now. The same with your mother and sister," he stated.

"You don't even care! Look at you. You are the reason they are dead! How could you do that to her? How?! How could you look at your own flesh and blood and see how gentle and sweet she was and *still* do that to her? She was my best friend, and you killed her! How could you?!" With all my flailing about, I fell off the bench and landed on my backside as I screamed and bellowed out all the demons that had lain quiet inside me for so many years. "It was too much! She was too soft! You should have given it to me. I could have taken the pain!"

My father's gray brows pinched together with a flicker of unease. If I didn't know him to be a complete monster, I would have thought he looked hurt at my words.

"You think you could have weathered the power better, but you're wrong, my child. Long before I had either of you, I chose your sister to receive my Artemi powers because she was the right fit. You think she was too weak. How else does one get stronger? By overcoming things we don't think we can. Look at you." He stood from the bench and walked to where I sat on the ground and extended his hand to me. "Do you think you would be as strong and fierce as you are now had you not been hardened by the events of your life?" He leaned in closer and barely above a whisper said, "Yet you are destined to change the realms far more than you could ever imagine."

I glared at him, refusing his hand. He let out a huff and sat on the ground next to me, somehow making me even more mad.

"I was destined to change the realms." If my eyes narrowed

217

any more, I wouldn't be able to see out of them. My fingers absently clutched at my pendant.

"Yes," he said with an unnerving stare at my sister's ashes.

I struggled to stand, nearly falling over again, feeling abnormally weak. The bond and tie were taking more from my body with every passing day, it seemed. "Enough bullshit. I don't want to talk to you anymore. Sever the tie and the bond between Eli, Mendax, and I now! They have no part in this. This is between you, me, and Adrianna," I shouted.

He looked to the ground, and his eyes fluttered closed. "I tried everything to stop you from coming here—everything in my power. I tried to hide and break the scrolls from the Fates before you could get them, I intercepted the scroll and included edible tickets that would send you back to the human realm, where you would be safe, but it was no use fighting fate. I even lost my dearest falcon to an accident when I tried to have it remove the scroll from Lake Sheridon."

"Why would you do all that to try and stop us?" I could feel my face reddening with frustration.

"Because the Fates are going to let Aurelius and Mendax go—" he began.

My heart instantly felt lighter. I knew we would all get out of this together.

"—and they are going to kill you."

Oh. Well, good.

I was aware that was likely never the response when you find out that you are going to die, but for me, it was the best scenario. It meant both princes could return to their realms and pick up where they left off—without me. I wouldn't be responsible for yet another of my loved ones' deaths.

"You welcome death," my father said, taking note of my small smile. "Why?"

"I have *long* awaited the day that I could be released from the pain and loneliness of this world and return to Mother and Adrianna," I said, feeling at peace for the first time in a very long time. It wasn't happening the way I had envisioned it, but Eli and Mendax would live, and I would get to rest in the Elysian Fields with my sister. I squeezed the pendant. I could almost imagine what it would feel like to hug her again. Was she still little, or had she grown up? I could hardly wait to see her again and tell her I was sorry.

"Adrianna is not resting in the Elysian Fields with the other unascended Artemi, I'm afraid, though your mother is there waiting," he said gently.

"What?" The word was a whisper.

"See the things you would have missed out on had you killed me upon first sight as you'd hoped to? There is far too much to discuss, Calypso." The corners of his mouth pulled up in a sad smile.

"How is Mom in the Elysian Fields? Humans go to heaven?" I asked warily, unsure if I should even be believing the things he was telling me.

"As I said: too much to discuss here. My hope in putting you back in this situation was not to hurt you but to let you grieve as you've never been able to allow yourself. Your anger and fury have stopped your ability to fully grieve them," he said softly.

I wanted to hate him. I had hated him, but I couldn't deny it was different now. Nothing about him exuded anything but wise and calm peacefulness. It was the same feeling I got with the animals. They never had bad intentions. Even when they bit, it was out of fear or hunger. As much as I had been trying to, I was unable to push that same feeling away now, even through my hurt and blame.

"Let me show you to your actual rooms. They are in the garden. I had a feeling you might enjoy it there." He offered me his hand again.

"If Adrianna is not in the Elysian Fields, then where is she?" I asked as I looked up from the ground.

He sighed and looked at the ground. "Because of you, your sister remains trapped in Tartarus."

As before, he went to remove his hand, but I grabbed it

before he could completely pull it away. I stood up and released him. "Because of me?"

His eyes were filled with sadness. I hated how much the almond shape of his eyes reminded me of my sister's. It felt nearly impossible to be upset with anyone who had any resemblance to her. He stared at my pendant as he gave a nod.

"The Elysian Fields are an ethereal place for those who have good, pure hearts. It's the place where the good go to rest and where the bad go to rot in misery. The same concept goes for Tartarus. It is where evil fae go to wreak havoc in happiness and the so-called good fae go to be punished. Eromreven is the place of arrival in Tartarus where it's decided what level you are cast to." He took a few steps toward the path before turning back to face me.

"I know what Tartarus and the Elysian Fields are," I grumbled at him.

He nodded, looking dejected. "Only full-blooded Seelie, Elven, and Hanabi royals and full-blooded Artemi are granted *immediate* access to the Elysian Fields."

"Adrianna is full-blooded Artemi. She should be in the Elysian Fields."

"She would be...except you still hold a drop of her Artemi power and a part of her soul in the ashes around your neck," he said softly.

No.

"You're lying." I clasped the pendant to my chest until the little white gold vines and the FEUHN KAI GREEYTH inscription dug into my skin.

"She is trapped in Tartarus until she can be reunited with that last drop of her power and the remainder of her soul," he said sadly.

My chest began to heave in a panic. "How? It's her ashes, not her soul."

A small tear ran down his face. "She, being so weak and gentle, as you put it, refused to leave you, even after she had died. The soul collectors had to go retrieve her, but by then, you already had a piece of her soul, completely encapsulated and unable to escape."

I couldn't believe what I was hearing. "Then I'll go to her. I'll give it all back!"

"That isn't possible. As of now, you are marked a Seelie royal by Prince Aurelius. You will join your mother in the Elysian Fields when you die." He glanced over his shoulder for a second.

"It was just a joke! Eli didn't even realize what he was saying!" I grabbed his forearms. It felt so weird to be touching my father and not trying to kill him.

He smiled, and a light sparked in his eyes. "Had either one of you meant it as a joke, it wouldn't have held in the eyes of the Fates. You may think you were being sneaky, but Aurelius was as aware as you were, and besides that fact, even if that didn't hold up, you are human. You would have then gone to heaven or hell in the human realm."

"But Mom…you said she is in the Elysian Fields." I let go of his robes and put my fingers to my temples.

He glanced back one last time. "I will tell you anything you wish to know, Calypso, but not here. Believe it or not, it pains me to be here as well."

"Then why do this?" I snapped.

"Because," he said, "you haven't grieved them. Instead of dealing with your pain, you found ways to hurt others as much as you were hurting. This was my only way of getting through to you."

CHAPTER 23

ELI

I hurried my pace as I followed the path Cal had gone down with that brown-haired woman. I needed to talk to her before tonight was gone. I hated feeling like we were in some kind of a fight. Of course I knew she hadn't meant to take her anger out on me; I wasn't upset about that. I was upset because I knew she was feeling a lot of things right now and she was being her usual self and trying to cut me out of parts of her.

I needed her to know that it was okay, that we were okay. I could only imagine all the feelings she was going through right now, and with us fighting off and on, I needed to make sure she was okay, to let her know that I was still here for her before she closed me out completely.

I rounded the corner and stopped, nearly tripping over my own feet when I saw the stream, the field. I would have recognized this view anywhere. This was what I saw every time I went to visit her in the human realm. This was the exact stream we would play all day in. It was where I first realized I was in love with her.

My feet moved faster through the familiar meadow where we used to chase hawks and falcons. Finally my eyes landed on the back of Cal's small house before they dropped to the familiar picnic table—

And landed on Zef and Cal talking.

Why would he make her relive this? He had no idea what he was doing. He was going to break her. He didn't know how she got—

I stopped myself from running to her aid.

What if he *did* know what he was doing? What if he could actually help her?

I saw a small spot of blood on his shoulder. She sat on the floor in a heap as they spoke. She was talking to him. Was it possible that was why he replicated this scene for her? I could hardly imagine anything that could break her walls down quicker than this place.

I moved behind a large tree at the side of the yard. It was one—or the replica of one—that I had pressed my back to so many times as I waited for Cal to come outside. I couldn't help but feel a little gross for listening in on their conversation, but I wasn't going to just leave her, not when she needed me the most, but I also didn't want to get in the way. So I stood and I listened.

And then I listened to the words that would change my fate forever.

"She is trapped in Tartarus until she can be reunited with that last drop of powers and the remainder of her ashes," Zef told Cal.

As they began to walk toward me, I realized my window of talking to Cal was probably gone.

I ran all the way back, not stopping until I was at the entrance of Moirai.

CHAPTER 24

MENDAX

I'M SORRY, BUT YOU CAN'T GET IN RIGHT NOW. THE FATES ARE busy!" the brown-haired woman from earlier yelled.

"They are about to be a lot busier cleaning the blood from these walls if you do not let me in to see them now." I took a few steps toward her. She barely even came to my shoulders.

She looked at the large green velvet curtain behind her. "If I were you, I would go back to your cottage before you ruin this for all your friends. Also, you shouldn't threaten people who already know that you are dying and have no powers," she said with a sarcastic frown.

"It's a good thing they aren't my friends then," I said with a wink. My hand shot out and latched on to a fistful of her hair. I slammed her face into the wall to the left, and her face ran with blood so red it was almost black. "And I promise you, I can do my fair share of damage even without powers." I threw her to the floor, making certain she hit her head again on the white tiles.

I moved to the green curtains. What an odd door to guard the Fates. I grabbed the heavy fabric and moved to shove it aside when a dense figure walked into me.

Fuck. I didn't have enough left to fight anyone else. I needed to see the Fates before it was too late for me.

"Please excuse me. I'm—" the man said as he stepped on my side of the curtain.

"Aurelius. Why are you here?" I asked as soon as his face came into view. "Where's Caly? Is she hurt?"

"What are *you* doing here?" he asked with a confused look on his clean face. The man never seemed to grow stubble. It made him look like an adolescent, though if I really gave it any thought, in fae time, he was an adolescent.

"Is she hurt? Where is she?" I repeated, louder. I knew I shouldn't have let her get that far away from us. Especially not here. I didn't trust the Fates or her father.

"No," he replied. "She is with her father in the garden."

"Why were you just with the Fates?" I asked. I considered blocking his path as he stepped out, but I knew he had slightly more strength than me right now.

"Surely the same reason you are, I suspect. Oh my suns! Mendax! What have you done?" he said as soon as the woman on the floor came into view.

"I'd be happy to show you again." I smirked.

Sometimes it amazed me that Caly, *my* Caly, could have even considered this sap as a lover. The two couldn't *possibly* be more incompatible. She was fire and venom with sweet sugar sprinkled on top, and he was a puppy that heeled on command and wagged his tail for a gentle pat and a kind word.

Which was why I was about to do what I was.

The other fae rolled his eyes. "You better get inside, because I'm going to help her, and when she comes to, I doubt you'll get the chance to see the Fates again," he said matter-of-factly. He had already bent down and scooped the bleeding woman into his arms.

"Bad dog," I scolded.

He glared at me before he carried the brown-haired woman down the hallway.

I pushed past the thick curtains, and darkness filled my vision. Dread coiled in my stomach at what I was about to do.

My eyes landed on two shadowed figures, and my mouth went dry.

I took a few more steps inside. My voice echoed across the expanse.

"Let me make you a deal."

CHAPTER 25

ELI

Y OU'LL BE OKAY. LET'S GET YOU CLEANED UP."
I carried the bleeding woman down a random hallway,
mostly just to get her away from Mendax before she woke up.
I knew he would never do anything like this to Cal, but it still
made me angry. No one should treat another person like this.

My ears perked at the distant sound of voices, so I took
another turn and headed in that direction. I continued to
follow the soft green walls, grateful to have a distraction from
what I'd just done and the agreement I had made with the
Fates. I didn't want to think about it right now.

The woman began to stir in my arms. I talked to her as
calmly and gently as I could in the hopes she wouldn't wake
and think that I was the one who had assaulted her.

"Anastasia, are you with me? I don't know if you remember
me, but my name is Aurelius. I'm the prince of Seelie—well,
I was until our castle got torn down…and my sister and the
Fallen took it over. I guess I don't really know what I am anymore. Anyway, I found you hurt and am taking you to get some
medical attention, okay?"

She blinked her brown eyes up at me for a moment.

"I'm not the one who hurt you," I added for good measure.

"I know. You remembered my name," she whispered. "You're King Felix's son."

My steps slowed for a beat. "How did you know that?" The distant voices were getting closer now.

"You run out of things to talk about when you're with the same people all the time. You get to know everything about them. There aren't that many of us here." She gave a weak smile. "Zef speaks only of his family since the day he arrived. He considers Felix, you, and Tarani family. Your father was a hero to many. I have heard so much about you, I think I could pick you and your sister out of a crowd."

I smiled, but my heart hurt at the thought of my father. "You must be close, you and Zef?"

"We are," she replied carefully.

A few more turns landed us in a large and brightly scented room full of banging and singing. It smelled like lemons and fresh herbs. Another few steps and I was hit in the face with bushels of hanging rosemary. I had obviously landed us in the kitchen.

"Anastasia!"

"What happened?"

The many people in the kitchen stopped what they were doing to come to our aid.

"Will you be all right?" I asked as I set her down in a chair to the side of the stove.

"Thanks for not leaving me there." She smiled. "You're my hero."

"It was nothing. Is there anything I can get for you before I leave?" Two of the ladies had already begun to clean the blood from her face.

She shook her head. "You should know they have already chosen you to stay with Zef's daughter. They will announce it tomorrow when the three of you meet for the performance."

"The performance?" I repeated.

She dabbed her swollen face with her fingers. "Yeah, but you didn't hear it from me. Thank you for your help, Prince Aurelius."

I left the kitchen and headed toward the garden. I still needed to see Cal. My thoughts somersaulted over and over. Happiness and nervousness soared and dipped as it all sank in. Everything that it meant.

Absently, I walked through the gardens. The sky had darkened, reminding me of how the human realm darkened at night and lightened in the day. It was nice to feel the coolness touch my skin. Whenever I had stayed in the human realm, it always excited me to wake up and see the sun. It made me appreciate it more.

I couldn't wait to see Mendax's face when he found out the Fates had chosen me. I imagined he would try and kill me. It was one of the few things I could predict about him. My imagination jumped to Cal's face, and it suddenly felt like I'd swallowed thorns. She would be devastated when she heard about Mendax, and I knew it.

I just wanted to help her. That was all I'd ever wanted.

"I swear to suns, Eli, if you come to me with any more shit news, I'll—is that blood on you? That's not Seelie blood. What happened?" Cal asked, walking up behind me, catching me completely off guard.

"Cal, I was just coming to find you." The moment I saw her, I knew I'd made the right decision. Her eyes looked almost hollow, like the life had been sucked out of them. I waved at my shirt, already feeling better about everything now that she was next to me. All I wanted was to see her laugh and smile again. "It is Anastasia's."

She looked at me blankly.

"The woman who checked us in—with the brown hair? Mendax beat the shit out of her."

"Oh my suns. What happened? Is Mendax okay?" Her tired eyes ignited.

"Yeah, he's fine." I recoiled at her lack of empathy. "I took her to get some help. She'll be fine too," I answered.

"What was he doing?" Her pretty blue eyes started to fade again.

I shrugged. "You'll have to ask him that." We began to walk as the awkwardness returned between us.

"What were you doing?" she asked. We paused to look at a garden bed of tulip-looking flowers that glowed against the dark as if fireflies were trapped inside. Tiny speckles of light rose from each one before drifting off into the other parts of the lush garden area.

"I was coming to find you," I repeated. "I don't like how we were earlier with each other."

"You've always been that way." She gave me a small grin. "Do you remember that time we fought because you couldn't come watch the solar eclipse with me?"

My shoulders lightened and relaxed a little. I smiled at the thought of our young stupid problems. "I had a war tactics panel, but that's not why you got mad at me."

Her brow wrinkled, and she let out a chuckle. "What do you mean that's not why I was mad at you? We had been planning to watch it on my roof for, like, a month!"

I shook my head and grinned. "You got mad because you dropped that notebook in the stream and it washed away, remember? I wasn't even there."

She laughed and dropped her mouth open in mock exasperation. I loved when she seemed light and unburdened like this. One day, I would make sure I made her feel that way every day.

"It was my first field notebook, and I was waiting in the stream *for you* when I dropped it."

A soft breeze had picked up in the garden that caused all the flowers and leaves to sway. Cal kept trying to hold the hair out of her face, but it continued to blow in her eyes as she missed one or two pieces. I moved in front of her and brushed the two or three pieces she kept missing into her hand.

"I found that notebook though." Happiness gushed through my veins at the memory of her face when I'd handed her the soaked notebook. She never knew it, but it had taken me almost two days in my fox form, trailing that stream, before

I'd found it. And I'd do it all over again just to see her happy. She deserved to be happy.

She smiled so wide, her eyes almost closed. "You did, and as I was saying, you couldn't stand the thought of us being in a fight, so every time after that, you would just show up if you thought I was mad at you."

I moved to the other side of the short grass path to look at—well, anything that was not that close to her. "You were never mad though, not really." I leaned over to smell a dark-blue bush. It didn't smell like anything, and I found myself a little disappointed it didn't have some sort of berry scent.

She joined me on the other side of the path. "You should know by now I could never really be mad at you."

"Promise?" I pressed. I *really* needed to hear she wouldn't be mad at me for what I was about to do...or at least that she would eventually get over it.

"Promise. You want to stay at my cottage for a little bit? I met up with my father," she said.

"You did? What did you guys talk about? I'll stay for a little while, but I think Mendax would have an aneurysm if I stayed all night." I couldn't help but laugh at the thought. He was going to have a lot more than an aneurysm to deal with soon.

Immediately, she let out a large breath and looped her arm in mine. "So that bitch that Mendax bloodied up? She took me to my cottage, but wait until you fucking hear what it was."

And so continued her detailed account of everything that had taken place between her and her father. I stayed in her new rooms into the wee hours of the morning. Occasionally, she would pause and wait for my opinions and comments. It felt just like the good old times and was *exactly* what we both needed before what was probably going to be one of the worst days of her life.

CHAPTER 26

MENDAX

A T THE NOISE OUTSIDE, I SAT UP AND PULLED THE STIFF WHITE sheets over my body.

A second later, there was a soft tap at the door to my bedroom. It was the annoying attendant.

"Sir, I heard you rouse again. Just wanted to check if you needed anything? I brought you a special breakfast brew. I'm aware it's several hours early, but you seem to be a light sleeper," the young attendant rambled.

"Leave it by the bed," I commanded, hoping I had cut off any further prattling.

He quickly rushed over to the table by my bed and set the stone mug of steaming liquid on a piece of cloth. I stared holes into him until he left. With the nuisance finally gone, I looked around for where he had laid the clean clothes. My eyes landed on the pile. All I wanted was a shirt for the moment, but I could already see that wasn't going to happen. If they thought I was going to wear a robe, they were fucking delusional and going to get an eyeful of my dick when I showed up naked.

I gave up on clothing for the moment and settled back into the soft mattress. It had felt like ages since my body felt the luxury of a decent bed.

But even with the decent mattress, I'd barely slept without her in my line of sight. As soon as our powers became inaccessible, I feared I might not make it another night. Initially, Caly was my main concern, but I quickly realized she was in favorable company, and they weren't going to let her die. Even an emotionally barren idiot could see how much her father loved her. He was a mess with her being here.

I hated not sharing a bed with her. The only reason I hadn't fought harder to keep her with me was the simple fact that I couldn't stand for her to see me like this—completely powerless.

I held my hand up and tried to draw up my smoke. Useless.

If my father or mother could see me now, they would probably try and extinguish me from their line. A small knot formed in my gut at the thought. I was the only one left in my lineage. If something went wrong today, then that was it for the Smoke Slayers—at least any that were known. When Caly and I left this place and returned to Unseelie, I wanted to have so many fucking babies with her—at least a dozen.

The thought of parting her pretty pink lips and filling her made my cock rise, stiff and ready for my queen. *Stars,* she was unbelievably beautiful. Especially when she got mouthy—fuck, I loved that mouth of hers. I gripped ahold of my cock roughly and ran my hand over the length. I could almost see her in front of me. I would lick her entire body if she were here right now. I'd make her strip while I watched. She'd stand there in all her beautiful, naked glory, waiting for her next command. Obviously, I'd make her wait *just* long enough that she'd start to get nervous and uncomfortable. Fuck, I loved to rattle her.

I fisted my cock faster, imagining her fully exposed and vulnerable, unsure of what I was going to do to her.

On your knees, I'd tell her.

She was very naughty, so of course she'd fight me for control. I loved when she fought me. Fuck. She'd likely tell me to fuck off or something threatening. I'd see the sparks in her eyes when she saw how impossibly hard she made me. Then I'd tell her to wrap her gorgeous lips around me and suck me off.

I threw off the sheet to pump into my hand.

I would wait until she was so wet, she was dripping like a filthy whore, and then I would tell her to bend over and give me her ass. Her cunt would be a gleaming, throbbing mess. I'd slide my cock all over her pussy until we were both covered in her slickness. She'd be crying out for me, so I'd slide my length into her, one inch at a time until she was spread out on the base of me. I'd go so deep inside her. I'd go slow at first—slower than she wanted. I'd want her frustrated and writhing on my cock, full of impatience. Then I'd reach around to the front of her and play with her clit. I would be able to feel her pulse and throb all over my dick as I pushed it in and out, fucking her until her eyes watered.

After my three fingers got nice and messy from her slippery cunt, I'd press her back down harder on the bed. I'd want to focus on that round ass of hers. I'd gently spread her cheeks apart. If she started to get bashful, I'd spank her and leave a stinging handprint as my mark on her. Then I'd take my three wet fingers and hold them over the tight little hole of her backside, just letting her know I was there. She'd start moaning as I continued to pump into her tight pussy, knowing every intimate, vulnerable part of her was wholly exposed to me. I'd kiss the back of her neck while I pressed two fingers into her hole as I continued fucking her. She'd moan and scream, making noises I'd never heard her make. Then I'd add the third slick finger, fucking her slowly so she was ready for my thick cock. I'd pull out of her dripping pussy while I held her hips. "I fuck every part of you because I own you. Every fucking hole is mine." It'd be almost too much for her at first, but then she'd find her rhythm. Just when she'd start tightening up to come, I'd bite her on the ass so hard, it would leave teeth marks. She would fucking *love* that. I'd wrap my other hand around her throat and press my thumb into her mouth. I would claim every fucking hole I wanted. She'd come all over my cock with a battle cry.

Fuck, I was about to come. I reached over to the bedside

table to grab the cloth under my tea. It was too late—I couldn't pull my hand away to move the cup, or I'd blow my load all over my own hand.

I rolled off the bed and grabbed the cup just quick enough to empty myself into the tea. The tip of my cock dipped in the warm liquid as it pulsed.

I dropped back on the bed in an exhausted heap just as I heard Aurelius's door close. I rolled off the bed and walked to the window. I saw the silhouette of him behind the curtain of his room. He was taking his shirt off. My blood began to pump faster.

That *fucker.*

It was morning, and he had just returned.

CHAPTER 27

MENDAX

Y OU WERE WITH HER," I ACCUSED.
Aurelius opened his bedroom door. I was already inside the cottage.

"Why are you in my room? Or my house for that matter?" he asked groggily. His lack of concern that I wasn't about to kill him irked me. Had he no self-preservation?

I shoved in past him and nearly gagged on the smell of her, it was so strong coming off him.

You cannot kill him yet. His life is still tied to hers.

I glared at him. "Have some tea. You look like shit." I handed him the stone cup.

He took the cup and let out a sigh. "I was with her. She had a tough time with her father and needed a friend. If you haven't noticed, she doesn't know how to deal with emotions and just gets angry. Look who I'm talking to," he grumbled before taking a sip of tea.

"I already advised you once against touching her, did I not?" I asked.

He sat down on the bench at the foot of the bed. "How do you know I hugged her?" he challenged.

I took a big breath in before slowly letting it go. "Because the creature hasn't given me a moment's peace since I met her. Her body, her voice, even the scent of her is like blood to a leech with me. I can't have enough of her, so my senses seek her out with a lupine whine of desperation. I know that you hugged her. A lot."

"And? They moved her rooms to the gardens. I've told you, you have nothing to worry about. We are friends. Now go back—"

"Believe me, I'm not worried…for me. You're not her type." I cut him off and walked to the door. "I hope they were goodbye hugs, because I'm going to kill you soon."

He rolled his eyes. "You're so sure that I'll be the one to die today? I really hope you have something dramatic up your sleeve, because I hate to tell you, but the Fates have already chosen me."

"It's a good thing you promised me a favor then, huh? The time and place of my choosing? Remember you gave me your word on the mountain?" My eyes searched his. He was telling the truth. "When did you find this out?" I asked.

He looked to the ground, almost as though he felt badly about what he was telling me. "Late last night, and I'm not giving you that favor. The woman you hurt outside the Fates' hall told me after I helped her. You really shouldn't hurt innocent people."

"You forget I don't care about innocent people or others in general." I moved to the door. "How's your tea?"

"It's good. You should do more nice things like this." He took a large swig. "Mendax." His tone was suddenly serious. "I don't know what is going to happen today, so I want to say goodbye to you. I'd like to say I'm sorry for how this all has worked out, but I'm not."

This was the trouble with Aurelius: he was a stereotypical Seelie through and through. It wasn't in their nature to be mean or deceptive, unlike my people. But this particular Seelie had been raised by a queen who contradicted everything Seelie. Even though all signs pointed to the latter, I wouldn't

257

have blinked twice to find out that he wasn't at all the flower-smelling, door-holding hero Caly thought he was.

The yellow-haired fae continued. "After getting to know you during this expedition, I still don't like you. Sometimes I'm baffled that Cal, or anyone for that matter, could love you as much she seems to." Two large vertical lines formed between his brows.

"If you aim to hurt my feelings, I'm afraid you will be disappointed." I walked to the window and looked over to my cottage. "I am barren of any feelings aside from the creature whose stench you wear like a fucking cape."

"You know, I believe that. I really don't think you care about anything or anyone but her." He rose from his chair and moved in front of me. "Then you will agree. Caly deserves happiness and someone who knows how to keep her safe. As a human, she is fragile and cursed with a short mortal life. Until I can find a way to give her all my powers, she needs someone with her who is going to give her the safest, happiest life possible. You want that for her too, right? Goodbye, Mendax."

For our kind, he was still young, but he carried himself with a confidence I hadn't ever thought appropriate until I saw how he fought me when he'd worried I had hurt Caly.

"If you think my time with Calypso is near its end, you are drastically underestimating the level of infatuation I endure of this woman. There is *nothing* I won't do for her—nothing. Kill me a hundred times, and every time, I will return with more determination than before—for her. Let this be my goodbye to you, the hero of Seelie. Say fuck you to Aether in the Elysian Fields for me when you get there, would you?" I clapped his arm roughly and moved toward the door, stopping before I stepped out. "You were never really her friend if you can't tell she is meant for me."

The door slammed behind my back, rattling the hinges as I stormed out.

I needed to see her so fucking bad it hurt.

My boots paused at the path's intersection in front of the

cottages. I inhaled, pulling the crisp morning into my body. My eyes closed as I reached for a thread of her scent. *Stars in fucking Tartarus*, I was such a fool for her.

I rolled my neck slowly from one side to the other, feeling the cracks and pops as I stood on the path. My body felt better today, as much as it could without my powers. I didn't feel like myself, but at least I didn't feel like my body was going to give out on me every few minutes. I thought back on the last few weeks of this journey. Had I not been struggling to keep Caly healthy, I would have had more of my powers. Images flashed through my head like a memoillusion cube of Aurelius and Caly holding hands and laughing. He was always watching me.

For the first time, I believed that the Fates must be as grand and all-knowing as they were made out to be, because had I had more of my power, I'd have killed the golden fae before we'd even left Seelie to begin this endeavor, and then I'd have lost her.

The heavy tread of my boots ground into the soil as I sharply turned to the right and proceeded with silent footsteps.

Out of instinct, my hands flexed, reaching for their deadly blankets of smoke. My pace quickened when the muscles of my shoulders flexed and no wings came. No power at all. Nothing.

Caly feels like this every day, and look at what she has done, I told myself. *You will be fine too.* It was all worth it if it meant I could keep her—anything to keep her. That was the deal I had made.

My feet picked up speed, and eventually I left the path all together and was running through the groomed flower beds, kicking dirt and smashed blooms across the pristine landscape as I hurried to my destination, every step slightly more frantic than the last.

When I had approached the Fates earlier, I knew I had only two things in my possession to barter with: Caly and my powers. I would only die without the first, and the second didn't matter without her...nothing did. Unsurprisingly, they weren't interested in just my powers but my...unique skills.

Apparently Caly's sister was some kind of anomaly within

the Artemi community, and they urgently needed her to ascend. I didn't know the details, and I didn't care.

Aurelius hadn't been the only one watching Caly and her father last night. I'd heard everything Zef had said about how Caly wearing the ashes of her sister and keeping the last drop of Adrianna's powers were keeping her trapped in Tartarus.

My heart pounded. It felt like a song in my chest as the building came into view.

I had known the Fates would decide to kill me. No matter who it was, no one wanted a hybrid Smoke Slayer and Impeller out in the realm, especially not one like me. But I had a bargaining chip, so I offered it.

I was the only one who would go to Tartarus when I died.

As long as Caly remained alive and safe and stayed bonded to me, I would go to the fae underworld voluntarily, taking with me the last drop of her sister's powers and the pendant with her soul. I would set Adrianna free from Tartarus so she could finally ascend like they apparently needed her to. And I would get to watch Caly from the pits of Tartarus as much as I wanted. They had agreed only after declaring that they were going to take away every one of her memories that involved me to prevent her from attempting to get to me. I would spend the remainder of my time as a liaison between the Fates and Kaohs, who I was already close with.

I needed to keep Caly in my life in whatever way I could.

I was going to slit Aurelius's throat the second they broke the tie between the two of them, before they killed me. I wasn't worried about Sunshine getting out of line with her while I was away. I knew she was as infatuated with me as I was with her. That was how I knew my hellhound would still figure everything out and come to me. I'd find a way. Whether she had a memory of me or not.

The things I did for fun turned most fae's stomachs, so one only had to guess what I would do for the woman I was bonded to and in love with.

Realistically, I was vulnerable and weak without my powers,

yet somehow, knowing I could still keep her, it only made me feel more lethal. I wasn't a killer because I had my smoke; I was a killer because I enjoyed the feeling of taking someone's life away from them. That would only be amplified now. Before Caly, my kills had been loose and haphazard. A taste of fun so I could enjoy the feeling of *something*. But with the hellhound bonded to me, I could feel everything she felt as if it were my own. It had opened up a cornucopia of feelings that I never could have otherwise experienced. When she laughed, I felt it in a way I'd never be capable of without our bond. It had become an addictive elixir in my veins that I would *never* give up. Even if I wasn't going to be a part of her memory, she would still be in mine.

I quieted my steps, pausing behind a bush to watch the large glass winged doors of the main building. My body pressed into the shadows, and even though I had no power to lend to them, they welcomed me in their dark embrace like an old friend, hiding me from view as the minutes passed.

Obnoxious birds chirped over the faint harp music. Three female Ascended Artemi walked out the doors and into the garden. I could feel their power like a punch in the temple as they passed.

Without a sound, I walked in the door behind them before it shut. The soft melody of strings sank into the marble at my feet as I silently passed through the empty entryway. The steps wanted to creak under my weight, but they were wise enough not to as I took them two at a time. Hallways and doors appeared as far and as high as I could see. Voices sounded down the opposite hallway. I took a few steps until I could press myself behind a drapery hanging off a nearby window. I closed my eyes as the small group passed and let the feel of their power wash past me.

They were demigods—half fae and half god or goddess. Until now, I had been convinced my powers were nearly invincible. I knew that Smoke Slayers were among some of the most powerful fae ever created—at least until I felt Zef's powers at the mountain. His were unlike anything I'd ever felt before in strength. Even here, in Moirai, the Fates were the only ones I'd felt top his powers. It was no wonder they took my deal to get Caly's sister out of Tartarus if she was supposed to be even more powerful than Zef.

I let out a quiet breath and moved down the hallway to the left. I could feel his powers radiating down the fucking hallway. It was the first time I could remember being unnerved since I'd killed my father. That day had changed me forever. It made me callous and cold. My father had been my best friend. Having to bear the duty of taking his life to protect mine and my mother's had been the day a switch shut off in me.

I didn't want that switch to shut off in Caly. I didn't want her to feel what I had felt. I was going to kill Zef for her so she never had to change. She could remain the perfect little hellhound that I loved.

I would do everything for her if she'd let me. Every hard thing she ever had to do again, I would do it for her for as long as she lived, because ironically, I wouldn't be alive, and she wouldn't know I existed.

My fingers gripped the brass knob and turned. I opened the door, ready to fight, but what I saw gave me pause.

The pungent smell of cut grass sat in my nose as I took in the lawn in front of a familiar dark house about twelve paces away from me. A falcon cried out overhead. My forehead creased as I saw a pale-blue sky where a ceiling would have been. It was as if instead of stepping into a room, I had stepped outside in front of another house.

A dark house on Arcanus Lane.

CHAPTER 28

MENDAX

I DIDN'T WASTE ANY TIME CIRCLING THE HOUSE. I KNEW ZEF WAS in there; I could feel him. My fingers pressed down on the black lever and pushed the large door open just enough that I could slide inside.

"What in the—"

The old man walked into the foyer before I had a chance to move. He had so much power radiating off him, it made my bones vibrate. He looked like her. That was going to be a problem for me, and I knew it.

"I need to talk to you about your daughter," I answered. Even without powers, my blood had already begun to excite at the prospect of a fight.

Zef's face softened a little at the mention of Caly, but he remained stern. "You shouldn't be in my quarters. The Fates have set the trial time for this afternoon. You should be saying your goodbyes, Smoke Slayer."

His face looked kind and weathered as he spoke, but there was something underneath that lit my skin up with electricity.

He hated me.

I grinned. "Don't be bothered, old man. I'll be sure to give Aurelius the goodbye he deserves once the time comes."

His blue eyes hooked mine so intensely, I had to search my memory of Artemi powers to see if he was about to get inside my head. I didn't think so. Like my father, I was an Impeller, but it didn't work on strong fae. Though with no powers, I doubt I could have stopped him anyway.

"You know, I have a few things I'd like to say to you about my daughter as well." He broke eye contact and turned around. "Come." His voice was gruff as he walked off.

I followed, looking for anything nearby to cover his face. I couldn't touch him when I saw even a little of her in his features. No flour sacks, no aprons, no coats, nothing. It was like he knew his best defense was simply not having something I could cover his head with and beat the shit out of him.

I followed him and stepped into a large sitting area lined with paintings and tapestries. The interior looked different lit up than it had when we had come. The room we were in was much darker than the entryway had been, with the main source of light being a great fireplace made of huge slabs of stone and large leather chairs placed in a half circle around the fire.

I smelled Caly.

Movement in the corner had me spinning, prepared for some type of an attack. The Artemi were supposedly a peaceful kind, but I had seen what they were capable of during the war between the Smoke Slayers and the Artemi.

"Jumpy?" the man asked with a hint of humor in his gravelly tone as he sat in one of the chairs.

Was she here?

The glass butterflies—at least ten of them—shifted from a vining plant on the wall and fluttered about the dark room. The white plants on the wall between the photos caught my eye.

"They are called the vines of accipere." He tilted his head in fascination as he watched me. "Every time I'm lost with missing my family, I look at that plant. It's been the only vessel of hope I've retained since coming here."

Unless the plant could hide his face so I could kill him, I

didn't give a shit about it. There was a blanket of knitted cream yarn in the leather chair next to him. That would work.

I moved impatiently to grab the blanket.

"The vine of accipere is the only one of its kind. It has—or had—something I needed. A type of material in the plant that has some of my very own features. I was able to make a present for Calypso from it with the hopes that I would get to visit her one day and make amends." He said the words so proudly, I almost felt sorry for him. Almost.

I felt my dimple indent. "If you let me know where it is, I'd be happy to give it to her, though I have to tell you, if it's not a weapon, I doubt she'll want it."

His stare hardened. "I've been waiting longer than she's been alive to give her this gift," he said coldly. "What is it you wished to tell me about *my* daughter?"

I still needed to see Caly before the trial; I didn't have time to draw this out.

Blanket, cover face, kill. I didn't need to speak to the fucker, but for some reason, I couldn't push the words away. "How could you leave that woman?" I felt myself getting angry. "I could hardly leave her for a fortnight without going mad. You—you had the chance to be with her every day...for years, and you squandered it. You wasted time you could have been near her."

He waved his hand calmly, but I could see the burst of pain in his eyes. "Believe me, I didn't want to leave them. No one wants to leave their family behind. I had no choice. It wasn't safe for me to be there." His tan face began to pinken as he flustered. "How did you find me?" He stood, shouting now. "You felt my power, and it was only me. You can't *begin* to imagine the impossibility of hiding me and Adrianna in the same place. It would have been so much more dangerous for them had I fought to stay!"

I smirked at how quickly he had started to unravel. "If I were that powerful, I would have stayed to protect them, taught them how to protect themselves from others." My blood was boiling inside me like molten lava. He had hurt her more than anybody, and he would pay for it. I didn't care if he was the most powerful fae I'd ever come across. He would die just the same as the others.

"There was no protecting them! Don't you understand how the Fates work? This was already in motion before they called me to ascend. You can't fight fate. The best chance I had of helping them was coming here and doing what I could to influence the Fates!" He stormed around the circle of chairs until he was in front of me. "Look around. You think I left them willingly? I would do anything for those girls! Anything! What did you do? Kill a few people and pine after her? Her mother sold her soul to Kaohs so she could go to the Elysian Fields and be with Adrianna when their time came. You know nothing about what this family has gone through!"

In his fit of waving hands, I took a closer look at the paintings layered across the walls. Each was a portrait of a blond girl I instantly recognized as Caly and another girl. There had to be a thousand small paintings tucked on the walls between plants and tapestries. They climbed so high up to the ceiling, I realized that it was also covered in paintings of his daughters.

"So all three of you were going to end up in the Elysian Fields and leave Calypso on her own again?" I couldn't understand.

"Remind me again, how many children do you have, Mendax? You act as if you know how to be a father." He shook his head. "You have no clue what you speak of."

"You may be her father, Zef, but I'm her daddy now." I smirked. "You're never going to hurt her again. I won't allow it."

"You think you can hurt me, Slayer? I left so that she could live a life untainted by the hate and cruelty of others, and instead I had to watch my daughter get piece after piece after piece get ripped from her until she herself had nothing left but hate and cruelty. And I had to watch it all from here—watch as the only thing that keeps her willing to live is the hatred she harbors for me, and all the while, I am unable to save or help her aside from talking the Fates into jamming the occasional gun. You haven't felt torment like this in all your life, and I pray to the Fates that you never do."

There was a muffled sound from somewhere in the room. Even amid my threat, Zef removed his eyes from me to glance in the corner of the room. Concern that hadn't been there just a moment ago widened his eyes and pinched the skin between his brows.

Ever the opportunist, I took my opening and began hammering my fists into the back of his head. He fell to the ground and shielded his head. Had he had a moment to think, he could have easily done something to stop the assault, but I didn't give him that moment to think. Every hit that landed was followed by another. "You—hurt—her, and—now—I'm going to—hurt you." I had become a feral animal, kicking and punching as I thought about Caly having to become so strong because she had no one there to keep her safe. "Never again," I grunted.

Zef rolled over in an attempt to jump away, but I stopped him. I was barely breathing as I let loose every little emotion in my hits and kicks.

"Tell her I loved her always," he rasped out from a ball on the floor. "Perhaps she will believe it from you. Maybe you can protect her more than I could." He wasn't even fighting me as he took my wild hits.

"Stop! Stop!"

I felt something on the skin of my arm, but it wasn't enough to snap me out of my fury—at least not until I smelled her again.

"Mendax, wait!" Caly attempted to pull me away from her father.

She didn't understand what I was doing. "You—I couldn't—you don't have to be the one to kill him. I don't want you to change," I panted, stopping briefly to look at her.

"Wait. I don't know if I want to kill him anymore!"

I struggled to process her words, still reeling from adrenaline.

247

Her palms on my chest took the brunt of my focus. Her round eyes were wide and vulnerable. I looked around the room, realizing she had appeared from out of nowhere.

"I was in the corner, behind the tapestry. I came to kill him myself, and then you showed up and—" She grabbed my arms and pulled me a step away from her bloodied father. "I—I heard everything." She paced in a small circle as she held her head in her hands.

She was the noise we'd heard in the corner.

Kaohs, she was fucking amazing.

"This is what you've been waiting for, is it not? Take over if you want to finish him," I said, still breathing hard. I could feel the doubt and confusion pulsing through the bond.

"No, Mendax, I'm saying that—I don't know. I—" She was so flustered.

"Figure out what it is you are saying, because once he gets up, it's not going to go well for either of us. Are you saying you don't want me to kill your father?"

Zef stood, calmly pulled a folded white handkerchief from his robes, and began to wipe the blood from his face with quiet mumbles that suggested he was more irritated than injured.

Caly's big blue eyes looked at her father as though she were seeing him for the first time, and I knew in that moment that she wouldn't want her father dead. A part of me was happy for her that she wouldn't have to go through what I went through with my father. Another part of me wanted to not listen to anything she said and go ahead and kill him anyway for making her feel any type of pain. No one hurt her and got away with it. Not now that she was mine.

He gave her a solemn nod, as if he was afraid to acknowledge her too much for fear of her changing her mind. Somehow the blood had already been wiped from his face, and he looked practically untouched, making me question if I'd even been the one to keep him down or if that had been his doing.

"I don't know what I want from you, but I don't want to be

248

responsible for killing you if I decide I need more information," she said with a firm chin.

The silence stretched as Caly and Zef watched each other with trepidation. Amid the tension in the air, you could feel something shift between the two of them.

"So you came to kill me even after our talk last night?" His voice sounded more full of interest than accusation. "What made you stop? I know you've been here at least an hour, no?" He moved toward her, and I cut him off, stepping in front of him.

His eyes roamed over mine, testing to see if I was actually prepared to stop him. Once he realized that I was, something passed over his eyes—possibly respect, possibly not—and he gave a small nod as he slapped me on my shoulder and stepped around me, completely unbothered.

"If you want my honest answer, the plants made me stop." She caught my eye, checking to see that I was calm and wasn't going to stop him before she moved toward one of the plants on the table under a large globe of glass. "I needed to know more about them. As soon as I came in here, I took too much time looking at the plant before Mendax came. How did you know I was here?"

He tipped his head toward a group of glasswing butterflies, and I saw two luna moths fluttering by. "They wouldn't leave the tapestry alone even though their king was in the room. Besides that, even though you only have a drop of Adrianna's powers, I can feel it."

Caly nodded silently.

"Of which…" He cleared his throat as he wiped a hand over his face as he tossed his bloodied handkerchief onto a nearby end table. "You need to give back Adrianna's animal power before you see the Fates."

I could feel Caly's pulse quicken.

"But…no. To who? I—" Her face reddened, and her lip trembled.

I moved next to her and crossed my arms as I silently waited for even a whisper of encouragement from her to have another try at killing Zef.

"I will fuse the drop of power back with the part of her soul in the pendant. You can have it to wear until the Fates decide on a way to get it back to her." Caly's father motioned us to the chairs around the fireplace, and I followed Caly's lead.

"But—" Her eyes gleamed against the flame as she struggled. "It's been a part of me for so long. I—it's the only way I can feel her. I don't know what to do if I can't feel her or the animals." Her voice cracked.

"I understand, but it's time. Adrianna can't stay trapped in Tartarus simply because you wish to *feel* a little closer to her. That's the hardest part of people dying…letting go of someone who you only want to hold tighter because they are gone, but it's also what stops us from grieving and learning to live without them." He pressed his thumb and forefinger into his eyes as if he too were trying not to cry.

After a few moments of silence, Caly put her hands under the hair at the nape of her neck and removed the white-gold pendant. She looked at it in her hands for a minute before pressing a kiss to it and handing it to her father.

"I'm going to neutralize the power and then return it to her soul in the pendant. You won't feel anything, okay?" He had scooted to the edge of his seat so he could easily reach her.

Caly nodded, tears rolling down her cheeks.

I felt her crippling sadness through the bond. It was shattering parts of me to watch her like this. I wanted to do something to make the pain stop, but I also needed the pendant to take back with me to Tartarus when they killed me in a few hours, though neither of them knew it.

I reached over and squeezed her hand. It felt like such a juvenile action, but thinking about her forgetting me made my need to touch her unbearable. This wouldn't be forever, and she would remain safely bonded to me. I would know every feeling she had, and even if *I* couldn't return to help her, I would make certain that she got any help she needed.

Zef closed his eyes for a moment, and I felt a flare of something. The Artemi's ability to take another's power was terrifying, and the fact that they did it with such ease was beyond unsettling.

Caly's eyes flickered closed as she tightened her grip on my hand. I was watching her unravel. She had spent her entire life trying to get to this point, and now she was being turned inside out. No matter what happened, I would be hers, and she would be mine. I'd happily spend the rest of my life reassembling her broken pieces. I'd prefer it that way. How else would I tuck in little shards of myself where her pieces were missing?

"I'd hoped to present this to you later, but—" He pulled out a glass pocket watch with a tiny flower inside. "I'm afraid we don't have much time before the performance."

"Performance?" Caly's eyes snapped open.

"Performance, trial…they unfortunately are the same," Zef said quietly. He rose from his chair with the pendant still in hand and walked to the wall with the white plant hanging from it. Caly watched him like a hawk as his hand reached into the stone pot and fished around for a moment, moving a few purple mushrooms out of the pot before removing one of the most unique blades imaginable from inside the plant. The symmetrical blade tapered into the sharpest, needlelike tip, except it wasn't steel; it was made of glass. The frosted handle looked somewhat normal, other than the fact that a glossy, clear butterfly figurine with unbelievable details attached to the base of the handle, just above the cross guard.

I heard Caly's intake of air in the silent room as she took in the blade.

The cross guard was made of two fronds from a fiddlehead fern that bowed out slightly before wrapping around the part of the blade closest to it. The green fronds were shiny and smooth, giving the impression they must be made of some sort of stone.

"That is the most beautiful weapon I've ever seen. It's similar to the one I grazed your shoulder with," Caly said, almost in a daze as she looked at it hungrily.

I resolved right then and there to steal it for her before we left this room. Just imagining her looking at me that way—even if it was while I gave her the blade—would be worth it.

The tense air between the two of them had melted into something I was completely unfamiliar with, but whatever it was, it was no longer hate.

Zef's worn face beamed brighter each time he looked at the way she looked at the weapon in his hands. He returned to his seat next to Caly with a barely contained smile. "It is. I finished it this morning. I'm glad you like it, because depending on what the Fates rule, it is yours."

CHAPTER 29

CALY

W HY DOES THE OUTCOME OF THE TRIAL DETERMINE IF I receive this present from you or not?" Had this blade been offered to me by anybody else, I wasn't sure that I could have accepted it. It was so simple and exquisite. But it felt significantly less hard to take from my father who had abandoned me and left my family.

"Give me your finger. I need to prick the end with the blade. It's the last and final step, and the blade is complete," Zef muttered softly as he gently took my hand.

Mendax sat up in his chair. "Unless you are handing her that blade to slit your throat, I strongly suggest you move away from her."

A soft chuckle came from my father. The surprisingly comforting sound poured inside my body and cozied up in my chest like a cup of hot tea.

"I can hardly imagine how Aurelius survived the journey with such a bewitched Unseelie at his side," he said. His blue eyes softened a fraction when I returned his smile.

My smile then went to Mendax at my side. Even in this very moment, I should be scared to death that I would lose him. The thought alone made my heart shiver with fear. If I couldn't get to Adrianna in Tartarus, then I needed to find a way to return her power so she could finally get to the Elysian Fields. At least Mom would be there waiting for her, so she wouldn't be alone. If anyone could help me find a way to get the pendant to her in Tartarus, it was Mendax. He had mentioned on numerous occasions that he and Kaohs, the keeper of Tartarus, were close. He would help me fix all this.

I smiled wider, and Mendax settled back into his chair like a guard dog waiting for the command to kill.

"I'm quite sure he wouldn't have had he not been tied to me," I replied as it dawned on me, and I snatched my hand away from my father, causing Mendax to leap out of his chair. "You must speak with the Fates before our trial. I am going to request they sever the tie with Eli." I swallowed, and it felt like shards of hot glass going down my throat. "But you have to make sure he remains alive."

The room suddenly felt too small and tight with me inside it. The news of Adrianna being trapped in Tartarus threw out every plan I'd had of taking myself out of the equation and instead left me with a horrible situation that I couldn't figure out. As soon as I said the words out loud, I knew the silence that met them meant it wasn't possible.

"I'm so, so sorry, honey, but I'm afraid it's too late." My father grabbed my hand again and bowed his head with a grimace. "Severing the tie will kill one of you, just the same as cutting the bond will kill one of you—whoever it is that they decide should die. The Fates are ruthless. We will be lucky if they even let you free since you are a human with no powers in a fae realm. Humans usually don't get the chance to go between realms and live to tell about it."

"But why?" My voice quivered.

My father let out a long sigh and gently squeezed my hand. It was strange how comforting it was to be sitting with someone I'd spent my whole life hating.

As soon as I entered the house to kill him this morning and saw the pictures of me and Adrianna climbing so high they covered the ceiling, I knew he wasn't the same horrible, hateful, and careless man I'd spent my life imagining him to be. I'd never thought for a second that he even knew who I was, let alone that he kept up with my life in the only way he could. It all made sense to me now why he had been trying to keep us out of Moirai. It had been impossible for me to believe anything but the worst, filling in the holes and empty cracks with all the reasons why it had been so easy for him to leave me. I'd never even thought that maybe he hadn't wanted to. The simple idea was followed with the little glittering thoughts that maybe I was harder to leave behind than I had always thought.

In this moment, I knew I never really hated my father. I hated the character I had crafted in my mind and called my father. I used every gap or unanswered question and filled it with a driving hate that was easier to live with than the pain of not knowing. The first whisper of grief I felt hit my softness so hard, I had to turn it into something hard that could protect me, and nothing builds a tougher wall than hatred. The truth is, I was a scared little girl who was left all alone and had nothing to play with but imaginary characters in my head. One of those was the character I had created for my father, but I never knew a thing about my father or his reasons for leaving me. I couldn't help but look at him now in a different light.

"The Fates play life like a game of chess. It is far beyond any of our comprehension how or what they do. I stopped trying long ago to understand them. The Ascended Artemi help carry out some of the finer details of their plans when it is needed, but generally they are so far ahead of our wildest thoughts that we only get in their way. Before you were even summoned, they likely already knew who was going to die. All this is just a big, entertaining charade for them." He held the tip of the beautiful blade up to my finger and waited.

I pressed my finger into the sharp tip of the blade, welcoming the prick of pain that followed. Crimson blood immediately beaded at my finger. Instead of taking the drop of blood, like I had expected, my father gently pushed the bloodstained finger back to me, signaling he was done before pointing the frosted tip of the beautiful blade up toward the ceiling.

At my side, Mendax wrapped his hand around mine again. I waited for the feel of his palm to encompass mine, but instead, I felt his hot tongue glide over my fingertip. I whipped my head to look at him and was met by his unwavering, delicious blue eyes on mine.

Mendax had the ability to make even the most minuscule of things, like a pricked finger, lust-filled and dangerous. He was walking sin with wings of smoke and the body of a warrior. If I couldn't be with Adrianna in the Elysian Fields, then I had to figure out what I was going to do if I was forced to live out the rest of this life, and I wanted Mendax by my side.

I wanted Eli to live. I *needed* Mendax to.

"There," my father stated, redirecting my focus to the line of crimson that had dripped down the middle of the frosted blade. "It is finished." He beamed brighter than the sun itself.

"My blood was for the dagger and not the pendant?" I asked, feeling the annoying prickle of curiosity crawl up my neck. Why was there blood inside it? What was special about this blade? I knew there was something. You could tell just by looking at it that it was one of a kind.

"Ah, yes, your sister's ashes." He set the blade in his lap and removed the pendant from where it had been tucked in his palm. His mouth straightened in a pained line. "It was nice to hold her again." The thin line of his lips stretched, and his eyes gained a hint of gloss. He opened the latch of the necklace and waited for me to put my head down before he removed his hands and sat back. "It's all done. Addy's last drop of power is infused with the soul mingled in her ashes. The Fates will waste no time in getting this to her, I'm sure. I can barely stand to think of that sweet girl in that hole of iniquity."

My lip pinched between my teeth, I looked away from him. I would find a way to make sure Adrianna got the pendant. That would be my only goal now. My blurry eyes snagged on a picture of Adrianna that made me stand from my chair.

Had I not thought about her big blue eyes every hour of every day, I wouldn't have even recognized the woman in the painting. The detailed black frame pulled the darkened edges of the portrait to blend into the dimly lit wall, making it appear as if she were almost floating. Her golden-brown hair stopped at her V-shaped chin, making her bright-blue eyes pop. She was looking to the right of the frame in a nervous sort of way that made my stomach tighten into knots, reminding me of my mother. "She is in Tartarus in this painting?" I looked to my father, now standing beside me.

"Yes," he said solemnly.

"How have you gotten all these?" I took in the painting again, trying to memorize every freckle on the bridge of her nose that hadn't been there when she was six.

"Being powerful has its perks," he said softly as he set the beautiful dagger on the table and stepped out from the chairs.

My eyes froze on the white vine whose pot he had pulled the dagger from and the little purple mushrooms he had removed from the pot. They had pointed caps that rose so high that they bent slightly at the tips. The plant itself lacked any color, which meant that it lacked chlorophyll, but then how was it growing?

"The mushrooms," I murmured, answering my own silent question.

"You are interested in the *Monotropa uniflora vitis*?" he said with marked fascination.

"They're getting their nutrition through parasitism, aren't they? The mushrooms?"

His face lit up once again, and a stirring of something landed in my gut. "You enjoy botany still. I always wondered if it was just a different side of your mask."

I felt Mendax's eyes slide over my body from where he still sat in the chair, and a chill crept up the back of my neck.

Tell him what else you enjoy, pet.

I dropped the mushroom I had picked up as I whipped around to see Mendax rise from the chair nonchalantly and give me a wink.

The bond. We can still use the bond here? I sent back.

Of course. The bond isn't a power. It's just us. He licked his lower lip and slowly raked his eyes down to my feet and back up.

"The plants use a structure called a haustorium to—"

"To penetrate their host plant, which drains nutrients," I added with a smile as I turned away from Mendax and back to my father. "It's a holoparasite, meaning that it cannot photosynthesize and depends on its host, the mushrooms, for food. The fungi draw sugar from the plant in exchange. That's why it's able to grow in this dark room with no sunlight," I said proudly, which was weird. I never cared about impressing anyone before in my life until about one and a half seconds ago.

My father clapped his hands together excitedly. "Perhaps some fae did get through your mortal veins after all," he laughed.

The expression fell from my face to the floor. "How is Mom in the Elysian Fields? Earlier, you said you had too much to tell me. Tell me now. How could she get in as a human? Were you two ever married? What—"

"Okay." My father held up his palms and spoke softly. "You deserve and have the right to know everything." He glanced at the door. "And I hope I am not foolish in the hope that we will have another, possibly many more, chances to spend time together. However, we are on limited time before the trial, and someone will be arriving any minute with your clothes for tonight. So might I encourage you to ask the most pressing of your questions for the moment?"

My brain was about to short-circuit with the number of questions I had. My mouth opened and closed as I tried to decide on the most important.

"Your mother and I were never married," he stated, no doubt taking pity on me.

"Were you in love?" I don't know why I asked it. It didn't really matter, but a part of me needed to know.

"Very much. She joked about getting my face tattooed over the skeleton's face on her chest," he laughed, and it transformed his eyes into happy, sparkling globes. "I told her that Kaohs would probably fight his way out of Tartarus just to remove it," he chuckled.

My expression fell. "What?"

Unholy fuck! Kaohs gave your mother a tattoo with a skeleton? Why have you never mentioned this to me, Calypso? Mendax shot through the bond.

My brows knit together. I didn't have time to deal with him being mad that I didn't tell him a detail of my life. Nosy fuck. "What do you mean Kaohs would remove it?" I asked my father. Unsettling tingles covered my arms as my nerves picked up.

"Your mom's tattoo? The skeleton holding skeleton keys?" Zef smiled wide.

Fucking stars, Calypso! Your mother was a—

I swatted the air at Mendax with a scowl.

"Yes, I remember Mom's tattoo. Why does that have anything to do with Kaohs?" My voice had risen an octave, but I was still trying to remain calm.

Zef's face turned serious as he tilted his head slightly. "She never told you."

"Told me what?" My voice shook. "She never told me what?"

Your mother was a changeling.

I whipped around to Mendax, who had moved to the chair next to the table with the dagger.

Changeling. Changeling. What the fuck was a changeling? I'd never heard the word before. My mouth hung open as I faced my father again.

There was a knock at the front door.

"Yes, leave them at the door," he shouted, keeping his worried eyes on me. "Didn't she ever tell you how we met?" Hurt threaded through his voice like a gust of wind.

"She never told me anything about you other than that you left us after Adrianna was born," I snapped. My chest was pounding so hard, I worried the Fates had decided to take me out early.

Realization seemed to dawn on the older man. "Oh my…"

"Your beloved mother was one of Kaohs's bond servants," Mendax said with the hint of a smile.

"I–I don't know what that is." I rushed to get the words out, needing one of them to tell me these details about the woman I loved so dearly.

"Your mother was stolen by Unseelie when she was just a baby," my father said softly.

My head snapped to Mendax.

He held both palms up and grinned. "As you know, I've always found humans detestable."

My father glared at Mendax but continued speaking. "Unseelie would occasionally steal a human baby, back when they could get through the veil, before they were sent to Tartarus. They would leave one of their own offspring in its place. When things were the worst between Seelie and Unseelie, they would try and balance the power by swapping out the babies of the opposing royal family with a human child so they would grow to be powerless, tipping the scales for the other side. No one wanted them, and they were sent to Kaohs in Tartarus, where he used them for cooking and cleaning until they were older."

"What did he do to them when they were older?" I asked Mendax.

His cold eyes danced with malice as one dimple popped. "I'm betting you can guess."

"Kaohs tattoos all his…favorite possessions. They aren't allowed to leave Tartarus or him, ever." Zef rubbed the back of his neck.

"But…then how did she get out?" I asked as I looked between the two men.

"I met Kaohs during the war. We were hoping to get his word that he wouldn't assist the Smoke Slayers." He glared at Mendax. "I'm sure you can already guess how that turned out. He had brought a few of his bond servants to the meeting, and your mother was one of them." He looked off into the distance, and you could almost see the memories dancing through his mind. "The moment I saw her, I was in love. I tried to leave with her then and there."

Mendax snorted. "I'm sure that went well."

"Your mother ended up making her own deal with the god of the dead. In exchange for her freedom, which included that she be granted access to the Elysian Fields, far, far away from him when she died, she would leave her soul with him." Zef suddenly looked exhausted and uncomfortable. "I took her to the human realm, where Kaohs cannot walk, and hid her and myself, foolishly believing I had outsmarted everyone and would get to live a happy, quiet life with my family until I was called to ascend."

"Wow," I mumbled in the quiet room.

Zef grunted in a way that reminded me of a small tantrum. He walked out of the room, and a few moments later, I heard the creak of the front door.

I stared at a line on the plaid rug and tried to process everything I had just learned. My anger at my mother was fleeting. I was nine when she and Adrianna passed. That information didn't seem like something you told your nine-year-old daughter, if ever.

"Are you all right?" Mendax moved the hair at the back of my neck and kissed the curve softly. "You want me to stab Kaohs when I see him tonight?"

I let out a deep sigh. "Unfortunately, I doubt stabbing him will help get my sister out of there. Wait—tonight?" I turned around and gripped his arm. "No. You are not dying, do you hear me? I don't know what to do, but I will figure it out. Neither you nor Eli are dying tonight or anytime soon!"

"I am the only one who can get to Tartarus, pet." He ran his fingers through the hair at my temple before gripping the sides of my face in his hands. After a minute of the most intense look, he whispered, "Never forget me."

I shoved his hand down and away from me. "Stop it!" Anger boiled so hot, I grabbed the beautiful dagger from the table and pressed it to his throat as I tried to calm my heavy breathing. He just watched me, a slightly sad look in his eyes. "Leave me and I will…I will marry Eli and fuck him three times a day." I pressed the frosted edge of the blade harder against his skin. I had never been more serious about any other threat in my life, and I knew he felt it through the bond…but I could also feel how serious he was about leaving.

"No, you won't," he said confidently as his eyes remained hooked to mine.

"I will. If you leave me tonight, I will become queen of Seelie." My heart was going to give out. I was sure of it.

The corner of his mouth lifted.

"I will." I swallowed deeply. My angry facade fell. "Please, you have to promise me you won't die tonight. *Please.* I need you with me."

"Oh my fates! Put the blade down, dear!" My father's voice came from the doorway as he reentered the room carrying a tall stack of folded red cloth. He tossed it on a chair as he grabbed the blade from me with a panicked look on his face. "You must be careful with this!"

I scrunched my face at him. "I thought it was mine."

He shook his head and moved it to a table so far away from me it was almost at the door. "I made it for you, but it's dangerous, and we need to speak with the Fates before I can officially give it to you, as I think it may interfere."

"Why?" This was turning out to be quite a day, and to be honest, a beautiful dagger might help make it a fraction less shitty.

"The blade is made from the blossom of the—" my father began.

"Oh my stars, if I have to hear any more about plants, I'm going to kill us all," Mendax said with a dramatic groan.

"Would you now?" my father said with a soft rumble of power flowing out from him.

Oh shit.

Mendax glared but didn't say a word.

"This blade gives its owner, you and only you, the power of anyone that it kills. I couldn't make you Artemi, but I could make this blade, and it is the next best thing. The plant was made so that only one bloom could ever be harvested, and I've gone to *great* lengths to ensure that another weapon of this kind can never exist and could never harm you," said my father.

"What if someone steals it and they use it?" Mendax chimed in.

Zef shook his head. "No matter who wields it or who they kill with it, the power can only go to Calypso."

I thought I saw a small grin from my father, but if I did, it was gone before I could focus my eyes on it.

"Obviously, I'm going to do everything in my power to ensure that you are safe tonight, but unfortunately, I'm not sure if there's anything to be done. They delivered your clothes for the trial. Could one of you take Eli his robes? Your tickets will arrive when it's time to go to the hall, so I suggest being ready as soon as possible. I'm so sorry. I wish I could spend more time with you, but I need to speak with the Fates and do what I can to help."

He handed us the pile of red fabric and sent us out the door and into the hallway of the main house.

"I need to talk to Eli," I said as I sorted through the red robes and ignored the fiery look Mendax was giving me. "Alone."

CHAPTER 30

CALY

R ED?" Mendax glared at the robe I handed him outside
his cottage.

"The color of the robe…that's what you're concerned
about right now?" I snapped at him. It felt like every drop of
tension I'd ever possessed had been stored up until my body
could use it in this very moment.

His eyes hardened a fraction as he towered over me. "My
concern has remained in the same place since it's developed."
He gripped my chin roughly and leaned down to hover over my
lips. "Give Aurelius his robes and have your chat, but be quick.
I need to spend time with you before…" His voice trailed off
as he ran his thumb over Adrianna's pendant around my neck.

"You promised me, Mendax. You can't leave me," I whispered against his soft lips as my eyes fell shut.

"Would you wait for me?" he whispered breathily.

"No," I snapped, starting to panic. Why was he even talking
about leaving me? He wasn't serious. This was Mendax. He
couldn't leave me.

"Then you'd come for me?" He grinned.

"No. Why would you talk about leaving?" I bit my lip until
I tasted copper on my tongue.

He watched my bottom lip intently. "Maybe I want to be everything to you…your hero and your villain." He let out a breathy laugh as if his words were all a joke, but I could feel through the bond it wasn't a joke to him.

"Please, promise me," I begged him.

"I promise." He pressed his lips to mine in a kiss I felt all the way down to the soles of my feet.

"Come on, get a room. There are fathers and best friends walking around here now," Eli said, coming up the grass path from his little house.

I laughed, even though I really, really didn't want to. Eli was always good at making me feel better when things got too hard. "You come on. I need to talk with you and give you your robes for tonight." I gave a final look at Mendax's handsome face and began to walk to Eli's front door.

I heard Mendax and Eli mumble something after I walked off, and I'd never been more envious of fae hearing, because as a human, I heard nothing but a few murmurs.

After moving inside, I tossed the remaining two garments down on the kitchen table and grabbed the one with less fabric.

The door to the cottage closed behind Eli. "What did I miss?" he asked with concerned eyes.

My fight not to spill to my best friend only held for another breath before I was sitting on the counter telling him everything that he had missed at my father's. He began to pace when I told him about my mom but stilled when I told him about the beautiful blade that my father had crafted to take the power of those that it killed.

"Holy shit," he said as he rubbed his face with his palms.

He had seemed really interested in the blade, asking me to repeat its description at least twice, but I was overflowing with things to tell my best friend, so I moved on after answering his questions.

"To make it worse, I think Mendax is going to try and get killed tonight. I can feel it through the bond. He's serious. I think he wants to be the good guy for once, and he's the only one who can get into Tartarus and return the pendant to Adrianna." My eyes began to well with tears for what felt like the hundredth time in this conversation alone. "I can't lose him, Eli. I–I have no purpose here without him. I know he and I can do anything together. He is friends with Kaohs. I know he can help me find a way to get Adrianna out of Tartarus and into the Elysian Fields where she belongs."

"And then what?" he asked. "What happens after Adrianna is free? What do you do then?"

I struggled to think about the answer as I took note of the details in the cotton rope rug beneath Eli's feet. "Then I…I guess I start the process of letting them go and attempting to live the life I couldn't while I was living as someone else."

Eli smiled, but it only touched his eyes for a second before it was gone, leaving his mouth sad.

"What's the matter?" I asked as I bumped my shoulder into his arm. I could feel something wild stirring from him through the tie. As a matter of fact, it was the first time I'd felt anything from the tie since being in Moirai. "Eli, they won't kill you. I won't let them. My father is talking with them right now. I… The only thing is, maybe we could let them sever the tie? That way, we can all live?"

I didn't even need to look at his face to feel the pain my words had inflicted.

"Yeah, I had a feeling you were going to choose Mendax. I was prepared." He laughed, but it sounded unrecognizable, like it came from someone who wasn't my best friend.

"No, I'm not choosing him, Eli. You saved my life, and I will be forever grateful for you. You know that. I couldn't have done anything without you as my friend. You've always been my hero when I needed you. Don't you want to live your life and experience things without worrying that you are going to accidentally kill your friend? Besides, without the drop of Artemi from my sister, we shouldn't even be tied together anymore, right? The Fates will have to let us go unharmed." I smiled and tried my best to make sure he saw that I meant it.

"I only saved your life and even had to tie myself to you because he tried to kill you, Cal, and I don't mind being tied to you. Even as only friends, I like being able to feel what you feel or when you're in trouble. I've always liked being your hero." He flashed his perfect teeth in his charismatic grin, and I couldn't help but smile back.

"Well, Mendax suddenly seems hell-bent on being my hero, so you're going to have to take that up with him," I laughed. "Maybe you could try out the villain for a change. I hear they have way more fun." I wiggled my brows.

I smiled, but something inside my mouth felt odd. Within a second, I was hacking and choking as something hard and smooth filled my mouth. Panicked, I looked to Eli for help, but he was no better off than I was as he tried to push his hand into his own mouth to grab whatever it was. I took his lead and tried to pry the oversized thing out of my mouth as I heaved and gagged.

"Here, here, tilt your face up," Eli said as he held my face and attempted to help pull the thing from my mouth after he had apparently had success with his own. "There it is," he said like a soothing voice as he emptied my mouth of the obstruction. "Another reason why I am still your hero and not Mendax. Feuhn kai greeyth, baby."

I bent over and hacked until I was certain my insides were about to come up. "What the fuck was that?" I shouted as I looked up to see him holding two large, thick red tickets with gold-foil lettering.

"These look like tickets to a show that starts in five minutes."

"A show? My father mentioned it was their entertainment…" My voice trailed off. A show? I thought this was a trial? "We should get dressed and quick. Where are we supposed to go?" I grabbed the smallest wad of robe and went toward the door.

"We are supposed to go to the concert hall. It's inside the main house and to the left behind the big curtains," he responded quickly as he grabbed his own red robe.

267

I froze at the door. "You've been to see them already..."

"Yes, and so has Mendax," he replied softly. "Cal, I love you. Go make sure Mendax isn't still choking on his ticket. I'll meet you both outside the hall."

I remained at the door for a beat as I watched him, then ran out the door and over to change with Mendax.

CHAPTER 31

CALY

T HE HEAVY CRIMSON ROBES FELT ITCHY AND SUFFOCATING
against my skin as I dropped my arms to my sides with a
heave, accidentally pulling a few strands of hair out as they fell.
I was trying to look somewhat presentable before we went to
see the Fates, but it was a struggle. My hair felt long and stringy
without having any conditioner, and my arms kept getting
stuck in the large, bell-shaped sleeves of the robe and halting
the progress of my braid.

I slammed my palms down on the washbasin in front of
the looking glass in defeat. All I wanted was to braid my hair
and not think about the fact that I was probably about to lose
the love of my life. My fingers tangled in the knotted strands
painfully, and I tightened my fist, ready for more.

My entire life had been calculated. There was nothing I
wasn't willing to do to get something done; it was second
nature to me. So why then, in the most desperate hour of my
life, was I unable to figure out what to do to ensure we all
walked out of Moirai alive? This whole time, I had been trying
to get to the Elysian Fields to apologize to Adrianna, and she
wasn't even there. I couldn't *count* the number of hours I had
spent trying to get where I was so I could kill my father, and

now, all I wanted to do was ask him all the questions I'd never had any answers to. Everything I had thought about him had been a lie spun by my own hatred and need to place my anger for my sister's death on someone. Hate and anger were so good at camouflaging vulnerable and weak sadness. I was alone, and I couldn't afford to be vulnerable or weak, but now—now I didn't feel alone anymore. I fought it at first, purely out of self-preservation, but the truth was I wanted a relationship with my father. I understood everything now, and I couldn't bring myself to hate him after seeing how he'd been hurting too.

"Let me help you," Mendax whispered from the doorway, startling me out of my tear-filled stare into the mirrored glass.

"How long have you been watching me?" I asked as I wiped my red nose on the giant hood of the robe.

Mendax moved behind me like a wraith and parted my hair down the middle with his pinky. He began to slowly comb through one side with his fingers. Tingles of pleasure tickled across my scalp, and I let my eyes fall closed—just for a second. His strong grip began to deftly pull and twist my hair into an impressively intricate braid.

"You know how to braid hair?" I asked, feeling like this was my final straw and that I may actually just be hallucinating all this after all.

His lips pulled up at one corner before twitching in concentration. I watched his every move through the mirror. He was somehow the most daring and horrifying man and the most surprisingly tender all at the same time. I supposed that was what happened though when your shell hardened—your insides softened even more with the protection.

"I frequently braid my stallion's mane. Your unruly mess is no different," he whispered with a twinkle in his eyes.

"Lovely," I mumbled with a roll of my eyes. I had to hike up the robe as it slid off my shoulder for the thousandth time. As Mendax tied a scrap of fabric around the end of one braid and started another, I couldn't help but notice how well his robes fit against his broad shoulders and long arms. It must be a trial outfit or something, because I had only seen the other men wearing robes like these. All the women I had seen, which, granted, were only a few, had more stylish dresses or robes than those of the men. Mendax looked like a god draped in the blood of his enemies in his scarlet robe. His long, black hair and pale eyes were strikingly beautiful against the vibrant red. He was stunning.

"Promise me you won't leave me tonight," my soft voice croaked.

"I promise," he answered just as softly as he swept his fingers over the back of my neck. Goose bumps erupted across my flesh at the simple touch from him.

"Why are you lying to me? I know you saw the Fates," I rasped as I watched him finish my last braid.

His harsh eyes caught mine in the mirror. "Because I'm a liar, among other things."

"Malum, there are other ways to get to Tartarus. You're friends with Kaohs. Please don't do anything stupid tonight," I snapped. I could already feel through the bond he was settled on something. I could feel his fear and excitement. It was unnerving.

In one smooth motion, he spun me around and lifted me up onto the ledge of the washroom counter. I swam in the large robe, and it easily made room for his body between my thighs.

"I'm going to Tartarus tonight. The Fates have already accepted my deal."

I felt the blood drain from my face. "What deal? No."

"They will sever your tie with Aurelius tonight but kill me." His palms tightened around my hips.

I couldn't breathe. My entire world was falling apart, and I didn't know how to stop it. "In exchange for what? You can't. You don't have to die. We will find another way. You are close with Kaohs."

His throat bobbed, and I watched his Adam's apple like it was a beacon. "In exchange for keeping the bond intact and you safe." For the first time, I watched Mendax's eyes grow glossy with unshed tears. "You won't remember me after tonight. They are removing me from your memories, but the bond will be in place forever. I will never stop watching over you, even when you don't know I exist." He moved his palm over the front of my throat and, with a quick and sudden tug, pulled Adrianna's pendant from my neck. "I can't make you any promises, but I think in exchange for my services, I might be able to get Kaohs to return Adrianna to Seelie. You could finally get your time with her."

"What?" I wanted to scream or cry, maybe both. The thought of getting to apologize to my sister finally was almost enough to silence my pleas—but not quite. I felt my face heat. "That's it?" I snapped with all the venom I could infuse into my words. I was furious. "After all this, you're just going to leave me too? You know, you are so full of shit! This entire, horrible journey, you have acted as if you would explode on Eli for so much as looking at me, just to turn around and forfeit yourself. Do you even care? Why pretend to hate Eli so much if you were just going to leave me with him?" I laughed. It was a laugh filled with venom and pain, absent of any humor.

Mendax leaned into me until my back was smashed against the mirror so hard, it fell from its place on the wall and off the counter, shattering into pieces on the floor beneath me. "Do—not—question—how—much—I—care," he ground out through clenched teeth. I could tell he had snapped. He stepped away and slammed the door shut so hard it fell from the hinges with a crack. He turned back around with an evil smile that made him look absolutely unhinged. "And who said I was going to leave you with Eli?" He stormed back over to me, and the glass crunched under his feet.

My stomach lifted to my throat when he grabbed my face in his hands. I'd never seen him like this. He was completely unbridled. I didn't know if he was going to say fuck it and kill me or fuck me. I wished I could say I wasn't scared of him, but the truth was he terrified me. Knowing he could crush me at any moment but instead chose to cherish me was intoxicating.

"What is going to happen to Eli?" I asked, suddenly very afraid for my best friend.

"I'm obviously going to kill him before I go." He smiled wide. "Now let's go. It's time." He bent down and kissed my gaping mouth before lifting me up and moving me away from the glass, not setting me down until we were outside on the grass. "Caly." His voice had softened. "I'll always be with you through the bond. Don't ever forget that."

I gathered up the fabric that pooled on the ground and followed Mendax up the path to the main house, completely at a loss. How was I going to stop this?

I racked my brain in a dazed panic until we entered the main building. The air smelled luxurious with a clean hint of saffron and cedar. Every clack of the floor sounded louder, and I realized for the first time since we'd been there, I heard no harp music playing in the background.

I moved to Mendax's side and squeezed his hand. No matter what ended up happening, I needed my last few moments with him to mean something more than anger. He stopped abruptly, and I tripped over the long robe. Mendax caught me and pulled me close. His face looked angry, and I wasn't sure what to expect.

"*Please* never forget me," he whispered before he bent me slightly and kissed me softly, running his tongue over my bottom lip and sending sparks throughout my body. If he thought I could ever forget him, he had no clue how in love with him I was. He was unforgettable.

"About fucking time. Are you late for everything?"

Eli sounded furious. What had happened?

Before I could look at him, Mendax began a fit of laughter that sounded unlike anything I'd heard. My eyes widened in shock at the sight of him laughing that hard. I hadn't even had a chance to look at Eli, but once I did, my laugh rivaled Mendax's.

Tall, muscled, and tan Aurelius, prince of the Seelie realm, stood outside the velvet curtain with arms crossed…in a beautiful crimson ankle-length dress with a train that billowed out. The stretchy fabric looked as if it were about to pop at the seams as he seethed at us.

"I think that you are wearing my robes," he said with a flushed face.

Well, I supposed that explained the size of the robe.

Mendax, laughing the entire time, blocked me from view as I swapped my robe with Eli's dress in the hallway. We didn't have time to go anywhere else to change, and Eli was so embarrassed, he was almost fully clothed before I had even stepped into the dress. Of course, this one fit me like a glove.

Mendax moved the velvet curtain aside, and we crossed the threshold—all together for the last time.

CHAPTER 32

MENDAX

"Tickets please." A young woman stepped from behind a small wood counter and held her hand out, palm up.

We handed her our tickets, and I fought the urge not to jam them down her throat just as they had been upon delivery. I was in the lead, so I missed the chance to see Caly's face when she realized we were in a concert hall.

The woman led us to the circular area of chairs in the center of the large hall. Lights as hot as the sun beat down on the area. Three darkly cushioned stools were in the brightest parts of the light.

"Stand here please," chirped the lady as she positioned us a few feet in front of the stools.

"What is this?" Caly asked. I could feel her panic through the bond.

"Quiet please," the old woman snapped, and I reached out to snap her neck before rethinking it and returning my hand to my side. I needed to make sure the Fates held up their part of the deal first. I needed to know Caly would be safe forever.

Caly's father walked out from somewhere in the dimly lit surroundings and nodded to us as he stood behind us in the dark. Heavy thuds echoed as he wheeled out a large gold harp with only a few strings. Aurelius cleared his throat, and the sound echoed through the concert hall. The hero offered to help Zef when he rolled past to which he silently shook his head and continued until he'd positioned harps in front of each of the three seats. He stepped back behind us, receding into the shadows of empty risers of chairs.

My breath stilled in my lungs as the three Fates walked the same path Zef had taken in a single-file line. I wanted to grab Caly and get her little mortal body out of the room as fast as possible.

The first sister walked meekly to the first stool. With the lights so bright, I was able to get a better look at them than I had the other night, and my nerves jumped as soon as I saw the familiar features of the woman in the first seat. The resemblance was striking, and there was no way they weren't related. The first Fate was the woman with wild brown hair who had greeted us the first day here.

The one I had beaten the shit out of.

I ran my fingers through my hair and tried to convince myself that it didn't mean anything. They would still hold up their end of the deal.

When I had come to see them before, the only lights in the concert hall were the flickering flames that spread across different parts of the walls. There had only been two of them, but I couldn't see their faces.

The first Fate looked up and winked at me, and it felt like my ribs broke with the pain that tore through my chest. They were going to kill Caly because of what I'd done. I'd assaulted one of the Fates.

Fuck!

The second sister, this one with blond hair and similar features, walked out proudly with a little excitement in her step. She bowed before sitting next to her sister at the harp with only half the strings attached.

The third sister came out with a completely different look to her. She had similar features in the nose and chin but looked tired and wise for as youthful as they all appeared. Unlike the others, who were dressed in red robes similar to ours, she wore all black with the hood of her robe being the only one that was up over her hair. Slowly, she made it to her seat with the harp full of strings.

The first woman stood and bowed before softly speaking. "As you may remember, I am Anastasia. I am the spinner." She pulled a white moth from the pocket of her robes and walked to the half-strung harp. "I create life," she said as she placed the moth on the top of the harp.

The bright light focused in on the little creature on the harp as it moved to its position above where the next string would be, almost dangling from under the top of the harp. The fuzzy-looking moth suddenly flew back to the woman, leaving a small white caterpillar where it had been.

I heard Caly's gasp as she watched the caterpillar twist and twirl, dropping lower and lower, leaving a string in its wake until it reached the bottom of the harp and climbed back up the string, making a tiny cocoon around itself and disappearing. The first sister sat back down with the mother moth on her finger.

The bench creaked against the floor as the second sister rose with a smile. She walked out from behind the harp and bowed gracefully. "I am Genome, and I am the allotter. I play the threads of life." She returned to her bench and adjusted the large gold harp. The lights from above shifted over her as she stretched her long fingers across the harp and played a tune that was similar to what we'd been hearing since we arrived. The woman lost herself in the music, and for a few moments, it was almost as if I had taken Caly to the orchestra instead of a death sentence.

After a few moments of her beautiful music, Genome sat back with a smile and watched as the cocoon broke open and a crimson-red moth emerged, fluttering its new wings as it stretched out on the string.

The third and final sister stood and stepped to the front, just as the others had. "I am Morta, and I am the decider of death." Her low voice echoed as she removed her hood. A black crow sat on her shoulder, nearly indistinguishable from her glossy, black hair. "I sever the strings of life." She turned slowly and walked to the harp where she stood for a moment before the crow on her shoulder flapped to the red moth on the string and, with a sharp snap of its beak, closed the winged creature in its mouth and cut the thread in half before returning to Morta's shoulder. She lifted her hood, shadowing herself and the crow once more before she sat.

My eyes snapped to Caly, afraid I was suddenly going to see her slumped on the ground dead, but I was relieved to see she remained standing quietly next to me.

The middle sister, the blond one, stood once more and cleared her throat. "You three have been brought here after you went against the rules of fate. Calypso, you were already tied to Aurelius through the theft of your sister's powers when you bonded with Mendax, the Smoke Slayer, is that correct?"

Caly shifted uncomfortably. "I suppose so, but I didn't ask for either—"

"Thank you." The woman cut her off. "As I'm sure you've figured out by now, the trial has already happened, and your fate has been decided prior to the present time."

The three of us exchanged panicked looks. My fingertips smoothed over the pocket of my robe, searching for comfort that never came.

"The trial has already happened?" Caly asked loudly.

"Yes. During your attempts to get into Moirai, we were testing the three of you for your integrity, compassion, and competence. All things that we feel are deciding factors in who should remain paired and whose thread should be cut."

The Fate looked to me, and for the first time since walking in the doors, I felt relieved.

"You should know that based on those three factors, we decided Calypso should die."

All the air left my body as I waited for what was going to happen next.

"But Mendax offered us a deal."

Oh, thank stars. I glanced to Calypso but had to turn away when I saw her big, round eyes filled with heartbreak.

"No!" she screamed.

The crow on Morta's shoulder cawed loudly, and everyone in the room went still.

"Mendax offered to take the last drop of power and soul to your sister in Tartarus and remain as a liaison to help fine-tune the process with Kaohs in exchange for cutting the tie between you and Aurelius and maintaining the bond so he may watch and feel you as frequently as he likes."

I heard the soft pitter-patter of tears as they hit the floor by Caly's feet.

"Of course, we would have to remove any traces of his memory from you, but as we've made clear, you'll still be able to see and feel snippets of each other through the tie—excuse me, the bond. I'm sure you understand that all this is for your own good." The sister nodded politely.

Caly's heavy huffs of breath were enough to kill me there without the help of the Fates cutting my thread.

"However, that's not how fate works." The sister in black spoke as she rose to stand, and I watched a coy smile crawl onto her face.

No.

No.

No!

"We have decided to take Aurelius up on *his* collaboration," she said.

"Wait, what?" I shouted.

The crow cawed again as it shoved its head out from behind the hood.

"What? Eli?" Caly said frantically.

"What collaboration? What will happen to Calypso?" I could sense the three of our hearts beating faster.

The first sister cleared her throat, looking between me and Aurelius. "As far as the tie goes, their lives are no longer dependent on the other's survival."

Aurelius locked eyes with me before he glanced at my pocket for a split second, then snagged my eyes again with a small nod. "You have the blade?"

My hand flew to the frosted-glass blade with the fern cross guard that held Caly's blood. I searched his eyes, making certain I understood his meaning. Relief and respect washed over me as I realized what was happening. "I have it."

The corner of his mouth pulled into a grin. "I knew you would. You've probably plotted this out a million times already. Bet you didn't expect me to ask for it though, did you?" His grin fell.

"What is going on?" Caly cried.

"Aurelius has removed himself with the request that he be sent to Tartarus upon his death," the first sister answered.

The crow cawed behind me, and I knew there was only a moment before it cut his string of life.

"Eli, you can't die! Stop this!" Caly shrieked. Her cries sent shivers through my bones.

I took a step closer to Aurelius.

"I love you, Calypso, and I always will. I've never seen you as happy as you are with him and"—he coughed as his own eyes filled with tears—"my family has done so much to take your happiness away. I want to do this." A tear rolled down his tan cheek. "I never wanted to run Seelie or be a prince. I just wanted to help you, and now I can. Use my powers as you see fit, Cal." He smiled warmly and looked away from Caly to me.

"No! Stop! Don't!" she screamed as she lunged for him.

"I need the pendant," he said to me with a tremor in his voice.

I pulled it from my neck and tossed it through the air to him. He clapped his palms together, catching it in midair. Caly was almost to him.

"Mendax, don't! Please! Stop! You can't!" she screamed.

The crow cawed.

I took the remaining steps until I was directly in front of Aurelius—then hesitated. I never hesitated.

"You would have made a terrible hero," he said with a warm smile that didn't reach his eyes. "Please make her happy. Oh! She really likes jokes with cats in them." Another tear fell from his reddened eyes. "Those get her every time."

He began to nod, and I shoved the blade down and onto the top of his head before he finished nodding. I always knew I'd kill the man, but I had no idea it would make me sad to do it.

"No!" Caly screamed as she knocked me out of the way, grabbing Aurelius and falling to the floor with him. "Eli! Please! Suns! Please, no! Please!"

She ripped the blade from the top of his head, but it was too late. His eyes fluttered closed against the golden, shimmery blood staining his face.

He had the ashes of Caly's sister gripped tightly against his chest, holding on to Caly with the other as he gasped for air. He lifted the pendant and tried to speak, but the words were garbled and incoherent.

"How can I do this without you?" Caly cried, holding tightly to his chest.

He whispered something, and I had to turn away to keep myself together.

"Feuhn kai greeyth." His raspy voice struggled.

Eternal love and friendship.

My palms flew to my ears to muffle the scream that tore out of Caly. I knew from the rasp of devastation in her voice that Aurelius was dead and gone from our lives forever.

I didn't immediately run to her and gather her up in my arms like I wanted to. The pain that radiated through her end of the bond was so overwhelming, I struggled to think or act. It was obvious now that those two really did have something more than just a friendship; it was a soul-connecting relationship created by pain and suffering and solidified with the mortar of something I knew I would never be able to understand. The pain that surged through the bond in that moment was easily more pain than I'd felt in all the wars and battlefields combined, and it buckled my knees to feel it coming from her.

281

I watched her in awe. This little mortal creature believed herself to be weak, yet she took this pain like a true warrior.

Zef rushed to her and gathered her wailing frame into a tight embrace, and for once, I was glad there was another man comforting her, for I could not have risen from my knees with this pain for all the power in the world.

EPILOGUE

M Y SKIN BURNED WITH THE COLDNESS THAT CIRCULATED LIKE icy steel over every drop of my flesh. My bones ached as though they were throwing a tantrum. Every ancient Seelie part of me knew I wasn't supposed to be where I was. For a moment, it felt like my body was about to combust with the icy sensation, but then I was relieved of the horrible feeling.

The presence of people whispered like a threat at my back as I hunched over the ground. Was that a horse whinnying? My fists tightened instinctually as I readied to defend myself. My hand clenched around something small and cylindrical. My mind sorted through random, unfamiliar images.

"Aurelius? What the...the fuck are you doing here?" Surprised blanketed the deep voice.

Where did I know that voice from?

I turned slowly to face the voice and was met with a pair of familiar brown eyes.

To be continued in book four of the Infatuated Fae series...

ACKNOWLEDGMENTS

Firstly, I cannot continue another word without thanking my amazing editors. If I could rent an airplane and write a Thank You across the sky, it would be to you, Christa and Gretchen. I can promise you there has never been a more grateful author to have been paired with you than myself. Thank you to my incredible publisher and every single one of you who have helped with this process. To my family, thank you for dealing with me during my writing chaos and for taking me to get ice cream when the emotions of this book hit me. But most importantly, I want to thank my readers. Without you I would just be that nerdy girl that had a creepy imagination and day-dreamed too much. Thank you for loving this series as much as I do.

With love,
Jeneane O'Riley

ABOUT THE AUTHOR

Jeneane O'Riley is a #1 bestselling author of whimsically dark and romantic fantasy books. Her love of storytelling began when she was a small child, dreaming up glorious fantasies to fall asleep to. As she grew older, her love of storytelling remained, but the tales became more dangerous and full of toe-curling tension.

She is a hobby mycologist and nature enthusiast who resides in Ohio, at least until she can locate a proper bridge to troll, or perhaps a large tree spacious enough to hold her smoke show of a husband, her Irish wolfhound, pet dove, and, of course, her three children.

See yourself *in*

Bloom

every story is a
celebration.

Visit **bloombooks.com**
for more information about
JENEANE O'RILEY
and more of your favorite authors!

bloombooks

@read_bloom

read_bloom

Bloom *books*